Good to the Last Drop

A NOVEL BY

Elissa Gabrielle

Peace In The Storm Publishing

Praise for Elissa Gabrielle
And
Good to the Last Drop

"Elissa Gabrielle writes with intriguing ease…Captivating her reader from page 1."
— Jessica Tilles, Author of *Fatal Desire*

"Elissa Gabrielle is the NEW VOICE OF EROTICA, RO-MANCE AND SUSPENSE who unleashes a SENSUAL and deeply ENTHRALLING story that will leave even the most inhibited readers of Erotica throbbing for more, but will Amber and Khalil's love affair
last after the HONEYMOON?"
—Disilgold Soul

"Elissa Gabrielle writes with passion, and brings the heat in this very sexy, hot romantic thriller...erotica at its best."
—Diane Dorce', Author of *Devil In The Mist*

"Elissa Gabrielle takes you on a VIVID, SEXY, AROUSING, and FUNNY ride with everything erotica fans ask for and much, much more.....stuff you ain't never thought of."
—George L. Cook, III, Author of *Let's Talk Honestly*

"With characters that come to life with every page, Elissa Gabrielle takes the reader to new heights of sexuality and drama. Her first-person accounts draw you into the story lines and let you know what you've been missing. Insightful, witty and engrossing. Few can get my attention with the first line, but she has managed to do it. Can't wait for the next journey."

—C.A. Webb, Author of *Destiny's Child*

"Captivating characters... page-turner....very funny and will stay with a reader long after the book is finished."

—Claudia Brown-Mosley, Author of
I Can Have My Cake and Eat It Too

"Her writing is erotic, stunning and explosive. She weaves a tale of intrigue and portrays relationships the way they really are. And just like you want your lover to be, it has a sensual side as well. When you pick it up, you won't want to put it down...unless you are "taking care of business." Did I mention it was hot? It IS!"

—Donnie L. Betts, Filmmaker, No Credits Productions

ISBN-10: 0-9790222-0-7
ISBN-13: 978-0-9790222-0-3

This is a work of fiction. All of the characters, incidents, and dialogue, except for incidental references to public figures, products, or services, are imaginary and are not intended to refer to any persons, living or dead, or to disparage any company's products or services. Although the author and publisher have made every effort to ensure the accuracy and completeness of information contained in this book, we assume no responsibility for errors, inaccuracies, omissions, or any inconsistency herein.

ATTENTION CORPORATIONS, UNIVERSITIES, COLLEGES AND PROFESSIONAL ORGANIZATIONS: Quantity discounts are available on bulk purchases of this book for educational, gift purposes, or as premiums for increasing magazine subscriptions or renewals. This is also available to various Book Clubs. Contact the Publisher for more information.

Peace In The Storm Publishing
P.O. Box 1152
Pocono Summit, PA 18346

Visit our Web site at www.PeaceInTheStormPublishing.com

Interior Designed by The Writer's Assistant
www.thewritersassistant.com

"A brother's character is defined by what he does when no one is looking. Feel me? And ultimately, everything you do in the dark always finds its way to the light."

– Shawn Fontaine

Good to the Last Drop

to the

A Novel By

Elissa Gabrielle

Amber

Ribbon in the Sky

Life couldn't get much better than this. I knew it was nearly impossible for it to become more splendid. As I look in the mirror, I think these thoughts to myself and glance over at my mother, Tracey Clarke, the love of my life. Her face is as round as a cherub and golden brown. Her hazel eyes filled with tears. Her perfectly straight, white teeth complete the most endearing smile. She looks at me with so much adoration and admiration. I know she's proud.

The French decorated room at the Manor was crowded on this Saturday in June. My mom is basking in her glory. My sister, Olivia, touches up my makeup. She adds more lip gloss, more than I've ever worn. Olivia has done it tastefully elegant even. She's finally decided to leave my face alone, well, after one more coat of mascara.

Keisha, my best friend, walks over and looks at me in the mirror. Our eyes meet in the mirror's reflection and I see a look on her face. The look is one of pride. She is proud her best friend is finally tying the knot. I love Keisha with all my heart. We look at each other with a certain kind of sister-friend-respect. To prevent myself from breaking down, I simply bow my head, and take her hand in mine. We both knew what it meant. Simply, I love you, my sister.

I stand up and walk slowly, nervously to the full-length mirror.

"Oh my God, what do I look like?" I say to myself.

"Do I look fat?"

I'd reached a fabulous size twelve for this day after coming down from an eighteen. My self-confidence was through the roof, but I still needed confirmation that all my hard work paid off.

"Oh, I hope I look good enough to be Mrs. Khalil Devereaux," I exhale just before I get to the mirror.

My dimples on my right cheek were deep enough to fit a quarter. I felt so excited when I saw myself in my Vera Wang gown—a strapless, beaded floor length piece of perfection in all white. I turned to the side to get a view of my ten-foot train, so elegant and so lovely. Just how I felt about myself on this very special day. My diamond earrings and choker glimmered and corresponded so well with my hazel eyes. They are my mother's eyes.

Olivia has done such a wonderful job on my makeup. I feel giddy as if I was on the red carpet headed to the Grammy's or BET Awards or something like that.

I cannot believe what Keisha has done to my hair. It flows and cascades down my shoulders to my mid-back. Those waterfall curls lay so beautifully under my crown and veil. Today is my day. A day I would treasure forever. It is the day I will marry my soul mate, Khalil.

"Momma, you ready?"

"Oh, Amber, I have never been more ready in my life."

Momma breaks down. She can no longer hold her feelings. They take complete control. Olivia sweeps in to wipe away her tears.

"Momma, it's alright. It's a happy day, Momma. It's gonna be alright," I say with a smile and a tear in my eye.

Olivia, who is now trying to repair some of momma's makeup, looks over to me and says, "I love you Amber. I am proud of you and so honored to call you my sister."

"I love you too, Olivia." I take a deep breath and hold it for a second. "Okay ladies, are we ready?"

Keisha, my maid of honor and best friend, gathers my bridesmaids. It was time, time for me to marry Khalil.

I hear music as the organist warms up. I step outside of my dressing room at the prestigious Manor in Newark, New Jersey. My dad was awaiting my arrival at the door. His eyes well with tears of joy as I walk toward him and take his hand. I am his first child to be married. Daddy looked handsome in his tuxedo. His salt and pepper hair and goatee to match complimented his caramel coated skin and bright eyes.

"You ready, Daddy?"

"Oh, I hope so." He leans over to whisper. "You make sure this mutha fucka treats you right. You hear me!?"

My dad is the biggest clown I'd ever met in my entire life. He always makes these off the wall comments that would have me rolling.

"Daddy, not today." I couldn't look at him for fear I would burst into tremendous laughter as I walked down the aisle.

We assemble quickly. All of my bridesmaids meet up with the groomsmen. My two flower girls in white satin and lace are also perfectly placed at their positions. We are ready and the ushers open the doors to the chapel.

My family, friends, colleagues and everyone Khalil and I knew are here. I look at Khalil. He smiles from ear to ear. He looks so happy. And I know at this very moment, I shouldn't be having horny thoughts, but he looks **good** in a tuxedo. The black tux atop of his ebony skin is turning me on. I cringe as I see his six-foot-five frame laced in all black and white. Why? He is the man of my dreams, and he looks gorgeous. The thought of him being mine for the rest of my life, to have his sweet ass for the rest of my life, gives my nipples a rise. *Lord, please forgive me for my lustful ways.*

3

Scott, my childhood friend, serenades us with his rendition of *Ribbon in the Sky* by Stevie Wonder. His version sounded more like the one from *Intro* –you know the R&B group from the early nineties. He is a fabulous friend and an even more fabulous queen. A pink boa adorns him around his neck. Scott sings in perfect tone and waves his hand in an off-beat-Mariah-Carey kind of way that seemed suitable for this most special occasion. His performance is flawless and his voice raises the hairs on my arms.

"Alright Daddy, we're up."

"Ok baby. But remember what I said."

He leans in again and kisses on my cheek. Then he whispers, "I'll kill Khalil if he doesn't treat ya right. Don't forget it."

Daddy's comment is enough to keep a smile on my face all the way down the aisle. *If they only knew why I am really smiling.*

Daddy releases me and kisses me again. Khalil takes my hand. I have tunnel vision. All I can do is look at my husband. MY HUSBAND.

"You look so beautiful baby. Oooh, I just love you, girl," Khalil whispers as he pulls me closer to him. He had that smooth voice. That radio voice. It resonated. Deep down.

"I love you so much, Khalil."

"Thank you for giving me one more chance to prove my love to you, Amber. Thank you for being my wife."

Reverend Green, who could pass for Gerald Levert's twin brother, winks at us and starts the ceremony. I listen but do not really hear the words. I just gaze into Khalil's soulful eyes. Half way through the ceremony, the Reverend taps me on my shoulder to let me know that it was my turn to say "I do."

I say it quick, too quickly, and my guests laugh. A little entertainment is fine. Even on this day. And even at my expense. Khalil is mine. Finally. Forever. *Laugh all you want! I got my man!*

Our parents did us well. And Khalil and I aren't too bad off, so we were able to afford the wedding of our dreams. Doves are released as we greet all of our attendees. It's a beautiful day for a perfectly landscaped outdoor wedding. It is an event. It is THE event.

"Alright brother! You did the damn thang, man," Shawn says as he walks over to Khalil; reaching out to shake his hand, give him a hug, a pound, showing him some serious black man affection. Khalil is overjoyed that Shawn was able to make it and to be Khalil's best man.

"Man, thank you for being here for me and for Amber," Khalil replied overwhelmed.

"I wouldn't have it any other way, Khalil. You my man. My brotha for life. You know that," Shawn says. He then turns to me, "Amber, you look absolutely gorgeous. Just stunning."

I blush, of course, but I kind of had the feeling that I'd looked better than I ever did in my entire life.

"Thank you Shawn. Come here, gimme some love."

Shawn and I embrace, for what seems like hours. Khalil joins in on our hug. This way, it doesn't seem like he is punking out had he hugged Shawn on his own. Khalil is a manly man.

"We sure have come a long way since our college days, right?" Shawn says.

"No doubt, baby, no doubt!" replied Khalil.

That's where we all met, in college. Shawn had been Khalil's roommate freshman year.

"Hey man, where's this surprise you've been telling me about? Gimme my surprise, man!" Khalil asks, his arm still gently around my waist.

Shawn smiles at the two of us. He turns his head to make sure no one else is looking. He then gives us a Terrence Howard I'm-so-good-at-being-bad grin. Shawn is easy on the eyes just like Khalil. The two could pass for brothers even. Shawn stood six-foot-two and weighed in at about two hundred and fifteen pounds, so he is in great shape. He too adorned a mouth full of pearly whites that looked like piano keys. Rich cocoa skin, deep, dark eyes, pretty full lips, strong masculine features, aligned his face perfectly

I pull myself from his baby browns.

"Yeah Shawn, what's the surprise? You have been hyping Khalil and me up so bad that I can't wait to get it."

Shawn was good for keeping us on our toes. He was always that way. Even in our college days. I could list a dozen different times where he'd have me so screwed up in the head behind one of his pranks. I love Shawn, as if he were my own flesh and blood.

Yesterday was his latest prank. He was running late for our rehearsal. He called Khalil with yet another story. Khalil had put Shawn on speakerphone so we could both hear him.

"Yo, Khalil."

"Wassup Shawn?" Khalil was stressed in his response.

"Yo, where you at again in Newark? The rehearsal dinner, I mean. It is off of Broad Street?"

Shawn had to come from Richmond, Virginia, so we really didn't expect him on time, but he made us nervous.

"Yeah man, we're right off of Broad Street," replied Khalil.

"Alright Khalil, I'm leaving Richmond now."

"What? Man, stop fucking with me!" Khalil yells at the phone.

As the words were coming out of Khalil's mouth in frustration, here comes Shawn with a big-ass smile. He never let us down, never. Especially when we needed him most.

"Wassup, baby?" Shawn says innocently.

"Shawn, you play too fucking much man! Good to see you. I'm glad you are here. It's an important time for me."

That's Shawn, always there.

"Amber! Khalil!" Shawn's voice brings me back.

We both responded in unison. "Wassup?"

Shawn said, "I'll be right back."

He walks away! Khalil and I just look at each other in disbelief and go back to greeting our guests.

Here comes this bitch. Oh how Khalil's mother gets on my last nerve. I mean this woman is never satisfied. Here she comes smiling in my face. *Shave your beard; it's your son's wedding.* Oh if looks could kill, she'd be pushing up daisies by sunset.

"Oh my baby done got married. My baby gone left me," she says with a whiskey sour in each hand with her drunken ass. "My baby, my beautiful baby boy.

"Oh, you look wonderful Amber, you really do."

"Thank you Mrs. Devereaux."

We both looked at each other with great disdain and fake smiles painted on our face. I knew she hated me.

Fingers tap on Khalil's shoulder. He turns around. It's Shawn. He is not alone. Shawn had an elegant woman at his side. What a sight! I mean I'm not the type of woman who is so insecure I can't compliment another woman. But damn, it's *my* wedding! And this woman who he must've just rented for the evening could've stolen the show had I not been so fine myself.

7

"Guys, I want you to meet Aaliyah, my fiancée."

I almost fell to the ground, I am so shocked. Khalil looks as if someone actually did shave his mother's beard; he was in so much shock. I said, "Your fiancée?"

"Yes baby, this is my fiancée. Don't just stand there y'all, say something, gotdammit!"

I lean in towards Aaliyah and say, "Girl, I'm sorry. I am really surprised. Girl, I'm Amber, so happy to meet you."

She walked over to me. Aaliyah had to be about five-eleven without those three-inch strappy sandals she was rocking. I instantly thought, *nice taste.* She had some style. You can always tell a girl's style by what type of shoe she's rocking.

Aaliyah wore a form fitting evening summer gown in turquoise that really brought out the green in her eyes. Lovely makeup. Very subtle, she didn't need much. She was beautiful. And for a woman to say that, she must've been . . .simply exquisite. And she had "good hair" unless she had a top-dollar weave. If it was, it was flawless. And this size twelve that took me a year to get into? Oh forget about it. She and her size eight dress which fit like a hand in glove probably went on effortlessly. But I wasn't a slouch either. So, it's all good.

"It's so nice to meet you Aaliyah." I smile at her with a real smile, not the fake, plastic smile I had given to Khalil's mother, "Welcome to the family."

I elbowed Khalil who seemed to still be in disbelief.

"Oh, very nice to meet you Aaliyah," Khalil stuttered while extending his hand with a puzzled look on his face. "So, when's the wedding?"

"Oh, Aaliyah and I don't know yet," Shawn beamed. "But what we do know is that we need and want you both to be there."

"Yes, we really do need you there with us," Aaliyah adds while turning to face me. "Girl I know we'll be spending a lot of time together."

"We will?," I question.

Suddenly Shawn interrupts. "Part two of the surprise!"

"We've moved to New York! Aaliyah has some modeling gigs lined up. I'm still into investment banking, so I can really relocate with no problem," Shawn says with a grin. "We'll only be twenty-five minutes away from you guys. Remember when I called you for the rehearsal dinner? I was on my way from our apartment in the city. "

"Word up, man? That's wassup," replies Khalil. Although he couldn't quite put things into perspective, Khalil is ecstatic that his man was moving closer. I could tell just from looking at Khalil's reaction. He figured they could kick it anytime they wanted now, so that is a good thing. As Shawn and Khalil walk off to talk their manly stuff, Aaliyah just stares at me.

"Amber, that dress is so fabulous," Aaliyah says, "And those eyes!! Are they your real eyes?"

"Girl, I was just about to ask you the same thing! Yep, they're mine. Somebody in the family had jungle fever at some point," I add with a giggle.

Aaliyah laughs, "I know that's right, girl."

I take Aaliyah's hand. "Come on girl, let me introduce you to family."

"Thanks for making me feel welcome, Amber."

"Hey bitch!" I hear and turn to see Scott walking my way.

Scott and I go way back like lemonheads and pumpkin seeds. Back in the day we were two parts of the group EnVogue. We'd have hairbrushes serving as microphones as we sung our asses off.

Scott is Diana Ross in male form. Like I said, Scott is the most fabulous queen I'd ever seen in my life. Scott's sense of style is impeccable. He is also easy on the eyes. He'd been into guys for as long as I could remember. Scott always played with me and all the other girls on the block when we were little. Jumping rope, playing hopscotch, doing our hair, and dressing Barbie's. He was never into sports and loved just being around us girls. Growing up, it was something everyone thought he'd grow out of, but he never did.

"Hey Scott, my baby. That song you sang brought me to tears honey." I have to give Scott his props. He is a talented singer, songwriter, and total artist.

"I know honey. You knew I wasn't coming up in here not showing my ass for my girl at that? Honey, please. You know girlfriend was going to represent for my baby," Scott replies with fingers up in the air waving and snapping on beat to his every word. It is almost as if he talked in rhythm.

"But listen here bitch; I ain't come here just to sang at your wedding. I came to find me a stallion honey, trust." *Another snap.*

"Oh Scott, stop it. You're too much," I respond blushing. I love Scott so much. Believe it or not, he'd pull in better looking brothers back in the day than I would.

Scott walks up to Aaliyah and me with a fabulous swagger. Looking in Aaliyah's direction and totally ignoring me, Scott moves in closer.

"Oh bitch! Stop the presses! Who…is…this?" Scott asks as he unwraps his feather boa from around his neck and throws his hand up as if to say, "talk to the hand."

"I'm sorry Scott, this is Aaliyah. Shawn's fiancée."

"Well would you look at this," Scott replies, eye balling Aaliyah from top to bottom.

"Shawnny done gone and outdone himself this time, hasn't he?"

Taking Aaliyah's hand, he continued, "How U doing?" Without waiting for a response, he continues, "Baby girl, mmmmphh, the dress...fierce. The shoes...fabulous. And the hair is to die for."

"Thank you." Aaliyah laughs a soft chuckle.

I jump in. "Scott baby, Aaliyah and Shawn just moved to the city from Virginia. She's a model so I know you'll be around to help make her feel like family, right?"

"Is that right?" Scott replied, still holding Aaliyah in his gaze.

"Well sweetie, anything you need, I'm the bitch to see. Hair, nails, shoes, bags, I've got the keys to the best in the city and some of the most fabulous agents you'll ever want to work with are close...personal friends of mine. Yes, we have got to get together so I can plug you into the underground world of queens, some of society's best."

"Queens?" Aaliyah sounded puzzled. "I'm not a queen."

Scott laughs and looks at me. "Would you please tell *Miss Thang* that I didn't say that...She did?"

"Scott please," I beg, "Don't start with all that drama queen stuff right now."

I look at Aaliyah and notice how uncomfortable she'd become. "Don't pay any attention to him; he's been this way for as long as I can remember."

"Excuse me," Scott says, throwing his boa back around his neck, "I simply meant that "us queens" only surround ourselves with the most gorgeous women, and I must say you most definitely fit the profile. Just ask Amber. I never give a busted bitch the time of day, Trust!"

Taking his card from his bag, Scott hands it to Aaliyah. "This is privileged information sweetie, only for the grown and sexy."

"Thank you, Scott, I'll be sure to remember that," Aaliyah smiles. "And thanks for the compliment."

"Honey, with those shoes you're wearing, I should say, Thank YOU." He turns to face me.

"Baby girl, always fabulous as usual." After kissing me once on each cheek, Scott walks away.

"Okay girl, it seems you've been approved by one of many," I tell her. "Now let's go meet some more family."

"You mean there are more?" Aaliyah jokes as we walk away laughing.

Khalil

I'm in Love with a Stripper

"You ready for that big day, baby?" Tony asks me.

"Oh yeah, Tony. Oh yeah."

Tony is my cousin on my mother's side. He is one of those fight-the-power-I-hate-white-people brothers, and he couldn't hold a job to save his soul.

"Yo Khalil, Amber got any sisters man?" Tony asks me with a smile.

"Puhleeeze, Tony. You need a job, first, Cuz."

"Awe, that's foul man. Real fucked up. You know you ain't right, yo."

"C'mon man, you know you ain't right for asking!" I tell him, "But seriously man, Amber's got a sister named Olivia. She's got her head on straight and is extremely focused. Shit, when we got our Bachelor's, she went on to law school. I think she's pursuing her Doctorate now. Y'all on different planets, baby. Like MC Hammer, baby, you can't touch that." I laugh because I know this is pissing him off.

"See K. Dat's what I'm talkin' bout. I need an intelligent woman in my life that can pay the bills," he says.

"Yo man, didn't you have that with that white stripper, Ginger?" We both look at each other and crack up.

All my boys have come to the private room they reserved for my so called *"last night of freedom."* They even had T-shirts made up with the newfound slogan. White Tees that had my name on the back surrounded by a ball and chain in red. The front had the words "Last Night of Freedom" in black and gold. They are too silly but good men nonetheless, all of them. Coming up out of the ghetto and witnessing how some other brothers lived, I am really blessed to have such good people around me. They know how to show a brother love.

Before the bachelor party, Shawn hooked up with Jamal, one of my boys from back in the day. Shawn didn't know anyone here in Jersey so he got with Jamal to help set things up.

Jamal and I used to run together in the Weequahic section of Newark. We'd been friends since the fifth grade. I lived on Shephard Ave, between Bergen and Osborne and Jamal lived around the corner on Bergen Street in an apartment building. We went to elementary together, then on to the same high school. I remember those days well.

Yeah, it was always going down at Weequahic High. Jamal was the wild type. Always trying to have fun and always into something. Never anything illegal, but he always got in trouble. So did I whenever I was with him. If he had a girl, I had a girl. If he skipped school, I skipped school. If he got his ass whooped, I got my ass whooped. That's how it was with the two of us. We used to call ourselves Tango & Cash. There was nothing that we didn't do together.

After twelfth grade, I moved on to Virginia Tech. Jamal and I managed to stay in touch though over the years. Whenever I'd come home for the holidays or semester breaks, he'd be right there at the terminal to pick me up, always with a different honey on his arm. He opted to stay local and went to Essex County College. There was no way you could get that boy to leave the hood. He was always too afraid he might miss something, not that there was much to miss.

I remember the day before I left for college; Jamal threw me the wildest party I'd ever been to. He booked this spot we used to go to called Club 88 up in East Orange. It must've been a private party because it was wall-to-wall Weequahic section. Everybody we knew came out to see me off. I didn't have to buy a drink the entire night. And since Jamal knew a lot of honeys, there was food everywhere. But that's how Jamal was when it came to me. He was always trying to have a good time, and he saw to it that I did too. His motto was, *"You only live once."* I couldn't have asked for better friends.

For my bachelor party, Shawn had rented a hotel suite. My boys had the bubbly poppin' and all the food you could imagine. I knew right away that Jamal had a lot to do with all of this. There was even a live DJ on the one-and-two's. It has to be at least fifty of us up in here. We got real *nice*, not drunk, that was for minors and there's a difference. We were grown and sexy at this stage in our lives. And we most definitely looked the part. After about an hour of eating, drinking, shit talking and reminiscing, the show was about to begin.

I don't know where they found these women, but I'm damn sure glad they did. These strippers have the best bodies I'd witnessed in a long time—that down-south booty, big ole country titties, fish and Grits thighs. Their bodies are whole, substantive. Now both Shawn and Jamal knew that I do not like any stick figures so they hooked a brother up. Word!

In walk these five thick, gorgeous women. I look over at Jamal, and he winks at me with a devilish smirk on his face. I'm sure the girls had their weave game going, but it was cool for tonight. I'm not complaining but I'm a natural man myself. I don't particularly care for running my fingers through tracks. No big deal, just my preference.

This one girl, Chyna, I'll just say *dayum*. She stood out from all the rest. She had the kind of ass that you could see from the front. Nice, round, phat, caramelized ass, just the way a big boy like me likes them. The string riding up the crack of her ass seemed to disappear as if it had just flown through the Bermuda Triangle.

Those big breasts in my face, and those asses I smack all night long, seriously have a brother worked up. But nothing would prepare me for what I am about to witness. And then Shawn grabs the mic.

"I want to thank you all for coming out and representin' for my man Khalil tonight." He holds up a glass of champagne and continues with his speech.

"Yo, K. We love you man, and we wish you a lifetime of happiness." Shawn jesters to the girls. "Now that we got that out the way…Ladies...do ya thang."

"Hold up! Hold up a minute, y'all." Jamal takes the mic from Shawn and staggers to the forefront. He always has to make himself known. He has a glass in each hand and takes a sip from both, then raises them in the air.

"Yo dawg. I just wanna say…that no matter what you do…or who you do it with, we'll always be boys," Jamal says into the mic. "Forget about jumping that broom tomorrow and focus on tonight. This one's for you, baby!"

As soon as Jamal leaves the center of the room, all five girls form a circle around me. They begin shaking their breasts and asses in my face. I immediately am rock hard. Damn! Then they begin to dwindle away onto the other guys. But Chyna and one of the other women stay on me. I'm sipping on my Chevaz Regal when one of them whispers in my ear.

"Khalil, we hear you got some secrets. Is that true?" I look at these two gorgeous creatures like they were crazy and almost choke on my drink.

"Oh yeah? What secret is that?" Chyna came right in my face.

"Don't be shy Khalil," Chyna says seductively through fire engine red lips.

"We know all about your fantasies."

I chuckle. Could they know? Could they really know about my secret desires? No way! Alright, man, breathe easy. It's just a bachelor party. Besides, who could have told them? I play along with their little game.

"Alright ladies, indulge me."

Indulge…they did. Chyna put the other one's face in her hands. I think her name was Eva. They kiss slowly and passionately in front of me. I was already hard but now I'm *swollen.*

"Oh shit!" I look at Shawn. He smiles and nods his head. I look over at Jamal who is front and center to see the performance. Then he yells at me across the room.

"Yeah baby! Get yours!" All I could do is smile. All the rest of the guys realize what is going down and stop what they were doing. They all just stare with their mouths open. These women are not just attractive. They are H. O. T. to death and could turn any man on.

Suddenly, the room gets quiet. Then the DJ, as if on cue, puts on T-Pain's *I'm in Love with a Stripper.* The bass echoes throughout the room and makes the floor vibrate. Eva and Chyna begin kissing. Everybody in the room goes nuts and throws money at our live entertainment. Eva turns. Her back is to Chyna and she slowly bends over in front of her. Chyna rubs her right ass cheek and then smacks that beautiful caramelized booty in my face.

If you're drinking, it'll make you dizzy. Oh, Amber is going to get it tomorrow. Imagine how backed up I'd be by morning. Chyna starts to grind on Eva's ass and reaches down to play with her nipples through her bra-like rhinestone top. They then get on the floor and put on a show I will never forget. Chyna licks Eva from her belly button to her breast and pulls her bra off with her teeth. She starts sucking her nipples to the beat of the song. I'd swear this shit must have

17

been rehearsed. Chyna takes her hand and starts playing with Eva's clit. *Right in front of me!* Eva reciprocates to my delight. And for the grand finale-Chyna straddles herself over Eva's face. Eva licks and devours her pussy, right there! In the flesh! In fucking Technicolor for all of us to see! Shit, is it live or fucking Memorex? It is such a visual turn on. I will definitely be jacking off tonight. I sing along with the music. Yo, I'm souped up, for real! My boys really got this shit off tonight.

Jamal comes over to refresh my drink. "You good, baby?" He yells over the music.

"Man Jamal, y'all really did big things here. Word up, y'all got this shit off!" I say with a big-ass-I-ain't-no-good grin.

"Well baby boy, I'm glad you enjoyin' yaself. But I got sumthin' else in the back I think you might like. That is...if you game." The look Jamal has on his face, I've seen many times. Too many times. I couldn't even ask what the hell he is talking about. I am tempted but afraid to even go there. Knowing Jamal, some gutter shit is about to pop off.

"Naaah, man, I'm not fuckin' with you. I'm gonna sit my drunk ass right here and enjoy this show," I tell him.

"Aaiight man. But if you scared, say you scared." Jamal laughs and walks away, disappearing into the crowd.

After the girl-on-girl show, I get up to take a leak. By now, all the guys in the room are grinding on the girls and singing along with T-Pain. I didn't realize how fucked up I was until I stood up. Everything and everybody is spinning around except for me. I don't know who it is but somebody helps me to the bathroom. Thank God for that person or else I probably would have pissed in my pants.

When I finally stagger back to the show, it was over and some of the other brothers had gone into private corners with the strippers to handle business. I start looking for Shawn so we could leave. He is the designated driver, and I am ready to bounce so I can lay down and get some sleep. I'm getting married in the morning. And I hadn't been this fucked up since college. I find Jamal instead and ask him where Shawn is.

"Oh, Shawn back here, Khalil," he responds while leading me to the bedroom. When I open the door, Chyna and Eva are waiting for me, all oiled down with nothing but those opened-toed stilettos on. Jamal quickly pushes me in the room and closes the door behind me. I lose my stance and fall on the bed.

They immediately start to undress me. I'm like, "Hold up, I'm getting married tomorrow."

"But you're not married now," Chyna says while sticking her tongue in my ear. Flashbacks of their previous show play in my head.... in slow motion. I'm in love with a stripper. I can still hear the song playing in the other room. Couple that with the many drinks that were constantly being refreshed, forces my dogism to the forefront and now it was on and poppin'.

They take turns taking my dick into their mouths and giving me the best professional I'd ever dreamed of. Sucking my dick simultaneously, as if they were dehydrated and trying to drink water. Two sets of wet lips, kissing, licking, sucking on my balls, down my shaft, the head, it some good-ass "bomb head." What really fucks my head up is when Eva puts a condom on my big toe and starts riding it. Yo! This bitch has got my foot in her pussy.

I start to laugh because I've never seen any shit like this before. Fuck man. I have never done any shit like this before. This shit is crazy.

Chyna puts a condom on the head of my dick. She unrolls it with her mouth without using any hands. She takes me all the way down like a champ. Then she straddles me backwards and mounts me. I'm fucking the shit out this broad. My thrusts in and out of her seem to repeat in slow motion. The visual of her pink pussy spread apart while moving up and down on my brown pipe makes me crazy. Couple that with Eva's face in Chyna's pussy while she rides me makes it impossible for me to hold on any longer.

The vision of all this ass is my face, jiggling, and shining, makes me wonder why white men love them some skinny white women, when shit like this is right here for the taking. I smack Chyna on her thigh. Although I have a condom on, one can never be too cautious.

"Aaiight baby, I'm there. Get up." I'm ready to explode. Chyna obliges with sweat gleaming from her forehead and says, "Let me get that for you."

She really messes my head up when she takes off the condom. I don't know why, but I don't even try to stop her. I can't imagine that she's about to let me release in her mouth, but that's exactly what she does. And....she keeps the change. I'm trippin' right now. In the midst of pure pleasure, I say to her, "Yeah, baby. Get your swallow on."

Chyna looks up at me with my juices sliding down her chin, swallow, and replies, "What?"

"You know, make it good to the last drop," I explain. Chyna and Eva laugh.

When it is all over and my high is coming down, I feel guilty as sin. I lay there in that big bed, covered in sweat, lube, and pussy juice, and flashback on all the times I did some real dirty shit behind Amber's back.

But just like Jamal always says...You only live once, right? *I'm in love with a stripper...*

Amber

Collard Greens

I pretty much feel that I am a genuine person at heart. I sincerely do. But certain types of people bring out the best and the worst in me. For example, my friends such as Shawn or my family such as Olivia bring out the best in me. However, some of Khalil's family, especially *Momz* as he so eloquently refers to her, brings out my inner bitch. Lord knows I've tried, for years in fact, to get along with this woman. She ain't trying to hear it. She'd rather see Khalil with some ebony princess, or probably even herself. Sometimes I wonder if she's really in love with her own son. Mrs. Devereaux. Mrs. Athena Devereaux definitely has some issues with color. I'm not dark enough, my hair isn't kinky enough, my eyes are too light, and I'm too tall. What else could she think of?

Khalil told me a long time ago how his mother felt about me. I really don't understand his reasoning. Would the information bring me closer to her? I don't think so.

I'm five-nine and can't do anything about it. My eyes are light, yes. My skin is like rich honey and my hair is what it is. It's a shame really. When I look in magazines, I know I am not the typical image that today's society deems beautiful. Now I've got to tolerate the *I'm-not-good-enough* vibe from one of my own. Where does it end? I credit her issues to the fact that probably no one will ever be good enough for her son. But still, her words sometime sting and cut deep.

While I admire the relationship Khalil has with his mother, it sometimes bothered me that he allowed her to manipulate almost every decision he made. Nothing is more attractive to me than a man who loves and respects his mother. You don't see that quality too often in men nowadays. I think it disappeared somewhere along with chivalry and monogamy, which is why I love the fact that Khalil has his mother on a pedestal. But *dayum*, gimme a break. There is a phrase called *taking the tittie out of your mouth*. It took me a long time to make Khalil understand that there was a way he could respect both his mother's wishes and mine without causing conflict. She just had to learn to follow her own spiritual advice: *Let go...And let God.*

I still had a couple days off from Divine Intervention left over from our honeymoon so I had some "me" time to bask in the ambiance of being Mrs. Khalil Devereaux before sharing it with the outside world.

I have time to reflect on my past and focus on my future. *"I's a married now,"* echoes through my head as I stare at my ring. It puts me in the mindset of that character, Shug, in *The Color Purple*, who's showing off her ring to her father as he rides by on the horse. Yes, I have definitely come a long way. Eight years ago, no one could have ever made me believe that some day I'd be Mrs. Khalil Devereaux. *Mrs. Khalil Devereaux.* I keep saying it to myself as if it's not real.

Eight years ago, I'd experienced the worst pain known to mankind. My heart was ripped from my chest and stomped on without warning and without refrain. A surgical procedure performed without anesthesia that left a scar the size of the Grand Canyon. I was wide-awake for what I like to refer to as my soul being put to death. It was the kind of pain that I wouldn't wish on my worst enemy. *Can't eat, can't sleep, can't breathe, and can't focus on anything else but the pain* kind of hurt. A single tear rolls down my cheek as I reflect on the past, which lets me know that although I've forgiven, I have not forgotten. But that was eight years ago. I wipe my tear away and focus on today.

Today I am a beautiful, healthy woman of thirty with a fulfilling career, a loving family, true friends, and damn sure strong in my spot. Today I am Mrs. Khalil Devereaux. My tears are suddenly replaced with a smile as I watch my ring sparkle against the rays of sunshine that are escaping through my bay window blinds. I walk over to the window and draw the blinds back to let the sunshine in and notice that Khalil is already outside waiting for me. I suddenly realize that I've got to put a cease and desist order on my journey down memory lane to prepare for our rendezvous with Khalil's family.

I am so glad I don't have to rush back to Divine Intervention. I love my job. I really do, and I always wanted to work there even when I was in college. Ever since I was a little girl, I'd always wanted to be a nurse. It was my life's goal, my passion. It was cool to settle in from the honeymoon and not have to go right back to work. I loved all of my patients, which is a no-no in medicine, but my heart and my head tell me two different things at times.

I enjoy seeing Khalil relax too. He made some nice lightweight paper a few years back when he closed a commercial deal. Now, he's getting his feet real wet in the consulting business. Newark has taken such growth in the past few years and many people are starting businesses and various entities right here. He has seen that and has successfully jumped on the bandwagon. He can talk his way in and out of any situation. He has a gift. His consulting firm should be called a *"get in where I fit in"* firm, because that's what he does.

I look at Khalil as he drives us to his Momz house. I'm in the passenger seat, chillin', listening to my girl, Jill Scott. *Beautifully Human.* It takes a beautiful woman to write such poignant songs. Her lyrics are heavenly. She brings a new dimension to the music world. She emotes a visceral reaction…not sampled tracks and misogynistic lyrics. Totally refreshing.

You don't hear originality in music too often anymore, except for the superstars that are obviously truly talented. Everyone seems to be so caught up in what the next person is doing that most artists' identities are aliases. Jill Scott brings something new and inviting to the table. You can tell she's not just caught up with entertaining her listeners, but she is actually involved with her music and wholeheartedly loving what she's singing about. I cross my legs, close my eyes and put my head back against the headrest. I'm smiling inside and wishing I could feel this way forever. Eight years was a long time ago.

"Damn baby. You still got that honeymoon glow to you. You are so sexy," Khalil says waking me from my thoughts.

"Why, thank you Mr. Devereaux," I respond and open my eyes and gaze into his dark brown eyes. *Sexy ass.*

"No, thank *you* Amber. You mean so much to me," Khalil says as he grabs my hand and kisses it. "I'm so glad you agreed to be my wife. I know I've hurt you in the past and now it's my chance to treat you as the honorable woman you are. I've come to realize a lot of things now and I thank you for giving me the opportunity to serve you. To be a good man to you. You deserve it."

I know Khalil is sincere in his words, his delivery of them even. I had been through a lot with him, yes. But again, eight years is a long time ago. Momma always taught me to forgive. Not so much for Khalil, but for myself. We've matured. He has definitely matured. Once you turn thirty, you get a new perspective on life. Well, at least some of us do. Like I said, some of us do.

We pull up to Mrs. Devereaux's house in Irvington. She's got a nice little place. She's been working for the city for so long; I know she's making a nice living. As Khalil parks the car, I think to myself, *Oh Lord, here we go.*

Here comes Kiana. Kiana, Khalil's younger sister, is twenty-seven years old and a reformed crack head. Well Khalil tells me she is reformed. Just in case, I close my purse and keep it right by my side at all times. The last time we had her at the house, it just so happened that my Donna Karan watch, my diamond earrings, and my platinum bracelet all decided to grow legs simultaneously and walk out the door. By sheer coincidence, Kiana was there the same day my stuff decided to go out for a stroll. I confronted Khalil about it. His response was, "Nah Amber, Kiana is strung out, but she don't do that to family." Yeah, ok. She's a selective chicken head. That was the most delusional statement I'd heard in a long time.

My goodness, there's Whiteboy. Yep, I said it. Whiteboy! That's what everyone calls him. Whiteboy is Kiana's on-again, off-again boyfriend. Ain't nothing like two crack heads in love. I imagine Kiana sucking on that glass dick and then sucking on his white one. The thought makes me laugh out loud. There's nothing funny about drug abuse, Lord knows I'd seen enough of it amongst family and friends, but this time, I just couldn't help myself. Through the grace of God, neither of their kids had come into the world affected by their drug abuse. At least there were no signs as of yet.

Kiana runs to the car. "Hey y'all!" She beams at us. Her face, however, is drawn in and a few teeth are gone. After so many years of *gettin' blazed, it has affected her looks.* From the pictures I'd seen, she used to be a pretty girl. But those days were long gone. Yes, the streets definitely had a way of leaving its mark if you allowed it. As she's smiling through the window on my side, I am reminiscent of Pookie from *New Jack City.* Sort of looked as if she'd been chewing on rocks. *Brush your teeth, please.*

We have come to his Momz house to drop off souvenirs from the honeymoon. I pray that we will only make an appearance and go. I'm in a serene state of mind and am not yet ready for it to end.

But Khalil also wants to see his nieces, Kiana's twins, Candelabra and Chandelier. Yes, I said it! Candelabra and Chandelier but everyone calls them Candy and Chandy. Nobody has time to be saying all that shit. They are turning one on Saturday. Khalil adores them, and I have grown pretty fond of them as well. They are very pretty little girls too. Short and plump with the thickest black hair. Looked like little chocolate baby dolls with rich, dark skin almost like whipped cocoa.

But *dayum*, Candelabra and Chandelier? What was Kiana thinking about? Did she have some sort of fetish for candles and light fixtures? Do people understand that what they name their children will stay with them for the rest of their lives, ultimately becoming their identities? Do they understand that their kids will never take on positions of power in this world with God-awful names like that?

Oh wait, let me take that back. I immediately think of Condoleezza Rice. Damn shame is all I can say. I know in this day and age, us folks name our children whatever we damn well please but Kiana must've found a way to sneak some last minute crack into the hospital after she had the twins. One last snort before she filled out the information for the birth certificates. Maybe she's a Liberace fan. Actually, I think Whiteboy may have had some influence in naming the girls. Damn shame is all I can say.

Khalil steps out of the car and greets "Pookie." Ok, let me be nice. "Hey baby sis." He greets her with a smile.

"Wassup big brother?" She runs up to Khalil and embraces him as if she hasn't seen him in years. "My big brother done got married! I can't believe it!"

Then she releases him and turns to face me. "Oh God, Hey Amber!" She gives me a hug.

"Hey, Kiana," I say and politely hug her back.

"I'm so happy for you, girl!" She squeals. "Oooh let me see this rock again."

She finally allows me to breathe by releasing her hold on me and takes my hand. She's so dramatic all the time. Everything always has to be so *extra* with this girl. I swear she could have won an Oscar for her award-winning performance today.

"Look at this ring! Damn, girl!" She yells pulling my hand to her face, "Two-and-a-half karats set in platinum? You must've been puttin' it on my brother sumthin' serious."

She releases my hand and gives me a look. "And look at you girl, ooooohh! What did you lose, about one-hundred pounds?"

"Something like that," I respond, thinking, *Can you say overkill?*

"Well whatever it was, you look good girl. Whiteboy, come over here and look at this rock. This jus' the kinda ring I want when we get married." *Yeah right*, I think to myself. The girl even dreams big. *And the nominees are...*

Here comes Bigfoot. I swear she could join the UniverSoul Circus as the bearded slave, the new character in their lineup.

"Oh look at my baby. My son done growned up." *Growned up?*

"Hi Amber, I see you've got a tan."

Here we go with the complexion thing again. I smile and say, "Hi, Mrs. Devereaux."

"Y'all come on in and get some food. I cooked your favorite baby." *Oh no, not those collard greens again.* Tasted like she took those greens straight from the ground and put them directly into the pot. *Whoa.*

Kiana, a.k.a. "Pookie" takes my hand as we walk into the house. I have to make jokes to get through this. I call *Momz's* house the "Thunderdome." It's wild. As I step in, I see that she hasn't changed a thing since the last time I'd been here. Actually, it looks like she hasn't changed anything since 1974. The burnt orange shag carpet is still in full effect. The cream-colored pleather sofa and love seat with the plastic covering still stands strong. The fake fireplace equipped with artificial fire log looks like no one has dusted it since Jesus wept. I get through the living room without cracking a smile or a comment, and for that I am grateful.

Kiana looks at me, and smiles. "Amber, you look so beautiful. Now that you're skinny, I see why Khalil hurried up and threw this rock on your finger. You always did have a pretty face so I guess he knew the niggas would be comin' for you real hard."

BITCH! I think, but with a comment like that coming from a crack head, you just can't take anything personally. *Wasn't she just at the wedding?* Maybe she doesn't remember it!

"Thanks Kiana," I reply quickly enough hoping she'll stop her drama but she keeps talking.

"Amber, we are like, really sisters now, right? I mean, with you marrying my brother and all, I can say you're my sister. And that means, if Whiteboy and me get married, you'll be Whiteboy's sister too. That is so hot." And she just keeps talking, "Word up! Now you are officially Candy and Chandy's aunt."

Needless to say, the look on my face was one of astonishment when I listened to her last statement. Whiteboy's sister? To say the least, being Whiteboy's sister was not something that I thought was "hot." I kept it nice with Kiana and Whiteboy, but I didn't trust them to save my own soul. I often wondered how Whiteboy made his way to Irvington, New Jersey. I guess crack will take you places.

Kiana still has a hold of my hand as she walks me into the dining room for our meal. Why doesn't this girl let my hand go? I hope to God she's not trying to slide my ring off. I suddenly wiggle my hand free and head for the dining table. *Oh boy, can't wait to get to those greens.* As the "Bearded Bigfoot" serves the meal, she asks Khalil to say a prayer. Khalil grins from ear to ear and I look at him with admiration. I'm so proud of the man he's become. Khalil clears his throat.

"Dear Heavenly Father, we ask that you bless this food and the hands that prepared it. We ask, Dear Lord, that you forgive our sins so that our prayers may be heard. Dear God, bless the people gathered in this room today, breaking bread with one another. Lord, I thank you for blessing me with my wife, Amber…"

The clearing of his mother's throat interrupts Khalil. He pauses momentarily and looks at his mother, then looks at me. He continues. "Lord, thank you for my wife Amber. Without her constant love, I don't know where I'd be. We ask that you cover us in your precious blood. In Jesus name we pray, Amen." We all say "Amen." When Khalil's done praying, he sits beside me and leans in close.

"I love you so much, Mrs. Devereaux." At that moment he wraps his arms around me and kisses me more passionately than he did when we said, *I do.* We hear the sound of his mother clearing her throat again but we don't care. Only a surgeon could have removed my tongue from dancing around in his mouth right now. This is my husband, and to hell with anyone who has a problem with that. I am Mrs. Devereaux now so "Momz" is just going to have to learn how to share that title. She has no choice.

Shawn
New York City

"You know what Aaliyah?"

"What honey?"

"I am so happy that we're here in New York. I think it was a good move for us," I tell her, "The pace is faster. More work for you and definitely big thangs poppin' for me. I get to chill with my mans-n-em more often. Now, we just gotta get you some women to hang out with."

"Yes baby, I agree."

"It is a good move for my career and yours. Khalil is cool, too. It's nice that you both have been the best of friends for this long. I'm looking forward to getting to know Amber. She seems really sweet. Khalil got him a good woman. And she is beautiful."

When I hear Aaliyah's words, I get a feeling deep, down within. Amber *is* beautiful. She is a warm spirit, a kind soul. Her beauty both physically and spiritually is empowering. She's modest about it too, which makes her more attractive. It was my shoulder she'd cry on back in college when Khalil slipped up.

I'd never seen any woman I know experience that kind of hurt before except for my mother. When my dad left when I was eight, my mom totally shut down. I didn't understand until I got older why she cried all the time. I realize now that most of her tears were shed for me.

Every dime my father sent to us, my mom made sure she spent on me. Haircuts, clothes, sneakers, school trips and anything else I needed. She took on two jobs just to pay the rent and keep a roof over my head and food in my stomach. It took her a long time to return to the outside world. A long time passed before she started to focus on herself again.

When Amber went through her ordeal behind Khalil and Shayla, I kind of knew what she was going through. Although I'll never be able to relate to what a woman feels when she experiences that kind of betrayal, I can honestly say it's nothing I ever want to endure.

Amber would skip classes and just talk to me for hours. She'd cry in my arms. She simply asked "Why?" over and over again. I never had an answer. We became so close during that time.

Khalil was going crazy, too. He'd beg and plead with her just to talk. Amber would have none of that. She felt there was nothing to talk about. He began using me to get messages to her. After a while I'd stop passing the messages. She reacted the same each time. She'd just bawl and look for lifelines I couldn't give her.

I felt so bad for her during that time. I eventually told Khalil to back off and give her space. And now, here I am eight years later, going through my own personal guilt about the bachelor party.

I knew, everyone knew, that Khalil had always fantasized about being a voyeur and witnessing two women to suck each other off, right in front of him. I mean, what man doesn't relish the thought? I have in my day. But with Khalil, it was different. It was sort of like an obsession for him.

I remember our college days. We hooked up and became the best of friends. Khalil and I were in a special program for gifted African Americans. We could basically go to school, earn our degrees for nearly half the tuition. This made life easier for the both of us. If it weren't for the program, neither one of us would have been able to attend.

Khalil and I met in our dorm room that we were assigned to. We remained roommates for all four years. Every night, me, Khalil, and some other guys would get together to get our study on. Every night, however, we ended up talking about women, busting nuts, ass and getting some "bomb head" jobs from wherever we could find it. The conversation always shifted to girls on girls.

One night in particular, Khalil, a little drunk from an early happy hour, informed us. "Yo man, I'm telling you. I'm ready to see some freaks eat each other out, right in front of me." His eyes glazed. "Can you imagine? Two fine, red-boned honeys just digging each other out?"

"Damn Khalil, you's a horny mutha fucka!" I laughed and tossed an old, funky gym sock at him.

"Shut up Shawn," he said getting serious, "You know you think about it. Don't be frontin' like you don't."

"Yeah Khalil, we all think about it, but damn, every night?" I said trying to keep the mood light.

"Well, I'm going to get me two women one day. They gonna sex each other out. Then they are going to get served while they are serving me. That's wassup!"

I'll never forget those words that came out of Khalil's mouth. So when Jamal called me with the idea of having two females do their thing at the bachelor party, I was down. It was his special time, and I wanted my man to be happy. But I never expected Khalil to fuck them. All they were supposed to do was fuck each other in front of him.

I should have known that Jamal was up to something. I saw him whispering to Chyna and Eva and giving them more money when they came in. All the girls had been paid already. If I hadn't been preoccupied with the lap dance I was getting, I would have seen Khalil going in that room and it wouldn't have gone down like that.

When I finally realized Khalil was nowhere around, I asked Jamal where he was. Jamal told me Khalil was laying down, wasted, in the bedroom. When I went to check on him, I heard the sounds of fucking through the door.

Damn. That's all I could say to myself before opening the door. I know my man is not going out like this. I opened the door and all I saw was my man living out his fantasy. One girl's tits in his mouth and his dick in another one's ass. I quickly closed the door and went to find Jamal. Jamal, however, knew what time it was and was long gone. He knew Khalil was ripped and that there was no way in hell Khalil could've fought that shit.

I felt real fucked up about it. Torn even. I knew that the girl on girl episode would make Khalil so happy, but now I was concerned with what this would do to Amber. Amber didn't deserve this. I hope she never finds out, because I'm not sure if their marriage could survive it.

"Hey, Shawn. Why don't we call Khalil and Amber and see what they're doing tonight?" Aaliyah interrupts my thoughts of guilt.

"Aaliyah, that's a good idea. I know they should've settled in from the honeymoon by now."

"Yeah, I'm sure Amber got her back blown out on their cruise. I know Khalil was happy to give her some quality pipe with how beautiful she looked at the wedding."

Why would Aaliyah say that? Hmm, I wasn't sure. I guess she feels comfortable enough to say it. Who knows? I head to the phone.

"Hello?" I hear Khalil's voice on the phone.

"Wassup, baby?"

"Yo, what da deal, Shawn?"

"Wassup with you and Amber tonight? Aaliyah thought it would be a good idea for all of us to get into something."

"Cool, I'll tell Amber we'll be hanging with you tonight. Let's meet at Delta's around seven. Cool?"

"That's cool, Khalil, but you've got the truck so why don't we all just ride together?" "No problem, man, I'll call when I'm on my way."

"Hold on Shawn, I want to make sure Amber's not around," he says and I can imagine him checking out the room. "Yo Shawn, how did you meet Aaliyah?" Khalil lowered his voice.

"Why you ask, man?" I ask not sure where this conversation is going.

"Just asking 'cause she looks familiar. Where is she from?" I sigh and say. "Khalil, promise me you won't get mad?"

"Aaiight Shawn, yeah, I'm listening."

"Shayla introduced me to Aaliyah."

Disgustingly Khalil replies, "C'mon Shawn man, wassup with that?"

"Khalil, Lexis is my God daughter and I do check in on her every now and then. Shayla briefly worked at this modeling agency as a receptionist through some sort of temp agency. She called me one day to tell me that Lexis needed fifty dollars for something at school. I agreed to drop it off. When I got to the agency, Shayla was at the front desk. Aaliyah just happened to walk by and the rest is history. Man, I couldn't take my eyes off her. So in true Shayla fashion, she noticed my interest and introduced us. We've been dating ever since."

"Aaiight Shawn, I see. It's all good. Thanks for taking the money to her." I hear relief in his voice.

"Khalil, you my man. You know I got your back, always brother."

"I know Shawn, I know. You just made a brother nervous, that's all. Here I am trying to figure out where I know this girl from and now you tell me you met her through Shayla."

"So where do you think you know her from?" I pressed.

"I don't know, maybe I don't know her, and maybe I know someone that looks like her. Shit, man, maybe it's nothing. Where did you say she was from again?"

"She's from Virginia."

"Virginia? Did she go to school with us?"

"Naaah, man, she didn't go there. Maybe you saw her around or something though. Remember, she is a model."

"Yeah maybe that's what it is, but I swear I've seen her somewhere before."

"Well she didn't come off like she knew you at all. As a matter of fact, she didn't know Shayla either, except in passing."

"Yeah aaight Shawn, I just wish you would have told me about *how* you met her, *when* you met her. We talk all the time, how did you manage to leave out something as important as that? All you told me about her before the wedding was that you were fucking some hottie," he says still a little pissed.

"Khalil, Listen. If it's any consolation, they are not friends or anything like that. They just worked together. And they didn't really *know* each other except hi and bye. Just coincidence Khalil. That's all."

"Hey man, let me go check on Amber. She's on the toilet. You know *Momz's* greens! Amber loves them just like me. She can't get enough. So she's on the toilet now. I told her *Momz's* greens ain't going anywhere!"

"Alright Khalil, I'll catch you later."

"Alright Shawn, tell Aaliyah I said…Wassup!"

Now Khalil knows good and damn well that his momma's greens tastes like grass. She can't cook. *What's wrong with that boy?*

Amber

Dance with me Baby

It is so nice to go out with Shawn and Aaliyah. The ride over to the city is filled with laughter and mostly Shawn and Khalil reminiscing about the past. We have the best time at dinner. Delta's is a hot spot in downtown New Brunswick, New Jersey. Candles dimly light the restaurant with great jazz music in the background. The best soul food that you can get in a one-hundred-mile radius. The kind of food your momma makes. It's good as hell. The staff, the atmosphere, and delicious food makes Delta's our favorite place to eat. I feel as if I've stepped into the scene of a really classy movie. I expect to get on stage any minute and rock the mic with some dope Jessica Care Moore type poetry. Me fantasizing again. The place is hot, the evening, even spicier.

Shawn looks at me from across the table. It's not just a look of joy that he's happy to be with his best friends. It's a look I can't quite figure out, but I think maybe its just pride. Proud that I've finally got a smile on my face and that I'm doing so well. I guess. I can sense that as much. On the other hand, each time I go to take a sip of my apple martini, Aaliyah is right in my grill. Maybe the two of them are just "lookers."

I signal the waitress to bring us another round of martinis. Khalil and I have some cash left over from our wedding gifts, so I am unafraid to splurge a bit. We truly do have the best friends and family anyone could ask for. Most of our wedding gifts haven't even been opened yet.

The first card we did open at our reception was from my mother and father. I remember the envelope it was in was so beautiful that I didn't want to open it. It was made of white satin and had the prettiest lavender chiffon ribbons wrapped around it. *To Mr. and Mrs. Khalil Devereaux* was stitched in lavender on the envelope. I had no idea it was from mommy until I opened it. No sooner had I opened the card to read it, that a single piece of paper fell to the floor. A check written in the amount of five-thousand dollars brought tears to both our eyes. I know how hard my parents had worked to be able to present a gift like this.

I can't forget about Scott's gift. Not only did he perform for free but also he gave Khalil and I an all expense paid trip to Cancun. And we'd be staying in a five-star hotel. The best part about it was we had two years to use it. We got so many nice things, I can't think of them all right now, but we really were lucky to have people in our lives that loved us so.

But the biggest surprise came from Khalil's mother. I'd expected she'd give us something like some of her collard greens, but nothing that I'd shout from the heavens about. I was wrong. An eigthteen-by-twenty picture frame made of platinum with diamond cuts around the sides. It was the most beautiful frame I'd ever seen in my entire life. The detailing on the frame was so exquisite, I gasped for air the moment I removed it from the box. It hangs just above our mantle in the living room, of course with our wedding photo inside. Yes, the Bearded Bigfoot really did surprise me with that one.

"Amber, one more drink and girl, I am done for the night," Aaliyah tells me. She did have three martinis so far and I ain't too far behind. I am just finishing number two. Ooh, I seem to be really feeling it right now.

The place is so dim, the music so soothing, the drinks-so syrupy sweet and powerful. This is my kind of scene. A mature crowd that is more concerned with having a good time than figuring about who they can rob once the place closes. Everyone is dressed to impress and looks so erotic. No white tees or hoodies at this spot. As live jazz plays, small tables set up in the most romantic way surround the band.

Each table is donned with a centerpiece and candles and encircled by black leather sofas. It's sort of like restaurant booths, which call for a most comfortable evening. A few lovebirds are out on the dance floor slow dancing to a beautiful rendition of one of Joe Thomas' classics, *Let Me Be The One You Love*. Mmmmm, I love this song. So relaxing, so sexy even. I glance at my husband and notice that he's just finishing the last of his buffalo wings. And those are his appetizer. His main course is fried whiting, macaroni and cheese, and cabbage with a side of candied yams and potato salad, fresh-squeezed lemonade and cornbread. Damn, my baby can eat. My head is swirling from the martinis I've had but it's a nice swirl.

I place my hand on his and ask him in the most seductive way. "Dance with me baby?"

"My pleasure, Mrs. Devereaux. Excuse us guys," Khalil says, takes me by the hand, and leads me to the dance floor. He wraps his strong arms around me and places his hands just above my ass. I lay my head on his shoulder and we dance to the music. Mmmm, his Versace cologne smells so good, I could eat him right here on this dance floor. I feel so safe in his arms. I know that this is where I'm supposed to be, in his arms. It seems like everyone has disappeared and we are the only two people left in the world. I whisper in his ear. "I love you K."

Without saying a word, Khalil begins caressing my neck with soft, gentle kisses, which eventually lead to my lips. Our feet stop moving and our tongues pick up where we left off, dancing to the beat of the drummer. His hands find their way to my ass as he rubs and squeezes it as only he could do.

We finally come up for air when Khalil takes my head in his hands and looks deep into my eyes. "I'm the happiest man in the world, Amber. Please don't ever leave me."

"I won't K." Shawn clearing his throat and tapping Khalil on his shoulder interrupts our mental love making. "Excuse me brother, may I cut in?" Shawn has the sexiest smile on his face. I chuckle at how he plays with Khalil like this. Aaliyah, who is also there and standing next to him, is looking at me with a smile on her face as well.

"C'mon Khalil, let Amber breathe," Aaliyah says gently pulling his arm. "I'll keep you company while my man borrows your wife."

We switch partners and continue dancing. Shawn smells good, too.

"What's that you're wearing, Shawn?"

"I don't know Amber. I've got so much shit on my dresser. I just picked up a bottle and sprayed."

"Boy you are a nut." I hit Shawn on his arm and laugh.

"Yeah, I know. So how are you doing Amber?"

"I'm fine Shawn."

"Yes, you are definitely *fine* girl, but that's not what I meant. How are you really doing?"

I laugh. Shawn has become so overprotective of me since we were in college. He took on the role of the brother I never had. He was a friend to me when I needed one most and for that, I am forever grateful. We formed an unbreakable bond back then. A bond that most people don't understand, but it suits Shawn and I just fine.

"Shawn, I'm good. Really, I am. I'm happy. I'm in love. And I couldn't ask for much more than this."

"Ok, baby girl, just checking. You let me know if you need me for anything, ok?

"I will Shawn. I promise."

I kiss him on the cheek and we head back over to our booth. Khalil and Aaliyah are already there.

Aaliyah leans in toward the middle of our booth to make sure everyone hears her.

"So guys, what's next? The night's still young."

Khalil had already started eating again and Shawn begins to help himself to some of Khalil's food.

"Not sure, Aaliyah," Shawn says, "But I do know I want to finish this first."

"Ok, Shawn, no problem." Aaliyah puckers her lips to give Shawn a kiss on the cheek.

"So, Aaliyah, where are you from? Khalil quickly changes the subject.

"I'm from Virginia, born and raised."

"Oh yeah, what part?"

"Well Khalil, no disrespect intended, but I really don't like to discuss my childhood all that much," she tells us. "It wasn't a very fortunate time for me."

"Ok no problem, just trying to make conversation." Khalil looks up quickly from his yams, "Besides, I'll just ask Shawn later."

We all bust out laughing in unison.

Maybe it's the alcohol and my mood but I follow Aaliyah's lips in slow motion as they float through the air and land on Shawn's cheek, right beside his lips. I feel myself staring and I can't stop. It's an awkward moment. As she removes her lips from Shawn's cheek, Aaliyah follows me with her eyes and settles back into her seat.

The waitress brings our drinks. I feel like I need to take a break for a moment when Aaliyah takes my hand. She says, "Come on Amber. The guys don't want to dance anymore, so let's go get our groove on."

The music has changed to R&B by now so I guess a little dancing won't hurt. I reluctantly stand up. My hand still in hers. As we walk to the dance floor, I notice that black halter jumpsuit Aaliyah is wearing is tailored to perfection. She fills it in just right. Her curly hair, swooped to one side and flowing down her shoulders, gives her a dramatic, yet, seductive look. It's a Cover Girl moment.

We are almost at the dance floor when I realize that her jumpsuit is so low cut that she can't possibly have on any underwear.

We start dancing to one of Maxwell's joints from his first album. Aaliyah moves with grace and confidence, the grace and confidence that only a model can have. Everything happens in slow motion. Aaliyah leans in to me. Her lips brush my ear as she asks, "So, how was that sex on the honeymoon?"

I am shocked that she would ask such a personal question. But it's ok, I guess. She's just free-spirited in that way, I assume. Nice enough girl, so I answer. "It was da bomb, girl."

She slowly moves back and smiles. The look in her eyes was one of mystery. I can't figure it out. I do notice, however, that my panties are wet. Maybe it was the dance that Khalil and I shared. I know I also could have possibly leaked in them due to the dancing and drinking. My delayed response, most likely. I can't hold alcohol. I'm on the ride of my life, so I feel it appropriate to really have a good time.

"Aaliyah, I'm headed to the bathroom."

"Ok girl, I gotta go too." She follows me.

We walk to the bathroom. And boy is it crowded. Aaliyah stands in line as I rush to the first available stall. I come out and Aaliyah goes in. As I wash my hands, I look in the mirror, admiring how dazzling I am. I see Aaliyah coming out of the stall. She comes over to wash her hands also.

By this time, the bathroom is so packed; there are wall to wall women. We actually have to squeeze our way out. I lead the way with Aaliyah right behind me. Then these two big-boned girls block our path. I have to make a sudden stop, so as not to walk straight into them, Aaliyah accidentally runs right into me. We are pinned between the big girls and the sink. I can feel Aaliyah's breasts on my back, her hands on my hips and her leg on my ass. It's no big deal. She's only trying to brace herself.

She leans into my ear. Her lips brushing my ear again, "I'm sorry Amber. I didn't want to fall."

"It's all good Aaliyah. It's crowded as hell in here." Aaliyah's still in my ear.

"By the way, you smell great. What are you wearing?" She asks.

"White Diamonds."

She pulls back from me, but still has a lightly hold of my hips. I turn and see in the mirror Aaliyah briefly glancing at my ass.

Once we get back to our table, Shawn and Khalil are done pigging out. Damn, these two could get thrown out of an all-you-can-eat buffet. We decide it's time to leave so we gather our belongings and head to the truck.

There is nothing better than a late night ride to New York City. The air is clear and the stars are shining bright in the sky. The New York City skyline is almost magical at night.

I adjust the rear view mirror to check my makeup. I want to make sure I don't look a total mess. I see that Shawn is all over Aaliyah in the back seat. She, however, is staring at me with a smile on her face. I quickly readjust the mirror and sit back in my seat.

Khalil puts in John Legend's debut CD, making the ride home a perfect one. He drives all the way home using one hand, while holding my hand with his other. The atmosphere at the restaurant coupled with the martinis has made me horny. It will be on as soon as we get home. Unless I decide to make Khalil pull over.

Khalil
Big Poppa

Sunday evening at the Clarkes. My in-laws. Mother Clarke, with her beautiful mature face and grace would serve a feast on this lovely day. The dining room table is meticulously decorated with the finest linens and china. Silver platters of Fried chicken, yams, collard greens, biscuits, prime rib, string beans, macaroni and cheese, dumplings all make the décor lovelier. I feel like I'm in a good episode of *Soul Food* where the entire Joseph family comes together to break bread with one another.

As I look into Mother Clarke's eyes, I see the woman that I will be married to in thirty years. They say that, if you want to really know who you are married to, who your wife really is, take a look at her mother. If this is what I have in store, I can't ask for much more. Mother Clarke is simply stunning in her golden years. She keeps her figure right with a routine of daily walks and lots of green tea. Her skin is like that of warm butter. Her hair, radiant, silky and long, frames her warm, friendly face. She dispels the myth that when you reach a certain age, one should cut their hair to rid that youthful look. Her shiny, lustrous, jet-black silky hair, coupled with her honey skin, hazel-green-gray eyes, depending on the day, make her easy on the eyes. Her inner spirit, however, makes her angelic. I've truly lucked up with Amber and her family.

Olivia join us. Same beauty. Same spirit. She is focused and determined. It's truly admirable. As I look around this dining room, I imagine Amber and me living this good. The Clarke's five-bedroom estate in Montclair is an architectural masterpiece. Huge foyer, hard wood floors, ten-foot ceilings, wet bar, in-ground pool. My life's dream.

In my early years, I could have cared less about working hard enough to live like a king. Amber changed all of that for me. She's been so supportive, so caring, so trusting, so Mother Clarke-like. Don't get me wrong; our condo in Society Hill in Newark is fine. Just enough room for us two. Close to Penn Station and close to the New Jersey Turnpike, so we are able to travel without pause. It's good that we're not that far from Rutgers because Amber may want to go back to school for her Master's. She's got that Clarke family drive.

Mr. Clarke, on the other hand, is a no nonsense kind of man. He is strict and stern about what he expects from his girls. Two daughters and no sons sometimes have that effect on a guy. He loves his family with his right hand and maintains discipline with his left.

I admire Mr. Clarke in so many ways; I just wish he could feel the same way about me. I don't doubt that his shoulder was one of many that Amber cried on back in the day. But I've grown up since then.

Mr. Clarke stands six-foot-two inches. He towers a good eight plus inches over Mrs. Clarke, his wife of thirty plus years and probably five-foot-six with heels on. Mr. Clarke is the kind of man who makes sure his home is in perfect order, first, before he goes out into the world to do whatever it is that he does. I respect that. Thirty years is a long time to hold onto the kind of love Amber's family has. Thirty years is a long time to hold onto anything nowadays. It makes me proud to be a part of it.

I glance at Amber. She loves to come home and seems to submit to her inner child whenever she's around her father. She always seems so comfortable when she comes home. Even her laugh is different here. Any opportunity we get to visit, I tell myself that this is exactly the kind of love and family that I'm going to give to her. I don't have any control over the past, but I plan on dedicating my future to making Amber happy.

Mr. Clarke blesses the food. He's cool but I know he doesn't care for me very much and that's my fault. Just shit from the past, I guess he can't let it go. I plan to prove to him that I am good enough now for his daughter. I wonder sometimes if I had a father like Mr. Clarke, if I would've become a different man. My dad was in and out of my life, for most of my life. Always with different women, leaving my mom for months at a time. Always for some red-boned honey. When he got tired of playing the field, he'd come home. My momz would always take him back.

"We ask that you bless the hands that prepared this lovely meal. Father, we pray that you will forgive our sins so that I prayers are heard."

Mr. Clarke looks at me after the *forgiving our sins* part. Is he throwing hints? Nah, I'm just taking things too personally.

"Ok good people, let's eat!" Mr. Clarke sits at the head of the table. We all start to chit chat about the wedding and the honeymoon.

"So Amber, how was the cruise?" Olivia asks as she so delicately takes a fork full of macaroni and cheese and places it between those luscious lips of hers.

Sinful thoughts, I know. I follow her mouth along with the words that come out of it. Her lips are so tender, so full. I imagine her taking me slowly as her lips part, and I begin to swell in her mouth. Amber's response to Olivia's question takes me out of my trance immediately. *Damn, I've got to get my shit together.*

"It was great! There was so much to do. I had no idea I would enjoy a cruise so much!" Amber answered with so much sincerity. "The water in Ocho Rios, Jamaica makes the Jersey shores look like crap! But you know I love Seaside Heights! But nothing compares to San Juan!"

Amber is truly an angel. We did have a good time on that cruise, not that we came out of our cabin all that often.

"Would you like some sweet tea, Khalil?"

Mother Clarke is the woman. Truly the matriarch of the family. Always there to provide whatever the family needs.

"Yes, thank you," I reply softly.

Turning to face her daughter, she continues. "Amber, you look thin."

"Thanks mommy," Amber responds with a smile.

"That wasn't a compliment baby. Are you feeling ok?"

"Mommy, I'm fine, just thought I'd lose a few more pounds."

"Well you know how I feel about skin and bones, Amber. Take some of momma's home-made dressing."

"Just a little, momma, ok?"

"Whatever you say Amber," Mother Clarke finishes while piling enough for an army onto Amber's plate.

The tight sounds of Notorious B.I.G.'s *Big Poppa* echoes throughout the dining room. Everyone looks startled.

"Khalil, I thought you turned your cell phone off?"

"I thought I did too, Amber." I excuse myself to retrieve my call.

Amber doesn't seem to realize that in the consulting game my cell phone always has to be on. I step into the foyer. The caller ID registers as a blocked number.

"Hello?" I answer the phone.

"Khalil?" A very loud and angry voice greets me on the other end.

"Yes?"

"Khalil, it's me, Shayla."

"Hey, Shayla." I am not in the mood. Not today. Shayla is screaming on the other end of the phone. I walk further into the foyer for fear that someone would hear her ghetto madness through my receiver.

"Khalil, you need to get down here to see your daughter. You do remember that you have a daughter, don't you bitch?"

"Shayla, no need to scream and call me names."

"Whatever, nigga. All I know is you ain't been down here to see your only fucking child. And now you all high and mighty! Livin' lawwge and thangs." She continues after a deep breath. "Your daughter needs you too, bastard. Yeah, I heard about yo' Donald Trump wedding. And you ain't sent no money down here for your chile? And why Lexis wasn't in the wedding?"

"Shayla, I sent you a thousand dollars last month!"

"A thousand dollars? You crazy, mutha fucka? That money came and left the same damn day! You know Lexis needs money for her recital. And speakin' of recital, are you coming? You thought about that, bitch, huh?"

I could see Shayla now. Thrusting that neck round and round, back and forth like a hood rat in rare form. I envision her popping gum and wagging her finger in mid-air as she tells me a thing or two.

"Shayla, I will be there. When is it again?"

"See that shit! You don't even fucking remember when your daughter's recital is?"

"When is it, Shayla?"

"It's next Saturday!"

"Alright, Shayla, I will be there. I am in the middle of dinner with Amber's family right now. Can I call you later?"

"Oh, you in the middle of dinner with Amber's family, huh?"

"Yes, I am."

"How is that fat ho anyways?"

I ignore that comment in hopes Shayla will get the message that I am not beat for her shit right now.

"Don't you even wanna speak to Lex?"

"I told you, I'm busy, I'll call her later."

"Busy?!"

"I don't need this right now, Shayla."

"Too busy to talk to yo own daughter?"

"Listen Shayla, I don't wanna hear this fu........"

"Hey Daddy." Shayla must've put Lexis on the line.

"Hey baby! How's daddy's little girl?" I reply, adjusting my tone and smiling.

"I'm fine. Are you coming to my recital?"

"Yes baby, daddy wouldn't miss it for the world."

"Promise?" Lexis asks sweetly.

"Of course, Lex. Have I ever lied to you before?"

"No, but mommy said that you were gonna be busy."

"Forget what your mom said, I'm gonna be there with bells on."

"Ok, daddy, mommy wants me to ask you if you're bringing Amber."

"Well, what do you want? It's your day."

"I don't care daddy, she can come. I don't really remember her that much. But mommy says she's a heifer."

In the background, all I hear is Shayla's big mouth yelling at Lexis. "He bet' not bring that bitch 'round this way. He might come wit her but he ain't gon' leave wit her, betcha that shit!"

Shayla is back on the phone.

"Well, go back to your dinner, bitch!"

"Shayla, I'll give Lexis a call tonight."

"Yeah, you do that. You do that."

There could not have been a more awkward moment. Just off my honeymoon from marrying the woman I want to spend the rest of my days with and this trick calls me. And to boot, she puts my daughter on the phone to make me feel like I'm the bad guy. She always tries to use Lexis as a weapon against me instead of just letting me love her the way she's supposed to be loved. It's not Lexis' fault that the two of us can't get along. She didn't ask to be here.

I met Shayla while at Virginia Tech. Shayla was from Virginia and decided to stay local for college. She was a freshman, while Amber and I were juniors. Although she lived locally, she she'd always say that life at home was no bed of roses, so she did reside on campus.

Shayla was a bad girl. I was instantly attracted to her. Amber was so angelic most of the time; I felt I needed to take a walk on the wild side. No big deal I thought at the time. All I'd planned to do was hit it a few times and step but Shayla had other plans. I've regretted meeting her ever since. Hindsight is always twenty-twenty. I wish I knew then, what I know now.

When Shayla walked into the student center that day, all I could see was how those jeans hugged her hips, like they were holding on for dear life. Her breasts sat up high underneath that tank top. Her breath-taking face and Halle Berry haircut made her fabulous. I was really digging the way she rocked those open-toed high heel strappy sandals with those jeans. You know, those come-and-get-me heels. That strawberry tattoo on her left breast piqued my curiosity instantly. The way she moved. That Coca-Cola bottle shaped body. That confidence in her stride. That MAC lip glass-the way it made her juicy lips shine. Her hips and legs and ass flowed together so divinely and spelled trouble for me. She wore a long, French manicure that day on her hands and pretty

toes and the smell of Versace's *Red Jeans* clung to my nostrils
as she walked by.

Our eyes immediately connected, and we began to talk.
She walked up to me and lowered her Versace shades before
saying a word.

"How are you, Khalil?" I was taken aback by the fact
that she knew my name.

"How did you know my name?" I said in a flattered
tone.

"Who doesn't know who Khalil Devereaux is?" She
replied with the most seductive tone to her voice.

"I'm Shayla. Shayla McNeil. Nice to meet you."

"Well, Shayla, the pleasure is all mine."

Shayla gave me this look that's hard to describe with
words. The best I can do is to say that she devoured me with
her eyes. Her sex appeal and sensuality amazed me, even in
those few minutes of speaking with her.

"So Khalil, wassup, can I call you sometime?"

"Umm, do you know, umm…?" Shayla cuts me off before
I can finish my statement.

"Yeah, yeah, I know you gotta girl, Amber right?"

"Right, Amber."

"She's a beautiful woman."

What the....? She's got me confused. Most women would
say something like "she alright" or "she cute."

"Yes, she is beautiful," I respond.

Okay, maybe she's not digging me, this is cool. If she
wasn't feeling me, my life would be much easier at this very
moment.

"But she ain't me, Khalil," she says with a smile, juicy
lips shining just speaking to me silently that she wanted to
work me over.

It's a wrap. Oh, she's definitely getting the business. Her confidence was an aphrodisiac.

Talking led to her inviting me back to her dorm room which led to some serious bumpin' n grindin'. There were family pictures all over the wall, from the top to the bottom. The fact that it seemed like her whole family was watching us quickly left my head. Shayla knew how to slay a dick like it was a part-time job or her life's goal to be able to please a man. Her passion and her conviction about satisfying me were fierce. She sucked me so good that I enjoyed my first orgasm within minutes. She rode me like a champ. And she gave me something that I have never had with any other woman...anal.

"You like this pussy, baby?"

"Hell yeah!"

"Well, I got sumthin' that I bet Amber ain't givin' you."

She slowly rose off my dick. Grabbing a bottle with the words, Anal-Ease written on it, she poured it into her hands and began massaging and stroking my manhood slowly.

"What you got planned?" I ask while in the midst of pure ecstasy. I'm almost certain of what's about to go down.

"Oh baby, I planned on givin' you some ass tonight and that's exactly what I'm gonna do!" Those words parted from her lips like a true porn star.

She poured the Anal Ease down the crack of her ass. I became even harder than I already was. She climbed back on top and rode me until I reached my maximum. After a few minutes of recovery, I fucked her in her ass. Glorious. She had to have had the tightest ass on this side of the Mason-Dixon Line. No porno I'd ever seen could top what I was into at that very moment. The way she threw her ass back at me, matching every powerful plunge I threw at her. I couldn't believe her ass was as wet as any pussy I'd ever been inside of. Damn, it was good.

The anal session provided me with power. I was in control. Control of my thrusts in and out of her anus. Power over her screams and moans. Complete control as to what movement I would make next. That power was awesome. She did more than stroke my ego. She made me feel superior. Shayla had me open. Wide open.

Now, I am with child, Lexis, my eight year old daughter. I love her dearly, but she was a mistake that I couldn't cover up or take away. I had my first child on Amber's watch, but without Amber. I'll never be able to live it down. Shayla will never let me live it down either. She blames me for her dropping out of college to raise our daughter. She blames me for all of the problems in her life. Maybe I should blame me, too.

I've learned to accept responsibility for my role, in some ways, I guess. Yes it takes two people to conceive a child. I'd told Shayla that I wanted to finish school and get my degree.

Shayla knew that abortion was the best solution for both of us but she had ulterior motives. Motives she thought would destroy me had backfired. She knew I had a woman. She told me she was on the pill or else I would have never indulged without protection. The hardest part about all of it was telling Amber. It was the hardest thing I'd ever had to do. Shayla thought it would destroy my relationship with Amber, and it almost did.

I had to fight to get Amber back and I was determined to make it work. Separated from Amber for almost a year was the price I had to pay for fucking with Shayla. I swore on my own mother that I would never hurt Amber again. I meant that. In my heart of hearts I know that Shayla is still troubled by the fact that I didn't leave Amber for her. And I know she's still upset with me for asking her to have an abortion. But it was the most logical thing for all involved. Or maybe it was the most logical thing for me.

"Who was that, Khalil?" Amber asks me as I walk back into the dining room. The look on her face tells me she knows whom I was talking to.

"Just a client, Amber." I tell her sitting back at the table.

"On a Sunday?"

"Yes Amber, on a Sunday."

Silence.

Amber
The Love Experience

Nobody likes to work. I don't think I've ever met a person that did. And on this Monday morning, it is hard to get out of bed. My nice, warm, cozy, king sized, recently christened marital bed! The alarm clock adds fuel to the *"I don't want to go to work"* fire, which is why the snooze button and me have become very close. I glance at the clock and it reads five-thirty a.m. Oh how I wish the clock said midnight. Then I'll have six more hours of sleep. I can't complain, at least I opened my eyes this morning. Thank God for small favors.

My beautiful man lay right beside me, looking just as delicious as he possibly can. Everyone says Khalil looks just like Boris Kodjoe dipped in black. Although Mr. Kodjoe is gorgeous, my Khalil is supreme. He simply is. His rich, ebony skin is majestic. He is so dark and smooth like a *Hershey's Special Dark.* That's my "special dark" right there. You can't see him at night, unless he's smiling. His black skin offsets that white wife beater to perfection. I give him a once over. His gray Sean John sweats make him look even more delicious as they loosely fit that track star behind he has. I can still smell his Armani Mania cologne. He's so sweet.

As for those size fourteen feet, they're even nice. I can see the sun trying to rise through my bedroom window. I could lay here for just a few minutes more, but it'll just be torture. I have to go back to work. I lean in towards his face and give him a soft kiss on his cheek. I move out slowly, and his sweet smells still lingers in the air. He sleeps as sound as a baby in his mother's arms. Doesn't snore much either. I love to watch him lay flat on his back. You can tell when he's really into some good sleep when that right knee gets bent into mid-air. It'll take a nation of millions to wake him up from one of those dead-to-the-world sleeps.

I slowly creep out of bed to take a shower. Before I can make it all the way out, there's my baby. His masculine hand grabs mine and pulls me back. "Where are you going?" He makes me tingle when he says it. He has a sort of smile sprinkled with a look of seduction. "Baby, I have to go in today. I told you," I reply in such a sweet and seductive voice.

"Come here," he commands.

That look in Khalil's eyes tells me exactly what's about to go down. There is something about the way he says "come here" that turns me on in my most vulnerable moments. It could also remind me of some our worst times. As for this newlywed-Monday morning, it was heaven sent. I smile and say, "What?" with all the innocence of a school girl.

"You know what," Khalil replies as his voice changes. It gets deeper.

"No I don't. What is it baby?"

We are playing the game. Khalil pulls me in closer to him. "Bring your sexy, succulent ass over here Mrs. Devereaux."

He smiles. I smile in return and I oblige. I love a man that wears the pants...well. That's right. Tell me how, when, who, where and why it's going down. I don't mind staying in my place. I can't help but to notice that he's bulging from his sweats. My mouth starts to water.

Khalil has this thing about massages. He believes that in order to please a woman, you have to thoroughly love her. He wasn't always this way, but over the years he has grown to be quite the lover. He massages my inner thighs with slow, deep strokes with his strong and powerful hands. He looks at me, "You're so juicy baby."

Khalil moans. It's his way of letting me know that I'm not in for a quickie. It's all in the moan. The moan represents his strong urge, his passion and desire to have his way with me. Not so much for his own pleasure, but for mine. I hate to think that this is probably part of the reason I've chosen to forgive him. But its part of the reason that he makes it about me...I guess as a thank you for forgiving him. The moan is intense. As intense as his strokes up and down my thighs. He even palms my ass and massages that too. He moans again. He's ready.

Khalil gives me sweet, wet kisses up my arm as he lay on his side in bed. He moves closer to my lips and pulls me in toward him. He grabs me gently by my hair, pulls me in closer and performs maneuvers with his tongue that make my pelvis flip. After a few seconds of it, I was moist enough to be penetrated, but Khalil has other plans. He lays me on my back and pulls my panties down around my knees. He loves to leave me partially dressed. I don't mind it at all. He then pulls my chemise over my head. And since I'm blessed with breasts that Tocarra would envy, he goes to work on them.

First with gentle licks around my nipples, then on to swirls with his tongue. Licks and swirls. Swirls and licks. He gets my nipples just the way he wants them…rock hard. He sucks on them softly, then blows them to keep them hard. Khalil continues to moan while he licks and caresses me, which turns me on crazy. There's nothing sexier than a beautiful black man, the man of your dreams in bed with you, loving you and making you feel so good about yourself. He really could stop right here, and I'd be totally satisfied.

He reaches over in true gladiator status and whispers to me, "Do you like this?" I know I must resemble *Janet-Jack-Me* when I respond, "Yes."

Khalil licks down my belly to my navel and grabs my hips. He massages my hips with deep, strong strokes. He then massages my inner thighs. He slowly pries my legs apart and feels the heat between my thighs. Our eyes meet. They are both filled with need. He proceeds to suck on my clit. He kisses and sucks it as if they were best friends. He makes his way down and enters me with his tongue. I can't describe it really, other than the fact that he "tongue-fucks-me." He's like a champ in it.

As if that wasn't enough to please me, Khalil flips me over, mounts me on my knees, and sucks my clit from behind. He again "fucks me with his tongue" from the back. The two entangle to the point where you can't tell where one ends and the other begins. His fingers join in to play. He slides them in and out and sucks my juices from them. After several moans, that turn into yelps, and finally into screams from me, he gets on his knees to penetrate me.

Khalil's dick was like the Rock of Gibraltar. He takes his left hand to spread my ass cheeks and opens me up. He slowly and gently rubs the head against the base of my pussy. He taunts me and makes me beg before thrusting into me. We both yell in unison all kinds of "oohs" and "aahs" upon initial penetration. His moans are intense and raise the hairs on my arms and make my nipples hard and ripe. Khalil is so supreme in bed. He then pulls out only to go back down and suck on my clit some more. Talking that good shit to me that makes me wild, he sucks my pussy with a passion. He licks my walls with a purpose. I'm crazy at this point. I reach back with my left hand and push his shoulders.

"Fuck me!" I plead. "Khalil, baby, I can't take it. Please."
He comes up for air listening to my pleas.

He says in a deep throaty voice, "Tell me you love me."
"I love you baby," I respond in a faint whisper.

"I said, tell me you love me," Khalil seductively demands a clearer response. He takes the palm of his hand and smacks me on my right butt cheek. He loves to give me a little sting to keep the juices flowing. I love it. I yell, "I love you!" in desperation.

Khalil gets on his knees again and thrusts into me to make sure he gets the full effect of what he's done. Sliding in me until he gets all of it in, down to the balls. And before we get into our heavenly rhythm, I silently apologize to my neighbors for yet another morning of the ruckus. Khalil knows how to get to my spot as if he has a mental road map of where it is and the best route to take. He calls it "the hot spot." He pulls completely out just to give me his dick all over again and goes deeper and hits my spot with continuous rhythm. He knows he's got me...*good.*

I yell in ecstasy, "Baby, I'm there! Please slow down." I look back at him. He's like a black stallion out on a mission. "You love it, don't you? Come on, Ma, cum all over me." He moans.

I feel like I want to sing his name in five different octaves. The visual I'm sure will replay over and over in my mind for the remainder of the day. He reaches towards me and moves my hair to one side.

Khalil says, "Let me see you." He likes to see everything. I yell again, "I'm there Khalil. Slow down. Oooh." He leans in again towards me and asks, "Do you want my tongue?"

Khalil knew that when I was "there" that a little tongue never hurt. He then puts his fingers in my mouth. I lick and suck on them until he pulls them away from me. He bites my lips and his tongue dances with mine.

Khalil takes those same fingers and rubs them in my juices. He tastes them.... My juices on his fingers. He makes me taste them too. It drives him crazy to witness it. The universe is all balanced and dancing to our rhythm. Famously, and in true Khalil form while reaching his maximum, he flips me over and whispers, "Come on, baby. Make it good to the last drop," as he straddles my chest.

Afterwards we collapse and lay there in total satisfaction. The sun comes up. I glance at him, sunlight caressing his near naked body. *Damn.*

"Khalil, I really have to get to work." I try to convince Khalil that we can't go another round.

"Amber, please I just need a little more. I wanna get my stance in it," he says jokingly.

"Stance in it?" I chuckle.

"You'll get some more tonight baby, k?"

Khalil gets a serious tone in his voice. He looks at me with eyes of sorrow. "Amber, I need for you to know that I love, admire and adore you so much. I do. And I know…"

"Khalil," I interrupt him. "I know." I rub his hand to reassure him and kiss him on his lips. I head to the shower.

There's nothing better than a nice hot shower in the morning to really wake you up, well aside from getting slayed by your new husband I guess. That man knows he does it for me. I turn on the CD player in the bathroom and enjoy the neo-soul sounds of Raheem DeVaughn's *The Love Experience.*

I lather up. I've always had a thing for very hot showers and exotic shower gels. Makes me feel really sexy. I'm in the shower, singing my ass off as I clean every inch of my body when I can sense that someone is near me. If you've ever seen or heard of the movie *Psycho*, you know damn well that this is not a good look right here. My heart races. Why? It's so silly, really. I have a big black man in the house with me, so whoever wants to slash me through my shower curtain will have to go through Khalil first. It's amazing how the mind can play tricks on you. Just to make sure, I pull the curtain back slightly and take a look.

"Khalil, what are you doing?" Khalil gives me an adorable, devilish smile. He's up to something.

"I was just coming in to give you a towel. You know, to help you dry off." I give him a *yeah right* look and smile. "I'm cool K, thanks honey."

Khalil leans his head further into the shower and puts his nose up against my arm and inhales deeply. "You smell so good baby."

"Thank you K. Now get out honey, I have to finish up." I push him on his arm. Khalil removes his head from the shower. I continue to bathe. After a few seconds, I hear the shower curtain open again. I turn around.

Khalil is in the shower with me, dick in *steel-bat-status*. I look up at him, "Baby, I'm almost done. I'm getting out of here." Before I say another word, Khalil lifts me up and spreads my legs. The music in the background with the hot, steamy shower makes for a tantalizing moment.

I'm caught off guard and wet all over again. I wrap my legs around his waist and place my arms around his neck to balance myself. He's shocking me at this very moment. His look is so intense. He wants some more pussy, I know it.

Khalil places my back up against the shower wall. The water cascades over us. He pushes my head to one side and bites and sucks on my neck so strong and hard. He is acting anxious as if he's never been inside of me before. Like he's ready to reach his maximum right now.

"Oh, Khalil. Baby, I have to ..."

He interrupts by placing his tongue in my mouth. I can still smell my pussy on his breath. His lips are sticky too. He nibbles my lips gently and licks and bites my neck. He grabs a hold of my breast and sucks on my nipple, tugging at it until it reaches its firmness.

I'm looking at him, he's gorgeous as he sucks with purpose, his shiny bald head, rich cocoa skin, even his diamond stud in his left ear is gleaming as the water beads from his smooth texture. He comes back to my face and I'm almost afraid of what he'll do next. Khalil licks his lips and reaches down to his manhood. He strokes it with his hand, and gives it all to me deeply.

"Amber, Oooh, you feel so good. Oh baby, damn, your pussy is so sweet." Khalil keeps his eyes glued to him sliding in and out of me, the more he looks, the slower he goes. With each motion, he gets deeper and deeper into me. He pins me to the wall. I can't move. He's got me wide open, dripping wet, and about to cum all over him. I feel as if I am going to explode, if I don't go crazy first.

I try to hold it all in. I don't want to arouse him any further. Khalil comes in closer to my ear. "Amber, don't give this pussy to anybody else. This is my pussy. You belong to me, Amber."

I exhale deeply, preparing to respond, hoping that the words will come out of my mouth. "I'm all yours, Khalil." He picks up speed, still watching as he goes in and out of me. He's talking that good shit to me, moaning and sucking any and everything he can get his mouth on. With one hand he caresses my nipples; it slithers down to my ass. He grabs a hold of it and smacks it, he gets deeper. I can't help myself, I'm there, and he knows it. I guess he knows *his* pussy so well.

"Ahh Amber, yes, that's a good girl, cum all over your dick. This is your dick Amber, cum all over it, baby." I cry out to Khalil, as he gives me the deepest dick I've ever had in my life and with one of his final blows, he delves into me, and whispers, "I love you, Amber."

I can't say a word; a single tear falls down my cheek as we both reach our pinnacle. *My God.*

Amber

Definition of a Ridah

I've reached my destination. Divine Intervention in Elizabeth, New Jersey. It is a convalescent center that I've been working at for years. I started as a certified nursing assistant and gradually, over the years, became a registered nurse. I started working here during my summer breaks from college. I finished out my degree in Virginia and came right back to work.

The elevator stops at the fifth floor, and I get off to a nurse's station. The nurse's station is full of flowers and balloons and so much love. It is a heartfelt welcome back to work after my honeymoon. "Hey Ma!" Keisha says with a smile. Keisha is my good friend and a better nurse, and you best believe that we are joined at the hip.

"Hi Keisha!" We embrace.

"Now, who thought of all of this?" I say with such a grin on my face.

"We all did Amber. We wanted you to come back from your honeymoon to even more love. You deserve it sweetie," Keisha says to me with that same sister-friend-respect we've come to expect from one another. She's my girl.

"Amber, you know Miss Beverly has been asking about you for two weeks. And they say she has dementia! Honey, she did not forget about you!" Keisha informs me.

Miss Beverly is one of my patients. She is an eighty-two year old black woman originally from the French quarters of Louisiana. Some of Khalil's family is from that region too. That's how he got the last name of Devereaux. Miss Beverly, to this day, is so beautiful. She's one of those Camille Cosby, rich tan skinned women with a heavenly glow in her eyes. Short, gray, curly hair that is baby soft. Skin smooth and silky like flowing honey.

I walk down the hall to get to Miss Beverly's room. My timing is perfect as she's just finishing up her breakfast.

"Hi, Miss Beverly!," I say in a soft and pleasant voice as I walk to give her a kiss on her forehead.

"Amber! Oh my Amber. You came home!"

Miss Beverly has been here a few years, so I guess she considers it home. But with dementia, you can never be too sure; she may actually think she's home, back in Louisiana.

"So, how are you feeling Miss Beverly?" I lean in to give her a hug.

"Oh chile, you know me, I ain't complaining bout nothing. I'm here. I'm still here."

"I brought you something from the honeymoon."

I reach into my pocket and pull out a seashell that I brought back from San Juan. In her younger days, Miss Beverly would visit San Juan quite often. It was one of her favorite places.

"Oh chile, you didn't have to," she says with tears of joy in her eyes.

"Miss Beverly, I know how much you love the beach and the clear blue waters of Puerto Rico."

"Yes, Jimmy and I would frequent there every summer."

Jimmy was Miss Beverly's husband. He died almost two decades ago, and she talks about him like he is here with us today. They had a magical, splendid love. Full of marital ups and downs. The key to their survival was that they stayed together. I've learned so much from Miss Beverly from talking to her over the years.

"How was the wedding sugah?"

"Oh Miss Beverly, it was dreamy. It was so beautiful and special to me. I've never been happier in my life."

"You know Amber, I told that lil narrow-tailed heifer out there to get me ready for the wedding. But she wouldn't. I had the right to smack her right in her mouth."

Miss Beverly had a temper. She was a sweet old woman, but don't cross her. She'd cut you!

I partially cover my mouth so that Miss Beverly doesn't see me laugh. She's too much, and I love her to death. She's like the grandmother I never knew.

"Oh Miss Beverly, stop it. I'm waiting for the pictures to come back from the wedding and I will have one here to you in a frame. Okay?"

"K, dear. You are so special Amber. I love you."

"I love you too Miss Beverly."

I walk into the bathroom to retrieve her brush set that I left in there. I come back to Miss Beverly and sit on the bed with her and brush her hair softly as she hums spiritual hymns. After that, I rub A&D ointment on her feet and ankles and put her socks on. I then check her to make sure nothing strange happened while I was away.

With these young nurse's assistants we have working here, you can never be too sure. We have to be careful. They don't get paid what they're worth, so basically, the patients are getting what the nursing home is paying for. Thank God she seems to be in good order. I pull out her lounging set. I bought this for her about three months ago when she complained that the clothes at the nursing home weren't "fly" enough for her.

As I prepare to change her clothes, I hear a voice that makes me cringe.

"Uh, uh! What you doing with my grandma?"

Oh Lord, here we go.

It's Miss Beverly's granddaughter. This big booty, weave-wearing, name brand having, loud mouth girl that gives every good black woman a bad name. She's gorgeous. But she has a God-awful aura about her. Very disrespectful.

"Hi. I'm just preparing to change her clothes," I say respectfully.

"Well, why she ain't got no top on?"

Duh. Didn't I just say I am changing her clothes?

"Well, I'm putting her top on right now. Then you'll be able to sit and talk with her. If you could just excuse us for one moment while I change her clothes please?"

"Uh uh. I wanna see what you doing with my grandma," she says loudly and rudely.

"Ok. Just slide over a bit so I can have enough room to change her."

"Uh uh, you fine just the way you is."

Momma said there'd be days like this.

"Loreatha! Stop being so rude to Amber! Err' time you comes in here, you speaking like that! Stop it! She takes good care of me!" Miss Beverly yells with conviction and an ole-time country twang that only years of living and experience could deliver. "If you and yo sistas did what you was 'posed to do, I wouldn't be here in the first damn place, now let Amber do what she do best!"

"Alright grandma. Just don't want nobody hurting you."

"Shut up fool! Ain't nobody hurt me but you and your damn foolish ass mother and sistas."

Miss Beverly's daughter, who is Loreatha's mother, left Loreatha with Miss Beverly soon after she gave birth to her. So Miss Beverly basically had to raise her. Her daughter was in and out of Loreatha's life. I'm not supposed to know this, but Miss Beverly and I talk a lot. We're very close.

Loreatha and I don't get along. She accuses me of all sorts of things. Such as trying to steal her grandmother away from her to trying to overmedicate her. She's really weird. I'm a professional, so I try to ignore her. It's hard because she is so ignorant and something I have to deal with on a regular. I finish changing her and start to leave Miss Beverly's room.

"Bye Miss Beverly. I'll check on you throughout the week," I say as I head for the doorway.

"Bye baby. Thank you for my sea shell."

"Uh uh. What sea shell?" Loreatha interrupts.

"Shut up fool."

I walk down the hall to see Keisha. Although I did speak to her briefly to let her know I was back, we haven't really had time for one another. Keisha and I have been friends for a long time. But other than work, we have absolutely nothing in common, except of course, our deep-rooted love for one another. We were both raised in Newark, but the environment seemed to stay with Keisha. She's intelligent, but hood when the opportunity presents itself.

"So how's Miss Beverly doing?" Keisha asks me with a knowing grin on her face. Miss Beverly can be a handful.

"Oh, she's alright. It's her granddaughter that I can't stand. I'm ready to get funky with her."

"Yeah, she tried to cause hell up in here last week."

I lean into Keisha and say, "I'm sure she did."

"Well your girl Miss Beverly was not trying to hear it last week. I went in there to change her clothes and brush her hair like you do. Amber, I thought she wanted to throw down! I walked into the room, and she gets out of her chair and gets in a stance.

I said, "Miss Beverly, I'm here to change your clothes. She says, 'The hell you is.' Amber, girl I tried not to laugh. Then she walked closer to me. Amber, Miss Beverly said 'What you wanna do?' Like she wanted to fight! I said 'Miss Beverly, I'm going to brush your hair like Amber does.' Then she says, 'When my Amber come back, then I'll get my hair brushed. Ok?' All I could do was look at her shockingly. As I'm leaving, she says, 'Bye, bitch!' By then, I'd had enough so I said…'*Bye bitch,*' right back at her. Amber, your patient is too much!"

I visualize Miss Beverly getting in a stance. I laugh so hard I double over, tears well up in my eyes.

"Keisha, you are nuts girl!"

"No Amber. Your patient is nuts." We settle down long enough to hold a conversation. "Amber, let's get together tonight."

"Okay Keisha. I don't think Khalil has anything planned for us. I'm down for it."

"I want to do a girls night out. Oh yeah, and have Scott come too."

"Well Keisha, it sounds good to me. You pick the time and place and let me know."

"Hey, Amber, why don't you invite Shawn's fiancée? What's her name again?"

"Aaliyah? Sure, I'll call her to see if she wants to come. That's a good idea. She needs some friends in the area."

Like I said, Keisha and I are the best of friends and total opposites. She resembles a ghetto-fabulous Naomi Campbell. Hair, flawless. She adorns a beautiful smile and smooth ebony skin. Strong features, deep dark eyes, full lips, high cheek bones. She's the type of sistah who can adapt in any given situation. If you're corporate, Keisha's corporate.

You should see how she handles some of the doctors around here. I think sometimes these lily white doctors and even some of the nurses in here look down on us black folks, mainly Keisha, because she's so dark. I think the doctors have this thing inbred, deep down, that she should be subservient. But when they talk that talk, Keisha talks it right back.

When family members come to check on their loved ones and start with the ghetto madness, Keisha's right there with the ignorance. She's like a chameleon, adapting when need be. And her gear stays tight all the time. Best believe, if she has on a BCBG watch, she has on the shoes and handbag to match. As for me, a Wal-Mart blouse, Payless shoes and a knock-off Louis Vuitton will suffice. We're like Burt and Ernie, Felix and Oscar. Completely different, yet the same in so many ways.

I walk to the nurse's station to call Khalil just to make sure he has no plans for us tonight. One thing I love about our relationship is that we always remain active. We're always on the run. We'd worked so hard throughout college to build the lives we lead today, that we treat ourselves every chance we get. Whether it's the movies, dinner, dancing, or a quick getaway to Atlantic City, Khalil and I know how to enjoy one another.

Just as I get to the nurse's station, Rhonda, one of the C.N.A.'s, calls for me. "Amber, you have a call." She looks just like Vivica Fox.

"Thanks Vivica," I reply with laughter. Rhonda laughs with me and hands me the phone. I pick up the phone to hear Chynk Showtyme's *Definition of a Ridah* playing loudly in the background. It could only be one of two people. Either Khalil or Shawn.

"Hello?" I ask.

"Is this Mrs. Khalil Devereaux?"

"Yes, it is. Proudly," I respond with a smile.

"Is this Mr. Khalil Devereaux?"

"Why yes it is," Khalil says in a deep sexy tone. There was a moment of silence between us two. All's to be heard was the background from Chynk Showtyme. We both start laughing.

I sigh in glee and say, "Wassup baby?"

"You...my doll. Amber, do you have any plans tonight?"

"I was just getting ready to call you to ask the same thing. Keisha wanted to have an all girls night out. I know she misses me." I continue. "I tentatively agreed to go with her. I figured we reach out to Scott and maybe Aaliyah to see if they wouldn't mind joining us."

"Amber, that's a great idea! I was calling you to see if you wouldn't mind hanging out with Aaliyah from time to time. Shawn said she has some modeling gigs lined up but until then, she's just settling into the apartment and kind of going nuts with no family and friends up here."

"I feel you honey. As usual I'm one step ahead of you. Catch up boy!"

"Do I hear a hint of sarcasm Miss?"

"Well...I...," Khalil interrupts me.

"Because all I heard this morning was "*ooh*" and "*right there baby*" and "*oh Khalil please*" and...," I interrupt him.

"Shhhh, Khalil. Ok, baby. You got me."

Khalil laughs on the other end of the phone and continues. "I love you baby."

"I love you too sweetie." I notice everyone in the nurse's station is practically down my throat.

"Excuse me, Khalil." I glance at everyone and say, "Listen, y'all don't have to be all up in a sistah's business like this."

They all laugh. I kindly excuse myself and get back to my hubby. "Sorry about that baby, I'm listening."

"Amber gimme some sugah, I have to run."

"Muuuuaaah!, bye baby." I hang up the phone and return to work, tending to some more of my patients. As I walk down the hall, I pass Miss Beverly's room again. Loreatha is on her way out at the same time. We barely miss each other.

"Damn, girl. You need to watch your step," Loreatha yells at me.

"Excuse me miss, I didn't see you coming," I respond with grace. *I do need my job.*

"Yeah, well, watch where you going next time." She sneers at me.

I smile and stare her in the eyes, "I will. Have a great day!"

It hurts to concede again to this ghetto trick. I hate to speak that way about my own kind, but she knows how to push my buttons. I don't understand where all of the hate comes from with her. She's always rude to me. I'll give her this; she's not a bad looking woman. Actually, she's very pretty, and she has a great figure. As long as she doesn't speak, she's just fine.

It's time to call Scott to see what he's up to this evening. "Hey Scott, is that you?" I spoke into my cell.

"Oh Hell to the no. You will not be wearing that hideous shit out in public with me." He had a habit of answering the phone while already in a conversation with someone else. He did this all the time, and it drove me crazy.

One time when I called, I listened to an entire conversation between him and one of his boy-toys about how he liked to be caressed and fucked and where he should lay when they were fucking and how he wanted to be talked to. I learned during listening to that conversation that Scott was a bottom. To this day, Scott still won't explain what that means to me. Five whole minutes had passed before Scott even realized I was on the other end of the phone. When he finally acknowledged it, he wasn't even embarrassed. That's the kind of guy he was, always up front, honest, and not easily embarrassed.

If the truth did somehow hurt, get ready to cry because Scott was sure going to tell you. He never pulls any punches or used the truth to beat you up. That was one of my favorite things about him.

Scott was real, unlike most frauds that smiled in your face, but you better not turn your back to them. Scott could tell a fraud a mile away. He'd quickly give some sort of reason why he had to leave or some lame excuse just to get away from the phony type. Either that or he'd tell them they were a fraud. Scott figured if he disclosed the fact that he is gay to today's hateful and judgmental society, then there is no valid reason anyone had to live through lies. I agree with him. Scott is one of the best people I know, gay and all.

If there were something going on that could quite hurt me, I could always count on Scott to tell me. If he were to know, nothing but death could keep him from letting me know. He'd often said I'd better do the same for him and I did. It was the kind of relationship we had. There was nothing we didn't know about each other. God blessed me with the best of friends when he sent Scott and Keisha into my life.

"Hellooooo......yoo-hoo.....Scott," I call out to get his attention. I can hear him snapping his fingers.

"I'm sorry baby girl, is that you? Just trying to teach this lame nigga some thangs. You should see the shit he has on right now, Amber."

"Who are you talking about?" I laugh hysterically.

"Nobody you know, *I hope*." We both laugh.

"Well, girlfriend, I was calling to see what you were doing tonight. Me and some of the girls are trying to get together and take Aaliyah out. You know, show her a lil bit of the city. You down?"

"But of course, baby girl, count me in. And I have the

perfect place, too."

"C'mon Scott, I don't feel like being around a bunch of fags tonight. What exactly did you have in mind?"

"Well that ain't never stopped you from being around the fag you just married. Fake-ass Michael Jordan." Scott teased with laughter in his voice.

"Oh, you got jokes right? C'mon Scott, stop playing, what did you have in mind?"

"Ok, baby girl. A friend of mine is giving a sex party and she says I can bring anyone I want. She knows I only associate with the upper class."

"Sex party? You trying to invite me to an orgy?"

"Baby girl listen, any orgy of mine, you would not be invited to, trust. I do not do pussies. Anyway, a sex party is for toys, you know, sex paraphernalia, and things of that nature."

"Ohhhh," I feel embarrassed. "Those parties where you can pick up little trinkets for the bedroom?"

"Yes, baby girl, so if you're game, make sure those bitches bring their checkbooks, ok?"

"Ok Scott, I'll call you back and get all the details later."

"No problem, just call me before five, it starts at eight, and don't wear anything that came from Wal-Mart please!"

"Oh no you didn't!" I laugh.

"Oh yes I did!" I hear another snap coming from Scott in the background.

"Well what do you suggest I wear girlfriend? Nobody's closet is as impeccable as yours."

"Wear that cute little Donna Karan number that you bought when we were at the Commons a few weeks ago." He says knowing my closet better than I do. "Or was that Willowbrook? Shit, I don't remember."

"Oh yeah, you're right, I forgot all about that outfit. It's nice enough so I think I will."

"Nice? Outfit? I picked it out sweetie and *trust*, I don't do nice outfits. People who shop at the Gap strictly use that term. I do creations. *Fierce* creations."

"Alright, Mr. Fierce Creations. What will you be wearing this evening?"

Scott was known for going all out when he dressed. He has to be the center of attention wherever he goes. You can always catch him in silks and leathers. Very rarely does he wear sneakers of any kind except to work out. He usually wore Stacy Adams, gators and shoes of the like. Armani and Brooks Brothers suits were his style of choice. His taste in clothing was exquisite and expensive.

Scott is tall and sculpted, around five-foot-eleven. He wears short dreads in his hair that are always nicely shaped around the edges. I think he must've gone to the stylist at least twice a week. He is a neat freak as most queens are. While Scott could be one of the girls, he is a bit rugged and masculine upon first glance. He's a perfectionist. Not what you'd expect listening to some of the words that come out of his mouth. And it shows in his physique. He stays in the gym. Weighing in at a muscular two-hundred-ten pounds, Scott has butterscotch skin complimented by a radiant smile, with a deep dimple in his right cheek. Sensual, dark brown eyes, framed by thick, well-trimmed eyebrows. Sweet and tender full lips, and a gorgeous profile combined with his sense of style puts Scott in a category all his own. Scott keeps himself groomed better than most women I know. A perfectly trimmed goatee, which looked sexy as hell around his mouth. Scott's a looker, make no mistakes about it. A gay version of Shemar Moore is the best way to describe him.

I always told him that he should go into male modeling. His reaction, "Oh no bitch! My magic is made behind the scenes, not in front of the camera!"

Scott gets in where he fits in. If he isn't singing and performing, he is styling and conceptualizing some of today's hottest stars. The hottest of women often tried to turn him out, but, as Scott always said, *he don't do pussies.*

"Well, baby girl, I don't know what I'll be blessing you bitches with this evening. Just know that I'll be fly as usual. Ain't nothing changed."

"Goodbye Scott."

I laugh as I hang up the phone. I quickly dial Khalil to confirm our girl's night out. Khalil said he didn't have a problem with it and that he and Shawn would be at the gym. He also said he'd be up waiting for round three.

Glory, Glory.

Shawn
The Loft

Aaliyah and I have a great spot downtown. We got lucky when we found this apartment. We happened to be in the coffee shop across the street perusing the newspaper for vacancies when the guy behind the counter told us that his friend was relocating. He explained that the apartment was a two-story, one-bedroom loft overlooking the city and was in great condition. He said he would call his friend to see if we could see it. Just so happened his friend was home and we were able to take a look the same day.

Aaliyah fell in love with it instantly, which meant I didn't have much say in anything. Beautiful hardwood floors accompanied by pastel, sponge-painted walls and ten foot high ceilings with sky lights made it very easy to secure my approval. It was perfect. Downstairs is this huge living room that Aaliyah insisted on painting a light olive green. I must admit our beige leather sofa set fits perfectly. Our fifty-inch plasma sits firmly on the wall right above my Aiwa sound system. A brother *gotsta* have his music.

I'm into black art so I had to throw my favorite piece on the wall. The black man bound by chains but breaking loose shows that the strength of the black man should never be underestimated. I ran into a peddler a couple of days before we moved in so I was able to replace my old eight-by-ten with the eighteen-by-twenty that's hanging now.

Yeah, that's me right there. You can probably slow me down but you will *never* stop me. And besides, I had to add a touch of "me" to the apartment with all the feminine shit up in here. Aside from the sound system, all of Aaliyah's corner-stand lamps, plants and African figurines could easily make a person believe that she was the only one who lived here. Opposite my man on the wall, hangs this sexy ass picture of me and Aaliyah taken at one of her photo shoots. She'd invited me down that day to see her in action. Of course, I was looking good as usual so she asked the photographer if he would take our picture.

Aaliyah was wearing a Chanel original. A backless, camel-colored, almost mustard, form fitting linen sun dress that seemed to hug all her curves and flared at the bottom. It tied around her neck and stopped right above her knees. The stars must've been in our favor that day because I was rockin' my silk, yellowish-orange Sean John shirt that accentuated my frame quite well. I had that Jamie-Foxx-tight-shirt look goin' on. A pair of crisp, clean Sean John blue jeans and some brand new Timberland constructs that matched my shirt perfectly and no doubt rocked a mean belt to match. Damn I was fine! My iced out white gold chain glistened magically against my dark skin and my Rolex hung just right around my wrist. Every time I look at our picture hanging above the bricked in fireplace, I tell myself how blessed I am to have Aaliyah. We really do compliment each other well. She's my soul mate.

Adjacent to the living room is the den, which Aaliyah and I agreed would be my baby. A man's touch, you know. Some place for me and the fellas to hang, have some drinks and whatever. Nothing fancy, just a wet bar, pool table, wide screen, stereo, desktop computer, Playstation 2, Xbox360 and a money green leather sectional. And I can't forget my black art.

This time I went for this piece I'd never seen before until I came here to the city. It's a card table with a green suede table cloth on it. Seated at the table are about five or so, dark-skinned, naked honeys having drinks, smoking cigars and playing cards with stacks of cash all over the table. When Aaliyah questioned me about it, I'd told her that I bought it because the green table cloth in the picture matched the sofa and to just think of it as dogs playing poker. I laughed because even she didn't go for that. But I had to remind her that this was my space so she had no choice but to fall back. A single door leads to the half bathroom right outside the den. A toilet, a sink, and a few rolls of tissue. Nothing feminine about this room. If it wasn't for the fact that me and the guys needed somewhere to sit, the leather sectional would be ghost. Like I said, a man's touch.

On the opposite side of the living room is the eat-in kitchen. We were lucky enough to have found an apartment that came with all the perks. A dishwasher, an in-wall microwave, digital range-top oven and a laundry room with a washer and dryer just off the side of the kitchen. Actually, the washer and dryer belonged to the previous owner but we got a good deal for it. The only thing we hadn't gotten around to was buying a kitchen set but we both agreed we had time for that.

Upstairs is the master bedroom, which Aaliyah took sole, decorating possession over. She definitely has good taste, but I made her promise to think of me while she did her thang in there. She opted for this leather contemporary set. Taupe leather headboard that reminded me of a *shrink's* lounge chair because it is that good, *rich people* kind of leather with the deep stitching along the seams. It is also a platform, which meant the bed skirts were out. Thank GOD!

The armoire that came with it is big enough to sit the forty-two inch plasma inside of which is also good and the dresser had a taupe colored, granite marble top with leather handles on each of the eight drawers that matched the headboard, and the two nightstands matched. What can I say? My girl has taste.

But of course, I just had to throw some black art up in there. Another of my favorite pieces where the strong shirtless black man has his arms wrapped around his queen while a fire burns in her belly. Yeah, that one was hot for the bedroom I said to myself while the peddler got me for another seventy-five bucks. He wanted a hundred, but I'm known for my ability to talk a mutha fucka down.

As I walk through the loft, I must say it's coming along nicely. Very comfortable. Easy access to Penn Station New York, the Path, Port Authority and any bus or cab we will ever need.

Although I am from Virginia, I feel right at home here in New York. Khalil would bring me home with him most summers during our college days, so I'm very familiar with the tri-state area. Even after college, I'd come up at least once a month. Khalil, Amber and I would have the best of times during our summer breaks. We were like the black *Three Stooges*.

New York is kind of hectic, but I'm loving it. Aaliyah has to get used to it. I told her that the career she has chosen demands that she travel, and she needs to get to know the world. It's a blessing to be able to make a living based on how fly you are. I was just going into our bedroom to check on my baby doll when my phone rings.

"Hello?" I talk into my flip.

"Wassup Shawn?" Khalil spoke. It sounds as if he is in his car.

"I spoke to Amber, and the girls are definitely going out tonight. She says she'll be calling Aaliyah to invite her."

"Word!? That's a good look right there. I know my baby will be happy about being thoroughly accepted by the family. Tell Amber I said thanks."

"I will Shawn. No doubt. I'll meet you in the City in about an hour or so. It's still early afternoon so why don't we get our workout on at the NY Sports Club. You know they have one not far from you."

"Sounds like a plan," I respond. I hadn't worked out since we moved here so this was right on time.

"Okay, I'll see you in a few."

"Alright brother. Oh, wait a sec, K. I have a dinner meeting this evening, and I need to get some proposals done. So, after we get our workout on, I'm going to have to shower at the gym and head on over to the investors meeting from there. Cool?"

"That's cool man."

Khalil is my man. He's coming over to the city so we can get our workout on. You know, do some lifting. We've always been into physical fitness ever since our college days. Both of us understand how the black man is known for his physique and sexual prowess so we played it up to the hilt in college. At the gym seven days a week serving as eye candy for most and enjoying our eye candy with some of the hottest girls there. I swear Virginia has some of the most beautiful women in the country. We had a ball. Anyway, we kept up with the ritual of keeping our bodies in shape. I walk into the bedroom so I can get ready for the gym. I know my sweats are in here somewhere.

"Where are you going?" Aaliyah asks me.

"Oh baby, I was just about to tell you that Khalil and I are going to the NY Sports Club to do some lifting."

"Oh," Aaliyah sighs.

"What's wrong baby?"

"Nothing, really."

"Baby, what is it? You can tell me," I lay down on the bed and put my arms around her.

"Shawn, you're all I have up here. It's just you and I. My first big photo shoot is not for another week or so. I guess I'm a little lonely."

I turn Aaliyah around, give her a kiss.

"Baby, we're going to do much better here. You'll make friends and the work will flow in steadily. I promise." I pull her closer to me. "You landed huge spreads with two of the largest magazines in the country. Be proud of yourself."

"I know Shawn, I just can't wait for things to pick up."

"Aaliyah, we haven't been here that long. No worries, okay?" I hug Aaliyah to console her.

"Besides, you never know what the day will bring."

I didn't tell Aaliyah that she would be going out tonight with Amber and some other girls. I want it to be a surprise for her.

Aaliyah's a model and likes to be in the middle of everything. I understand. She's used to having the spotlight. Some days when there's nothing going on for her, she's going nuts. I told her that New York is such a huge city, full of culture, entertainment, and opportunities. I guess she just has to get used to the fast pace.

I'm proud of her. Right before we left Virginia, she landed two spreads in *Elle* and *Essence*. *W*hich is *huge*. She even got the cover of *Elle*. The shoot should happen in a few weeks. I don't know how she managed it, but she must've worked her butt off to do it.

Amber
Welcome to the Brickz

The first day back at work from a vacation is always rough. I passed out more meds than I have in weeks. Talking with patients, checking I.V.'s, blood pressure and everything else that goes with being a nurse took its toll on me today. In addition to the looney family members and the near death of Miss Ida on the fourth floor, I am beat. I did promise Keisha that we would go out tonight. Scott has something planned, and I still have to call Aaliyah. What I really want to do is lay down and nap.

I walk through our condo, picking up after Khalil. He's a bit of a mess at times. Funyons on the floor, and dishes in the sink. I'll have to speak with him about this. He knows better. But that's my baby. Let me get out of these scrubs and shoes. I just want to rest my toes for a few minutes. I need to call Aaliyah.

I stretch out across my bed in nothing but my bra and panties. I am so comfortable at this point. I can smell the fragrance in the air and throughout the sheets from our morning of love making. Whew. Sends chills through my body just thinking about it. That man knows he's got some quality pipe.

Khalil bought this huge plasma television for the bedroom wall. It's ridiculous. I go through the channels to find something good to watch. I turn on *VH1 Soul* to catch a good video. *Can't Be Without You* from my girl Mary J. Blige. I love her. I played this CD to death in the truck. It's all scratched up now. I need to get a new one.

I call Aaliyah. The phone rings for a few seconds. Yep, I'm calling Shawn's house. All I can hear before anyone says hello are the sounds of Chynk Showtyme. He's an underground rapper from the Bricks that Shawn and Khalil are listening to. Shawn and Khalil are true hip hop connoisseurs. I am not too far behind them. In our early thirties, we had no choice but to love hip hop. Hell, we are hip hop. We've lived it since its underground inception to mainstream acceptance. From the Sugar Hill Gang to Common. From the Fat Boys to The Jungle Brothers. From DJ Red Alert to DJ Clue. I'm still waiting for Jay-Z to come out of retirement and Rakim, the God Emcee to bless us with a new joint. Been too damn long. Yes, we definitely are hip hop.

"Hello?" Shawn answers.

"Hey blacky." I laugh because I know I'm the only person that can get away with calling him that.

"Hey baby girl, I thought you'd be calling." He snickers into the phone. "How you doing?"

"Hi, Shawnny, I'm doing ok. What about you? Everything okay over there in *lovers land*?"

"As well as any man could hope for, baby. I'm just getting ready to go work out with your husband."

"Oh, okay. Well you two have fun. Where's Aaliyah?"

"She's right here baby, hold on. Honey. Come and get the phone. It's Amber."

I can hear Aaliyah yelling in the background like it was Publisher's Clearing House on the other end of the phone.

"Hello. Hi Amber!," Aaliyah says excitedly.

"Hey girl. How are you?"

"I'm good Amber. Wassup?"

"Keisha, Scott and I are going out tonight to one of Scott's parties. I was calling to see if you would be interested in joining us."

"Hell yeah girl! I'm going nuts. I do want to go. What time do I meet you?" Aaliyah yells to Shawn in the background.

"Baby, I'm going out with Amber tonight!" I hear him say, "That's good baby" in the background.

"Shawn, can you turn that music down, please! I'm sorry for yelling in your ear, Amber. Shawn has that music up so loud. Let me take the phone into the bedroom."

"No problem Aaliyah. I hear Shawn is playing *Welcome to the Brickz*. Trust me girl, I've been listening to that CD for a while now. It's hot."

"You're right Amber, I love it, especially this song. But does he have to make my eardrums bleed?"

There's a brief silence on the phone. I guess Aaliyah is walking into their bedroom to get away from the loud music. Suddenly, I hear her singing in my ear, the lyrics to the song. Mmmm, I'm sorry Amber. I always get so caught up in that song."

The sounds of Chynk Showtyme fade away; I guess she's reached her bedroom.

"Sorry about that Amber. Should I have Shawn bring me to you?"

"Umm, you know Khalil is coming there to work out with Shawn, so maybe he can bring you back with him, and I'll get you home. How does that sound?"

"Perfect. Shawn wanted to write some proposals tonight so I don't think he wanted to make his way over the river."

"Okay Aaliyah, I'll speak to Khalil and get the details together."

I go back to flicking the channels for a few minutes more. I don't have much time to waste. It's almost two-thirty. Scott wants to leave at five.

I call Khalil. Again, the bass is blasting on the other end. I yell above the music, "Khalil, turn down that music, damn."

"Oh Amber, baby, c'mon, rough day at work?"

"No Khalil, I just want to know that you can hear me."

"Yes, baby, I can hear you. What's up?"

"Well, listen. Call Shawn and touch base with him. I told Aaliyah that I would ask you to bring her over tonight so we can go out. You should be home by six-thirty, right?"

"Yeah, I should be. But I thought you were leaving at five, Amber?"

"No, Khalil, I'm moving slow. Scott will just have to wait. His little party doesn't even begin until seven or eight."

"What party, Amber?"

"Scott invited us to a sex party."

"A sex party? What do you mean?" Khalil sounded like he had a bit of an attitude in his response. He's such a secure man, but I think I hear just a tad bit of jealousy.

"Khalil, it's a party where you go to get toys and things for the bedroom. Oils and lotions. Eat, drink and buy products, that's all. Why?"

I can hear Khalil laughing. "Ha, baby, I was just joking." Sounded more like a sigh of relief to me.

"Are you okay with it, Khalil?" I 'm just asking because I don't want any drama when I get home.

"Yes, baby. I'm fine with it. I just thought it was some type of wild party. I know Scott, and I know that he's a freak. And I don't want anyone drooling over my baby. Besides, you've dropped like fifty pounds, right? I don't need anyone pushing up on you."

I understood what Khalil meant by those words. And I caught a serious attitude. I like to call it a "smatty." My smatty is on real hard at this point. He was never jealous when I carried the extra baggage. Now he's jealous? I'm still the same person. Khalil does flaunt me more now. I've always been a modest person, but, in all honesty, I've always been fly too. Always been a looker. I just thought that my beauty came from within. I know now that it also comes from my outer appearance. I reserve my comments and get back to the conversation.

"Okay Khalil." I make my anger obvious.

"What baby? I'm just saying….baby? Hello? Amber?"

I hang up the phone. I'm tired and not trying to deal with Khalil's nonsense right now. I love my baby, but sometimes…

I get out of bed to shower. I pass the mirror and glance at my new sculpted physique. I am impressed. And as usual, grinning from ear to ear. My pink lace boy shorts and bra to match compliment my honey skin so well. Here comes the real test. Let me take off the underwear and reveal what's really going on under here. *Oh my. Not bad sistah.*

I walk into the bathroom and pull the shower curtain back. I turn on the hot water and walk out of the bathroom to the closet to pull out my Donna Karan number. I stroll back to the bathroom and finally get in the shower. The water running over my body feels so nice and warm. My Victoria's Secret shower gel has the bathroom smelling so sweet. The sensation from the water and gel gives me goose bumps and makes my nipples hard. I get out of the shower and begin to dry off when the phone rings. I reach over to pick it up.

"Hello?"

"Mmm Hmm. Well you better know honey that I ain't about to come home to this funky ass house. This shit better be clean when I get back. Comprende'?"

I smile because it can only be one person… Scott. He's speaking to whomever again while on the phone with me. He's incredible.

"Yes, Scott. I'm getting ready. But I won't be ready at five. More like six-thirty."

"Oh, see I told you five baby girl. But six-thirty is fine. I won't even spit fire at your ass today. It's not that far so we will get there on time."

"Well gee, thanks honey. I'm about to call Keisha now, and Aaliyah will be riding back from the city with Khalil."

His mood changes on the phone.

"Hello? Scott? Are you still there?"

"Yes gorgeous, I'm still here. Hmmm."

"Hmmm, what Scott?"

"Well, you know I'm not the type to hold my tongue but…"

"Oh boy. What? Scott!"

"What the hell are you thinkin' 'bout, lettin' *Miss Thang* ride alone with your man? Last time I checked, she was a dime, and ain't no way I'd let her around any of my men. And they **GAY**."

I laugh at Scott's last comment, but I hear where he's coming from.

"Scotty, look. I don't have a problem with Khalil being around other women. I'm very secure at this stage in my life."

"Humph, it ain't Khalil you need to be worried about!"

"Alright, Scott, I'm hanging up now. I'll call you when I'm leaving. I guess I'll bring Aaliyah and Keisha with me and then pick you up?"

"Oh! No! Bitch. Not in that F-150. I don't do pickups. Let me know when everyone is there and I'll pick y'all up. Kisses."

"Bye Scott." Before I could set the receiver back into place, my phone rings again.

"Hello?"

"Hey girl, it's me. Just checking in to see what time we're getting together." It's Keisha. She's my girl twenty times over. One of my best friends in fact. I can't wait for us to get together tonight. If Keisha weren't a nurse, she could part-time it as a comedienne. She's so funny. But a good woman at heart.

"Hey Keisha. I was just about to call you. We're all

meeting here, and then Scott will take us to the party."

"Oh, Scott doesn't want to ride in your truck, right?" Keisha says knowingly, and we both laugh. Keisha knew that Scott was too fabulous to get into my load.

"Nope, he sure doesn't. He said he'd pick us up here at my house."

"Oh okay. So Aaliyah decided to come? That's good; it'll be good to see her. She's so damn pretty; it makes you sick, right?" We laugh again.

"You know Keisha, she is pretty, but I'm not *sweating her technique*. But it is a lil sickening ain't it?"

"Okay, girl. I'll be at your house around six. Is that okay?"

"Yes Keisha, that's fine. See you soon."

I hang up the phone and decide to get a little nap.

I really earned my money today.

Khalil
The Work Out

Feels like the good ol' days. Shawn and I getting our workout on. We worked out religiously in college. Shawn spots me as I'm pressing. I wave to him to come over.

"Shawn, how long have you known Aaliyah?" I ask out of curiosity.

"Not sure Khalil. It hasn't been that long. Sort of like love at first site. Why do you ask?"

"I just can't shake the feeling that I know her from somewhere, man."

"Khalil, we've been through this. I don't know where you know her from. She has never mentioned it to me that she knows you so I wish you'd let that go."

"Aaight man, I'll leave it alone." We continue with our lifting.

I move from the weight bench to the bike. Time for me to get my blood flowing. I notice the woman on the bike beside me is staring. I don't want to be rude so I smile and say hello.

"How are you?" She asks and smiles and responds with sweat dripping all over her body. I notice how her fuchsia colored biking shorts seem to be painted onto her petite frame. Her sports bra top is drenched with perspiration. Her hair is pulled back in a pony tail, and that too, is soaking wet. She's cute, I think to myself. Too thin, but cute.

"I'm fine. Yourself?" I continue with small talk. I don't know what else to say to her.

"Couldn't be better. What's your name?"

"My name is Khalil, and yours?"

"Nice to meet you Khalil. I'm Tina." We shake hands.

"I've never seen you here before. Are you new to the club?"

"Yes, I am. I came with my friend Shawn. He just moved to the area so we figured we'd check it out." Shawn comes over and nudges me. "Shawn, this is Tina. Tina, this is my friend, Shawn."

"It's a pleasure to meet you, Shawn." She grins at us.

"Likewise, Tina." Shawn says and then turns to me and gives me the *time to go* look. "C'mon Khalil. The treadmills are free."

"Alright man." I shift focus back to Tina. "Well, it is nice meeting you Tina."

"The pleasure is all mine Khalil. Hope to see you around the club more often. I'll leave my number with you, if you're like to give me a call sometime."

I walk away smiling because Shawn looks so serious right now. We get on the treadmills, and he shakes his head at me.

"What, man? I can look, can't I? I'm married, I'm not dead." I laugh at him. He's always this way. I must admit that if it weren't for Shawn, I probably would have ended up in much more trouble than I did.

"You need to get your mind right, Khalil."

I don't respond. I've heard this speech too many times before. We decide to cool down and take a breather.

"Shawn, I need to take a trip down to VA this weekend. It's Lexis' recital. Shayla wants me there. I have to go and support my baby girl. Jamal already said he'd go. I wanted to know if you were down to ride too?"

Shawn gives me the pity look again. The *shame on you for fucking up all those years ago* look. The look that makes me want to run away with my tail between my legs.

"Yeah, yeah, yeah Shawn, I know. I wouldn't be in this situation if I had some self control. Is that what you're going to say?"

"Well I *was* going to say that but you said it for me." Shawn grins as he ups his speed on the treadmill. "I'm game brother. I need to see my God-daughter anyway. And I need to make sure Shayla doesn't rip you a new one. You sure know how to pick 'em, Khalil."

"Yeah Shawn, I know. I know how to pick 'em. Excuse me for being human." I up my speed to match Shawn's. "Everyone can't be "*Mr. Good Black Man*" like you. I just didn't understand back in the day how you could have so much self control."

"Listen, Khalil. I know women if nothing else. And if you want to keep a good woman, you have to be willing to reciprocate the same.

"Amber was the first woman, or should I say the only woman that I've ever heard you say you love." Shawn adds more speed to his treadmill.

"On the right hand, you loved Amber to death, but on the left hand, you were fucking Shayla in her ass. I tried to tell you back then to ease up with Shayla but you wouldn't listen. That girl had you sprung."

"I know man, don't remind me." I match his speed.

"Well, I think you need reminding, so I'm not finished. You couldn't see past all that ass she was giving you, and you never stopped to think of the price you'd eventually have to pay in the end."

"C'mon, Shawn, I don't wanna hear this shit from you. I hear it enough from Shayla."

"See, that's your problem, Khalil. You didn't want to hear my mouth back then, and you don't want to hear my mouth now. What was it you called me...a cock-blocker? At some point, you're going to have to listen to somebody so it may as well be me. Now I'm not trying to come off as this perfect brother or anything. We both know I've done my dirt.

But we also both know I was never claiming any one woman as my lady while I did my dirt. I never purposely hurt anyone. Any woman I dealt with knew what time it was with me from jump. I made sure of that. If they chose to stay involved with me past a certain point, it was their prerogative to do so. I didn't hide anything because I never had to." Shawn slows down to a slow jog.

"It's all about honesty, man. And character. A brother's character is defined by what he does when no one is looking. Feel me? And ultimately, everything you do in the dark always finds its way to the light." He wipes his face and head.

"Man, Shawn, what is that? Some righteous Fruits of Islam talk? Man, go head with that."

We laugh and finish cooling down. We have to make it a quick workout today. As we head to the locker room, Shawn adds his final thoughts.

"No, man, but seriously. Are you gonna be cool being around Shayla this weekend?"

"What do you mean by being cool? I don't have a problem with Shayla; she has the problem with me."

"Look at what you did to the girl, Khalil." He stops by the fountain. "I'd have a problem with you, too, if I was her. Have you not yet accepted any responsibility in this mess? You have a child in another state and you do not communicate with your child's mother at all, except to get some ass when you go down to see Lexis. You think I don't know that shit K. But I do."

He just won't stop.

"Shayla is always gonna be in love with you. You know that, and you take advantage of it. Stop sleeping with her when you go visit your daughter. You're giving Shayla the wrong impression. You're married now. Do Amber right this time. Have you told Amber yet that you have to take the trip?

Besides, you have absolutely no idea what your daughter likes and dislikes. For all you know, any Tom, Dick or Harry is raising her in the street."

"Well that's not my fault Shawn." I try to defend myself.

"C'mon Khalil, we weren't raised that way and you know it. We come from good, solid, strong families. The kind that stick together through whatever. From holiday dinners and summer vacations. Be a man and a father."

I cut Shawn off. I heard enough. Not only was he right but he was striking every nerve in my body. The sweat dripping from my head was no longer coming from my previous workout. The truth hurts like a mutha fucka.

"Alright Shawn, I got you! Say no more." *Please,* I think.

"No, you don't *got* me K. You have no idea what it's like to know who your father is but not know him at all, do you?" He grabs my arm. "You have no idea what it's like to know your father has this whole other family that doesn't include you! Well guess what, I know how it feels!"

"Yeah but Shawn, that's different. Your father was married to your momz when he left. Shayla and I were never together."

"Never together?! Then how the hell did Lexis get here if you two were *never together*? You think Lexis cares about some damn marriage certificate? All Lexis knows is she has a father named Khalil. Is that good enough for you?"

"No, it's not Shawn. What do you expect me to do? Shayla won't let me get close enough to Lexis to form any kind of bond with her. I don't know what to do, man!"

I am angry, frustrated. Both at Shawn and not at Shawn at the same time. Everything he said was true and it cut deep into my soul like a knife. I hated him for saying it. I hated myself more.

"You know what you are, man?" Shawn will not let up.

"No, Shawn but I'm sure you're gonna tell me."

"Damn right I'm gonna tell you. You're a dead beat dad, K. That's what you are and the sad part is that you don't even know it."

"Now see, you're wrong for saying that. I send Shayla money each and every month without hindrance. And anytime Shayla says she needs anything for Lexis, I don't question it. I am far from being a dead beat dad!"

"You really think because you send her some change, it makes you a good father? Let me tell you something Khalil. My father sent my mother money for me all the time but that didn't fill the void he left."

I can see the pain in his eyes.

"You know I've got brothers and sisters that I don't even know. By now, I probably have nieces and nephews, too. It was just me and my momz. Just like its just Shayla and Lexis. Yeah, my momz got herself a boyfriend when I was growing up but I was old enough to know he wasn't daddy. She tried like hell to make it feel like a family for me, but *she* was my family. Man, Mr. Khalil Devereaux, you've got a lot of growing up to do."

He sounded disappointed.

"I'm grown, Shawn, in case you haven't noticed. I've settled down and married the woman of my dreams. I'm taking care of my home like a man is supposed to do. And I'd never make the same mistakes again that I made with Shayla. I was young back then and in college. I'm not trying to justify anything but I was wildin' out back then. I was doing shit that could never happen now."

"Oh really?" Shawn laughs. "I bet Chyna would say differently, now wouldn't she?"

"Look, man, I don't want to talk about this anymore."

I just want this fucking conversation to end.

"I hear where you're coming from and I got you, so let's drop it, aaight?"

"Oh now you don't want to talk anymore, huh? The truth hurts like a mutha fucka, doesn't it?"

"Damn man! You just won't let it go!!"

"Alright, alright, Khalil, I'm done. I love you man. You my boy and it's my job to let you know when you slippin', feel me? And you're gonna make sure there won't be any slippin' this weekend, right?"

"Yeah, I feel you. Just don't come down so hard on a brother next time, aaight??"

"Whatever man, just as long as I got your attention. You just make sure you stay focused this weekend. It's all love baby. It's all love."

We head to the showers. I look to make sure none of Scott's friends are around. Shawn catches me, and we bust out laughing. Like close brothers, we know what the other is thinking. We do this every time we go to a local gym. Once we spotted Scott in a steam room laughing and giggling with some other guys at another local gym, from that moment we knew what time it was.

Once we're done showering, Shawn reminds me of the girl's night out tonight.

"Khalil, can you give Aaliyah a ride back to your crib? I told you about my meetings I have to get to. I have no time to chauffer her high-yellow ass across the tri-state."

I laugh. "No problem, man, I can bring her over but how will she get home?"

Shawn sighs. "Aaliyah mentioned that Amber would bring her home. I think that's how it's going down. But I'll be done with my work by the time they're done partying, so I can come and pick her up if it's a problem."

"Sounds good Shawn. I'll get the truck washed, and swing by and pick Aaliyah up."

"Alright brother. Oh yeah K, listen. Since you're actually paying attention to what I have to say today, pick me up one of those slammin' corned beef on rye sandwiches from the Four Leaf Deli, you know the place you always took me to when we came home from college. I've been craving one of those for the longest."

I smile and reply, "They closed man. But I can get you one from Cooper's on South Orange Avenue. I know, with the works…cole slaw and Russian dressing."

Shawn gives me a pound and says, "You know I love you man. I'll see you later."

Khalil

Bump-n-Grind

Standing off to the side while the short Spanish guy applies the Armor All to my tires, I inspect my truck thoroughly. You have to do this before you pull out of the car wash or else you'll notice everything they missed once you're miles away. Sort of like when you go through a drive-thru at McDonald's. "Yo man, get this spot right here." I point to a smudge left on my driver's side door. Ever since I bought my 2006 Escalade a couple of months ago, I practically live at the car wash. All black with beige leather interior and fully loaded with navigation, wood panel trimmed dash, air conditioned and heated seats, On-Star, Bose sound system with XM satellite radio, Dolby surround sound DVD players in each head-rest, third row seating capabilities, and twenty-four-inch rims make this baby my home away from home and the second love of my life. Finalizing all the details of my car wash, I take the cloth from the small man and apply the finishing touches to my Cadillac.

"See this right here man. You have to make this shine," I say to the dude as I wipe the Cadillac emblem on the grill.

I stand back and take one last look before I pull out. I notice two women staring at me and I quickly nod. I make a fast getaway.

Broads like that can get a brotha in trouble I say to myself as I step on the gas. *Gold-diggas!* All they see is a nice ride. They can't possibly be checking *me* out. I'm fine, but I've looked better. A white wife beater, blue jeans and some white Air Force Ones couldn't have possibly made those tricks drool the way they were. I'm on my way home from the gym so I know I'm not looking that good. Has to be my ride.

Those ladies don't see a hard working, independent brother with responsibilities and major bills. They just see a nice ride, and all they wanna do is ride. I begin to laugh. Yeah, I bet they do wanna ride 'cause one of them looked like those fake ass Minolos were hurting her feet.

I suddenly think of Amber. We have been together for so long I feel she completes me. I never had to worry about Amber being a gold digger. She's been with me even when I had nothing. She's helped me get to where I am right now in my life. I never questioned whether her feelings for me were genuine. I already knew. If anyone else in my life somehow faltered, I could count on Amber to be real.

I toy with my wedding band. I shouldn't have made that comment about her weight. I didn't mean it in a bad way. I just wanted her to know that I did notice. She's always looked good to me, but now she looks even better. Maybe I could have said it differently.

I pick up my cell to dial Amber to reassure her of my love, but before I can dial, my cell rings.

"Hello?" I answer. I don't recognize the number on the display.

"Hi...Khalil?"

"Yes, who's this?"

"This is Aaliyah. I was just wondering what time you were going to be here."

"Oh, hey Aaliyah, I'm on my way over there now. You ready?"

"That depends, Khalil."

"Depends on what?"

"Depends on what I should be ready for."

Dead silence on my end of the phone.

"Khalil, are you still there?"

"Yeah, I'm here. Just didn't know how to take that last comment from you. Let me speak to Shawn."

"Shawn's not here. Remember? He has meetings today."

"Uh, okay. I should be there in about ten minutes so come outside."

"I've got a better idea. Why don't you come inside? Real women never wait by the curbside for their rides."

Before I can respond, I hear a dial tone on the other end of the line. The line goes dead. I   I feel uneasy about the conversation with Aaliyah. Maybe she was just being facetious. Yeah, that's it, I'm just being paranoid. She couldn't have possibly flirted with me just now.

I pull up to the front of their building and beep the horn. No response. I wait a moment thinking she must be coming out, but still no Aaliyah. I beep the horn a second time. Nothing. I pick up my cell and call. No answer. I get out of the truck and walk to the door and notice that it's open.

"Aaliyah." I call out but no response. "Aaliyah, it's me Khalil."

I let myself in.

I notice Aaliyah has bought yet another lamp that has been dimmed to a seductive setting. R. Kelly's *Bump-n-Grind* remix plays in the background softly as I sit down to wait for her. "Damn, they're really hooking this spot up," I say to myself not noticing Aaliyah coming down the stairs.

"Thanks, I'm glad you approve Mr. Devereaux. I didn't hear you come in," Aaliyah says as she approaches me wearing only a towel.

"C'mon now, I thought you were ready Aaliyah," I respond feeling very uncomfortable. *Why in the hell would she come in front of me wearing only a towel with a body like that?*

100

"It'll only take me a moment to slip into something. Why don't you have a drink while you wait for me?" She walks up to me and points toward the den as if I don't know where the alcohol is in here.

"Naaah, I'm good. Just hurry up before you end up catching a cab." I'm heated at this point.

"Suit yourself Sweetie, but I'm going to have one."

Aaliyah walks into the den and returns with two drinks and me gives one. I catch a whiff of a fragrance that's permeating from her body. It's the same stuff that Amber smells like when she gets out of the shower.

"Here Khalil, it's only White Zinfandel, it'll relax you."

"Aaliyah, what's up with you?" I ask feeling disrespected along with my best friend. I am now becoming agitated.

"Nothing. I just wanted you to be comfortable while you wait for me."

"Comfortable!? You come out here in a towel and you want me to be comfortable?"

"I never heard you come in Khalil or else I would have never come down the stairs this way."

"Okay, so your door just happened to be open when you knew I was coming?"

"What are you implying Khalil? You think I'm deliberately trying to seduce my fiancé's best friend?"

"I don't know what to think. All I know is any grown ass man in a position like this one right here could easily come to the conclusion that you were trying to..."

"Trying to what, Khalil?"

"Listen Aaliyah, I'll be outside. If you're not out there in five minutes, I'm leaving."

"Khalil. Please don't do that." Aaliyah moves in close to me and invades all my space.

"I promise I'll be ready in five minutes."

Damn, she's fine and if Shawn wasn't my boy and Amber wasn't my wife, I'd fuck the shit out this broad. I feel my manhood swell. I grab the drink from her and down it in one swallow. I quickly walk toward the door. I call to her over my shoulder not wanting to look back, "Hurry up Aaliyah or I'm out!"

I hear Aaliyah singing along with the stereo as I walk out the door. *"I don't see nothin' wrong..."*

I make a dash for my truck. What the hell was all that about? Could my man's girl be a trick? Do I dare tell him what the hell just happened in there? Maybe it was nothing I say to myself to calm down. Moments later, I see Aaliyah walking toward my truck no longer in a towel but a low cut yellow ensemble. I pop the locks for her.   I hope like hell she'll be quiet during the ride to my house, but as soon as I finish my silent prayer, she took a stab at conversation.

"Listen Khalil, I don't want you to have the wrong impression about me."

"What impression is that Aaliyah?" I try to keep my eyes on the road, but I can't take my eyes off her cleavage. This dress hugs her body in all the right places and makes it hard not to stare. And her come-fuck-me heels are not helping me at this point, which all of a sudden reminds me of Shayla. And damn, she smells just like Amber.

"You know exactly what I'm talking about, Khalil, don't play stupid."

"Okay." I figure my one word response will shut her up but I'm wrong.

"Okay, what?"

"Ok, Aaliyah, whatever you say, no hard feelings alright."

"Hard feelings about what?"

Aaliyah places her hand on my thigh and has a sincere look on her face. She looks at me innocently like she's done nothing wrong. If I didn't know any better, I'd say I was the crazy one.

"If I've offended you in any way, please let me know, Khalil. The last thing I want to do is make enemies."

"Naaah, Aaliyah, I'm cool. I'm just not down with being alone with my man's girl and having drinks with her while she's half naked and listening to music, that's all. But nothing happened, so it's all good. Just don't let that happen again."

"You're right Khalil, it was naive of me to parade around my own apartment wearing a towel. It was wrong for me to listen to music while I got dressed. And I should've never offered you a drink while I was having one myself. How stupid of me."

"Are you trying to make me think I was imagining things back there, Aaliyah?" She is pissing me off! Ain't a damn thing crazy about me. If I didn't know anything else, I know when a broad is throwing pussy at me!

"I think that once you step outside of "Khalil's little world," you'll find the answer to that question." She has the audacity to throw up the quotation fingers when she makes that smart ass comment about *my world*.

I stare at her dumbfounded, in true disbelief after she says that and watch with my mouth agape. She reaches forward to change *my* radio station as if she hadn't just insulted my intelligence. Oh, she's good. Her poise and confidence is killing me. I laugh as I think to myself; If this wasn't my man's girl, I'd break her back in, slap that Mac lip glass off her mouth, and make her catch the fucking bus.

Amber
I Was Born This Way

It's six o'clock. I'm finally ready for our girl's night out. I love the way I look in this dress. Scott sure knows how to pick them. This black Donna Karan surplice dress feels just as sexy as it looks. It's form-fitting and hugging my new body like a glove. The halter ties behind my neck and this strapless bra I found is even managing to hold these thirty-eight double-d's of mine in place. The full skirt ends with a four-point hankie hemline right at my knees.

I have on the cutest black ankle strap, open-toed sandals that I got from Payless. I lied and told Scott that I picked them up from Nine West. He'll never know the difference if I don't take them off. I decided to go with a Bohemian curly look today for my hair with a natural makeup. My black clutch is fierce, and yes I got it from Payless too. It has some sort of C-shaped emblem on it so Scott will probably think it's a Coach bag. Seems that we're going to be overdressed for a simple sex party, but knowing Scott, we'll be dressed just right.

I look out the window and just as I am making sure the vertical blinds fall back in place properly, I see Scott pulling up in front of my house. Today he's chosen to drive his pearl, cream colored Lexus RX330. I can tell he's been to the car wash; his tires are shining more than the ice he's wearing around his neck.

Scott gets out of his truck. He knows better than to blow the horn for me. I chuckle as he walks to my porch. The man switches better than any runway model I have ever seen. "My God, he is so dramatic" I say to myself out loud.

While Scott may switch, he is definitely a fine, light-skinned man, smooth like whipped butter. He's wearing a Gucci outfit; I mean "creation." It's just a little tight for my taste. I mean, I don't like a man to sag his clothing, but a little room doesn't hurt either. Scott always said, "I'm never going to wear this more than once so it may as well fit just right."

Scott hates when people bought their clothing two to three sizes too big. He thought that was strictly for children because they're constantly growing. As a man thirty-five years of age, he didn't have use for leaving room to grow. He'd done all the growing he was going to do. Scott also feels that wearing creations more than once is passé. I guess this is why he shopped all the time. Nordstrom's is his second home, and everyone who worked there was on a first name basis with him. Actually some are on an intimate basis with his platinum American Express card.

I head down the stairs to greet my friend. He's going to bust a blood vessel when I tell him that Khalil hasn't gotten here with Aaliyah yet.

"No you are not standing on my porch looking at yourself in your lil mirror." I joke.

"Hello to you too, baby girl." Scott places his mirror inside his Gucci bag and kisses me on both cheeks. We head on in the house.

I smell Scott's Jazz cologne, and all I can do is admire his gear. I follow him with my eyes from the bottom to the top and give him a once over. I, however, have trouble getting past the Gucci moccasins. The moccasins are in beige and ebony original Gucci fabric, with brown and green calfskin trim, and topped with a red and green signature buckle in the middle. He had to have paid no less than four hundred dollars for those babies right there.

Scott knows I'm checking him. He turns to face me again with all the grace and confidence of a supermodel. He tips his Gucci frames so I'd notice those, too. He wore those classic aviator sunglasses with the black metal frame and gray gradient lens, laden with the Gucci logo alongside the temple. The diamond cut Movado watch also catches my eye as it almost appears to float in mid air against his shades. The detailing on his Gucci cotton pants gives them an air of retro style. The belt loops are set a bit below the top of the waist, reminiscent of the vintage Hollywood-waist style, and there is a small V-shaped notch at the back, for a dash of flair. Scott is fabulous, and he knows it.

"If you're done with your once over," Scott says with a smile, "Is the gang all here?"

"Actually, it's just me and Keisha. Khalil is bringing Aaliyah as we speak."

"Ok...see...You bitches are getting on my last nerve already, and I am too pretty to have that happen right now." He snaps his fingers. "You better call Big Daddy Kane and see how much longer we have to wait."

"Alright, Scott." I respond laughing. We enter my living room. Keisha is seated at the bar already on her third Grey Goose martini.

"Damn bitch, I'm loving that outfit. You have got to let me rock that one day." Keisha says in a slur.

Scott looks disgusted. Keisha didn't properly acknowledge him.

"Amber would you please tell her?" Scott commands more than asks.

I immediately start laughing and glad Scott has arrived.

"Keisha, Scott doesn't wear outfits, okay? He wears creations."

"Oh, please! All I know is he's wearing some clothes created by Gucci, and my apple bottom ass would look gorgeous in that shit."

"Amber, is she drunk!?" Scott asks with his hand on his hip and pointing at Keisha. "Please don't come around my people acting all ignorant and shit. I would never be able to live it down."

I take a look at Keisha and she does look a little tipsy. Without saying a word, I politely take her drink from her hand.

"I am not drunk, Amber. Scott knows damn well that I have a nice ass. He just doesn't want to admit it, but I bet if this same ass were on a man, he'd suck it." Keisha stands and strikes a Playboy-like pose in the middle of the living room.

Scott sets his Gucci bag on the table, removes his shades, folds his arms and takes in the effects of Keisha all in her Prada "creation." He knows it's from Neiman Marcus. He saw it yesterday. Her white halter-type bustier cut top allows for a clear visual of her belly button and her matching low rise capris seem to hover perfectly above the crack of her ass. The three and a quarter-inch, honey colored, leather spiral-strapped Via Spiga sandals wrap around her petite leg flawlessly, traveling up to just below her knees. Her jet black hair flows down her shoulders and glisten against her ebony kissed skin. Keisha is dark, majestic even. She has the kind of skin color that scares white people. Some would say she is regal. Her Via Spiga shades match her bag and sandals perfectly and make her look as if she is one of Charlie's Angels. The rhinestone belly chain ties firmly around her mid-waist and makes her flat belly look even more inviting. Keisha does look good.

"Yes, I guess you're right. If your name was Keith instead of Keisha, I'd probably give you a sample." We all laugh together. Scott takes Keisha's drink from me and finishes it.

As I search for my cell phone to call Khalil, I hear a key in the door. Khalil walks in. He has a strange look on his face. Aaliyah follows close behind. She seems in a glorious mood.

Khalil must have an attitude about me hanging up on him earlier. Oh well, he should learn to think before he speaks. Now that I am married, I have set in my mind that I'll take some things from Khalil, but the years of his nonsense have grown me a thicker skin. So bullshit is no longer allowed. I guess he'll find that out soon enough.

"Hey, everybody." Khalil acknowledges Scott and Keisha.

"Amber, I need to talk to you." He walks up to me and leads me by the hand toward the bedroom. He appears to be in a very serious mood.

"Can't this wait, Khalil? I've already made Scott and Keisha wait too long." Without even responding, Khalil picks up his keys and leaves out the door. Aside from Aaliyah, everyone in the room notices his attitude and turns to look at me.

Of course Scott couldn't resist.

"Oooohhh...uh uh, baby girl, is the honeymoon over already?" His voice seems to have elevated two octaves.

"It's nothing Scott, trust me. Nothing that he won't get over."

"You sure, Amber?" Keisha jumps in. "I've got my straight razor in my bag and a whole lotta strength in my *slap-a-nigga* arm."

"That won't be necessary, Keisha. Like I said, he'll be just fine." I turn to Aaliyah who is staring at me from the bar and has already made herself a drink.

"Hey Aaliyah, you look lovely." I say.

"Oooh Yes, girlfriend, I believe *tight* is the word," Scott agrees walking to Aaliyah and taking her by the hand. Forcing her to stand up from her barstool, Scott circles Aaliyah to get a better look. "I absolutely love this dress. Is this from Nordstrom?"

"Thank you Scott, but no, this is from the Chanel line," Aaliyah replies.

"Chanel? Really? I'd say this definitely makes you a member in my circle of trust. How much did this set you back?"

"Oh I didn't pay for it, it's one of the perks I get from my modeling gigs. They let us have what we want after we've modeled them."

"Oh, so you mean it's second hand?" Scott retorts. He releases Aaliyah's hand as if she has some incurable contagious disease. He brings his hand over his mouth and chuckles lightly.

This is my cue to change the current path of this conversation. Scott doesn't hold back when it comes to his comments, especially about fashion. Sometimes he needs to be interrupted. This is one of those times.

"Scott, would you look at the time? It's six-fifty-five. Where exactly is this party being held at?"

"Oh shit, you're right, Amber. It's in Scotch Plains, so we've got to roll now." Scott picks up his Gucci bag, takes out his mirror, smoothes over his eyebrows, puts his shades on and heads to the door. "You ladies did remember to bring your checkbooks, correct?"

"I got shotgun!" Keisha blurts out. "I look much too good to be holding down anybody's back seat today."

Scott turns to face Keisha and, without a second thought, snaps his fingers and states, "Bitch, please! You can ride in the trunk and you will still look good because you're riding with me, ok?"

We laugh all the way to the car. As we all pile in, Scott blasts one of his favorite songs and begins to sing along. *I Was Born this Way* by Sylvester. None of us seem to have a problem with his current choice of music. It was the jam back in the day so we all join in. The sun is shining, and it's about seventy-five degrees outside. A beautiful summer evening. We look good enough for *Lifestyles of the Rich and Famous.*

Aaliyah is sitting a little too close to me for comfort. I slide over to add some space and place my purse between us to give some much needed room.

"Amber you look really nice today."

"Thanks Aaliyah, so do you."

"And thanks for inviting me out tonight, I was going stir crazy sitting in that house."

"No problem Aaliyah, call me anytime if you're feeling bored. I don't mind you coming over to the house."

"Okay, Amber, I'll hold you to that." She moves in closer to me and leans her head in toward my neck. "Mmmm, that smells good Amber. What are you wearing?"

"Oh, it's Estee' Lauder's *Beyond Paradise*. I fell in love with it the first time I smelled it in one of those magazine inserts. It's nice, right?"

"Yes it is. I'm going to have to tell Shawn to pick up some of that for me. I love that soft, fresh, yet seductive scent."

I look up and my eyes meet with Scott's in his rear view mirror. I hate to say it but he doesn't miss a beat.

"Awwww, hell no, girlfriend. Why are you all up on her like that? We don't do cloning around these parts, okay?" He continues. "One Amber is all we need in a lifetime, so please, do me a favor and get your own identity."

Scott always had this way of protecting me even when I didn't need protecting. He used to do the same thing with Keisha until she told his ass off. It was almost as if the two of them would compete for my attention. If I were with Keisha one night, I had to be with Scott the next. They used to drive me crazy until they both realized that I'd never take sides and that I loved them equally. And, ever since Keisha let Scott have it in her own ghetto fabulous way, he accepted her as one of the family. He had no choice, because I honestly believe Keisha would've ended up whipping his ass.

"Scott, shut up!" I say before Aaliyah could get the fireworks going.

When I look at her, she has a smile on her face. Keisha's in the front seat laughing her head off.

"It's okay, Amber. I'm sort of getting used to Scott's personality. He doesn't hold back. I like that."

"Girl listen," Keisha said between giggles. "All you gotta do is put this queen in *Her* place. I promise you, *she'll* back off. Until you do that, its gon' be open season on Aaliyah."

Scott interrupts. "Well right now, I'm already in my place. Behind this wheel, and, if Miss Thang back there gets too out of line, she'll be left on the side of Route 22 hailing a cab. And I doubt seriously, she'll see any cabs around these parts."

"Now that's the second time today I've been threatened with catching a cab. Looks like I'm going to have to get my own set of wheels if I'm to survive in this family." Aaliyah says.

We all laugh and small talk ensues for the rest of our ride to the party. Somehow I don't think Scott is feeling Aaliyah too much and something tells me it has nothing to do with competing for my attention.

Keisha
I Need Love

Finally, we're here. Scott and this damn sunroof was 'bout to make me slap his ass. He knows damn well that this ain't the kind of hair to be blowin' in no wind. *Fuckin' fag.* He does this shit on purpose.

"Take the locks off the doors so we can get out, stupid!"

Scott looks at me and puts that damn finger up. I should grab that shit and break it.

"See bitch, you'll be walking home tonight." Scott says to me while he's switching his high-yellow ass off.

Amber and Aaliyah laugh at us, but shit, I ain't playin'. I'm mad as hell. I gotta walk in here lookin' like Macy Gray, all frizzed up 'n shit. Scott's just mad 'cause I'm the real thang, and he ain't. Fuckin' fag.

Amber gets out of the car and walks over to me. She begins smoothing my hair back into place.

"Keisha, you'd look fine if you just fixed your face and stop snarling like that."   "C'mon Amber. You know he had that sunroof open like that on purpose. Soon as I asked him to close it, he opened the shit wider."

Scott laughs. He has the nerve to be grooming himself in his little mirror. Amber grabs me by the hand and leads me to the front door. She knows I'm 'bout ready to spit in Scott's face. I don't know why I always insist on being around this mutha fucka. He gets on my last nerve.

"Calm down, Keisha. Why do you always allow him to get under your skin this way? You know if you feed him, he'll keep growing."

"I don't know Amber. But one of these days it's gon' be a misunderstandin'."

"Well please, let's not do that tonight, okay?"

Amber always gotta be the peace maker.

"Scott, come over here and apologize."

"Puhlease! Who that bitch think she is, Bernie Mac? She'll be okay. Here KeKe, you want my mirror?" I can't help but laugh at his punk ass. We are all laughing. If I didn't love him, I'd probably be in jail by now for murder.

Scott walks to the front door and rings the bell. A tall, sexy, *foine* ass brotha opens the door. Damn! Baby got it goin' on too. Got the Mitchell & Ness jersey thing poppin' with the fitted to match. Some Roc-A-Wear jeans with the new air max on. Got the *bling-bling* hangin' 'round his neck and the Sidekick on his hip. Mmmmphh! And he a red bone thug, just like I like 'em. *Dat's what it do.* Something tells me I'm going to have me some fun up in here, *yes sir.* Especially if there's more where he came from. Scott interrupts my drooling with that high-pitched ass voice of his. Always tryin' to be a soprano.

"Hey Bobby. I didn't know you were coming out tonight. You should have called me and maybe we could have rode together."

Now why the fuck he gotta sing instead of talk?

"What's up, Scott?" They do that European shit and kiss at the air on each side of their faces. *Ain't this a bitch!*

"Come on in y'all. Everyone's inside and they're just getting started. I hope y'all brought y'all checkbooks."

Would you look at this shit? Oh, I gotsta get my gaydar looked at. Amber, Aaliyah and I are behind Scott and *Barbara, I mean Bobby* as we walk in the door. We can't help but crack the fuck up. Scott turns around. He gives us a dirty look as if to say we better not embarrass him. Oh I intend to show my natural black ass up in this here spot tonight. Mutha fucka wanna open up sunroofs 'n shit, well payback is a bitch! And I'm still trippin' over this homo-thug ass brotha that let us in.

We walk into the house and there are wall to wall people. And no they are not playin' L.L.'s, *I Need Love*. Damn. Looks like the BET awards up in here. From chandeliers to red fucking carpets. They even got caterers walking around serving champagne.

"Excuse me." I'm trying to get this waitress' attention. She don't seem to hear me. "*'Scuse me.*" I say it a little louder this time. I know the bitch hears me. She walks over to us in her little French maid costume and gives us all drinks. I sure as hell hope they're paying her a grip to wear that bullshit. Lookin' like a damn French poodle with that fake ass blonde hair.

Scott leads us further into the house. A short, young woman approaches us and introduces herself. *Dayum*, she 'bout black as me. She's cute, but she can't be no more than four feet tall. And she got heels on.

"Hello Scott. Ladies." She nods at us and more European kissing between Scott and the lollipop-kid.

"Hey, Pam. These are my friends, Amber and Aaliyah." Scott introduces her as the host of the party. She shakes Amber's and Aaliyah's hand, then Scott points to me.

"And this right here is Kizzy." Scott looks at me and busts out laughing. Even Amber and Aaliyah have smiles on their faces. "No, no, I'm just joking. This is Keisha."

Okay, he wants to play. Well I got sumthin' for twinkle toes. The dwarf pretends to ignore Scott's ignorance and continues with her hospitality.

"Nice to meet you all ladies. Come on in and make yourselves comfortable. Feel free to take a look around and the person with whom you'll be placing your orders with will be out shortly."

"Ummm, excuse me Pam. But is everybody in here gay?"

I figure this question will fuck Scott up. It does.

"Keisha!" Scott yells.

"What!?" I ask like I don't have a clue.

"It's okay, Scott." Munchkin laughs. "No, Keisha. But even gay people like to spice it up in the bedroom from time to time. I don't discriminate when money is involved." She continues. "Especially since *the house* gets everything for free. There's something here for everyone. I'm almost positive you'll leave with a few things of your own. I'll be inside mingling with other guests so just let me know if there's anything you need."

She glances over at Aaliyah. "Excuse me. Aaliyah is it?"

"Yes, it is."

"I just can't help but feel like I know you from some place. Where are you from?"

"No, I don't believe so. I'm not from Jersey, I'm from Virginia." Aaliyah explains.

"Oh, okay. I just asked because I'm one of those people that never forget a face."

"Well I do model. Maybe you've seen me in something."

"Well that must be it then. I'm a fashion editor for *Elle* magazine. I knew you looked familiar. You've just landed the next cover, right?"

"Yes, I did." Aaliyah has this big smile on her face. Probably 'cause somebody besides Shawn done noticed her ass.

"I guess congratulations are in order then. And I must say you are a very beautiful woman, even more so in person. I'm sure we'll be seeing a lot of each other. Have you relocated here to Jersey?"

"Thank you, Pam. But no, I don't live in Jersey, I've just moved to the City."

Okay, enough of this damn small talk, I needs me another drink. These two bitches need to go get a room.

"New Jersey, New York, it's all the same thing girl. Well, let me let you all go and see what we have to offer. And Aaliyah, be sure to touch base with me before you leave the party, alright?"

"No problem Pam, I will."

Finally. We walk away. We all start looking at the merchandise.

Scott sees some more of his "people" and says, "Okay bitches, you're on your own. Time for me to circulate. I refuse to be seen hanging around *straight* people all night."

He walks away and fades into the crowd.

Amber, Aaliyah and I are browsing at the displays that are set up on every table. Body lotions, body oils, body sprays, and body gels. Big dicks, little dicks, huge dicks, *monstrous* dicks. Damn, they even got curved dicks. Strap-ons, boodie-balls, nipple clamps, clit clamps. Asshole clamps? What the hell? Is that a pussy? I walk over to get a closer look. Now I know gotdamn well...

"Amber! Lee-Lee! Look at this shit right here! It ain't enough to just sell dildos anymore? Now *we're* being cloned?"

"Please don't call me that Keisha." I ignore Aaliyah. I'm too busy tryin' to see what this fake pussy is about. We stare at the replica with our mouths open. We pick it up, one by one, and examine it. The shit even got fake pubic hairs on it. I'm buggin' so I sniff it then stick my finger inside of it.

"*Eeeel*, Keisha, stop. I can't believe you just did that." Amber jokes. "Put it down."

"What? That's what it's for, right?"

I drop it on the table, and we continue looking at displays. I feel like I have been sucked into a pornographic website. All these people in here are the pop-ups. Shit, I ain't clicking on nothing. Fuck around and have me in another room, butt naked and doin' the "give-it-up". Ain't nothing *but* freaks up in here! I don't know how Amber let Scott talk her into coming to this wild event. This is beyond me.

"So Keisha, what did it feel like?" Aaliyah asks.

"What you talkin' 'bout Aaliyah?" I know what the fuck she talkin' bout but I wanna hear her say it. Damn freak.

"You know. The pussy. What did it feel like?"

"You picked it up and held it, didn't you? Why you askin' me what it felt like?"

"I know, but I didn't stick my finger in it, you did!"

"Well ain't you never stuck your finger in yo' own pussy before?" I'm laughing at Aaliyah. Looks like somebody wants to know what it feels like to take a walk on the wild side. Nothing else after that. Should have stuck her own damn finger in there. Fuckin' freak. I don't know, Scott has me wondering about Aaliyah now, and she hasn't done a damn thing. Amber nudges me.

"Be nice, Keisha."

"What? Stop doing that Amber. Keep nudging me 'n shit. I *am* being nice." We continue browsing. I see a waiter, I mean a caterer, coming with more drinks. I signal to him, and I take two glasses. Amber and Aaliyah look at me while taking only one a piece.

"What? I don't know when he gon' bring his ass back out here." They both laugh like I just said sumthin' funny.

"Keisha you are so ghetto."

"And so are you Amber. Wasn't too long ago when yo' ass was drinkin' forty's from the bottle right along with

117

me. You just happened to go off to college and come back white." Amber almost snorts up her drink laughing.

"Come on y'all, let's go over where the food is. I'm hungry." I lead the way.

We head to the corner where they placed all of the food. We see platters of crabmeat, lobster, chicken, shrimp, baked potatoes, Mac & Cheese, tuna salad, baked beans, they got it all. Chips, dip, crackers, bagels, pigs-in-blankets, all different kinds of cheeses, breads, celery sticks, salad dressings. The works. Even got a section just for pastries. Cakes, pies, cookies, donuts, Danishes, strudels. Damn! I'm gaining weight just looking at this shit.

I grab a plate and help myself to some lobster, crabmeat and baked potatoes. Humph, I may be ghetto, but I got me a suburban appetite. Amber and Aaliyah tryin' to be cute. Sitting here sipping on some gotdamn bottled water and eating salad. Dem two bitches can go right ahead and watch me eat. I'm fuckin' this shit up. It's free too? Shit, you ain't gotta tell me twice. And I betta not hear their stomachs growling later, either. I'm going to burp loud as hell if I do. While we're eating, Scott sees us and comes over.

"Hey girls. Are you having a good time?" I ain't answering 'cause my mouth is full, but Amber does. She ain't got shit in her mouth anyway.

"Yes Scott, this is really nice."

Nice? It's a fuckin' freak ass orgy going on up in here.

"How about you, Aaliyah? Are you enjoying yourself?"

"Yes I am Scott. Thanks for inviting me. Did you find anything you like?" She asks.

"Yeah girl. I saw this ring that I want."

"Ring? What kind of ring?"

"Girl, it's a ring that goes around your dick, honey!"

Scott excitedly demonstrates for us like we really give a fuck about a dick ring.

We ain't got no damn dicks.

"You slide it over your dick all the way to the base. It gets tighter when you're getting ready to cum. It's supposed to keep you from cummin' fast."

Amber doesn't understand what the hell he's talking about.

"Well how does it know when you're getting ready to cum?" *She's such a saint.*

"Because Amber. The more excited a man gets and the closer to ejaculation he becomes, the harder and larger he gets. As the dick gets larger, the ring traps blood in. This again makes it larger."

I figure this is my cue to say something. "Well, why don't you see if you can use it on your tongue. That way, the harder it gets for you to shut up, the more it will tighten."

"Fuck you, Kunta!"

Everyone laughs. Scott fades to black. We're done eating and decide to have some more drinks. As we continue to browse, Aaliyah gets our attention when she sees something she likes.

"Amber, look at this one. Oooh, I want this."

Amber takes it from Aaliyah and reads the card attached to it. Says it's called a Beating Heart. Looks like a thong with no damn crotch if you ask me. Instead of a crotch, there's this little heart shaped thingy that feels like gelatin. Even Amber looks confused.

"What the hell is this?" Amber had to ask. Of course I can't help but jump in.

"A pair of fucked up ass panties." More laughing.

"No, Keisha. You're crazy. Something is really wrong with you." Aaliyah laughs and begins explaining. "See the picture on the card? That's how it's supposed to be used."

I look at the picture. A woman is wearing these fucked up ass panties. But actually it looks kind of interesting. "Oh, okay. You put this on like a regular thong, and this little heart shaped thing sits on top of your clit?"

"Yes, Keisha. See, Amber. You put your legs through the straps and the heart shape sits on your clit. And this button right here controls the beating. Here. Feel the vibrations." Aaliyah gives it to Amber. Amber passes it to me.

"Ooooh. I think I can get with this." I tell them. "Fuck around and wear this shit under my clothes to work and be smiling all damn day. Every time Miss Beverly pisses me off, I'll just hit this damn button and start smiling. They won't know what the fuck is wrong with my ass."

We all crack up. Amber actually coughs up her drink this time.

"You're stupid, Keisha! Look what you made me do." She says with a laugh.

"I ain't make you do shit. You probably was thinkin' the same thing."

Aaliyah writes down the information she needs to place her order. We move on. I'm thinkin' she must've been to one of these parties before. She actin' like she knows what to do.

All of a sudden, the music stops playing, and everybody gets quiet. *What the fuck?* See, I knew this was the gotdamn Twilight Zone. The midget lady reappears and asks for everyone's attention. Looks like all the caterers are now out on the floor, walking around to everyone, refilling drinks.

The midget speaks. "Hello, everyone. For those of you I haven't met, my name is Pamela, and I'm your host for this evening. First I'd like to thank you all for coming, and I hope you've been enjoying yourselves. Now, without further ado, I'd like to introduce my friend Eva, who'll be going over each and every item, including demonstrations. Next to each display, you should see order forms that need to be filled out if you wish to purchase that item. So, having said all of that, drink up! And here's Eva."

Oh, little Webster think she slick. Tryin' to get us all liquored up with free alcohol so we can go check-writing crazy.

"Hello, everyone. My name is Eva, and I specialize in adult entertainment. What I'm passing around right now are my business cards. If you read the cards, you'll see that my partner Chyna, who couldn't be here tonight, and I, run a business called *Selective Succulence*. We do all sorts of things, from birthday parties to bar mitzvahs. Office parties to bachelor parties and so much more. Please feel free to give us a call if you're interested and by all means, do tell a friend."

Dayum! I ain't gay or nothing, but this bitch Eva got it going on! Pretty, light skin. Long, black pretty ass hair. Bad ass shape and ass for days. She don't got no bra on either 'cause her shit sittin' up just as perky. Sexy, aqua looking green eyes. I know they probably fake, but she making that shit work, for real. I ain't mad at her either. *Damn, could I be gay?*

I look at Amber and Aaliyah, and I can tell we're all thinking the same damn thing. This bitch better work! I think probably everybody in this room is. I look around the room, and even the gay ones are drooling. *Dayum!* Check out her gear. She got this tight ass baby blue Burberry halter dress on. I don't even care for Burberry too much 'cause I don't like all that plaid 'n shit, but her shit is nice. She only has the Burberry detailing around the edges. And her wedged heel Burberry sandals look like they were custom made to go with her dress.

This a bad bitch right here! I gotta give it to her. As she makes her way around the room, she's holding everyone's attention. It's like we all hangin' on to her every word. Even the gotdamn caterers have stopped serving. Now they been in the back all damn night, I know they seen her ass already, so why the fuck they actin' like that? Somebody betta come over here and serve me. Shit, I'm sittin' here questioning my sexual preference so I *know* I needs me a drink.

As I wave to the hired help for more drinks, Scott comes over and sits with us.

"Guys, isn't Eva gorgeous?" None of us say anything. "I know y'all been looking at her, don't act like y'all deaf."

"We hear you Scott." Amber speaks up. "Yes, she's very pretty. Do you know her?"

"But, of course, I know Ms. Eva. And if you think she's gorgeous, wait 'til you see her partner, Chyna."

I already know the answer but I gotta ask anyway. "Is she gay, Scott?"

"Why? You thinking about hollering at her?"

I knew this mutha fucka was gonna get smart. "No, I'm not, you back-door-bandit. I just figured since *you* knew her, she must be."

"Well I know you too, Celie. Are you gay?" Again, I can't help but laugh. Amber and Aaliyah are doubled over. I can't *stand* this nigga. Oooooh!

"Fuck you, Scott. The only thing you can get me on is my complexion. So what, I'm dark. But I'm a bad bitch, and you know it. And if I was a light-skinned bitch, we'd be just alike."

"Now I don't know what in the hell would make you think that sweetie." He snaps.

There he goes, snapping those damn fingers. Bastard don't know he just set himself up. "C'mon now, Scott. You know we got a lot in common. We both dress fly as hell, and we both suck dick."

Even Scott laughs. I stick my tongue out at him then finish my drink. We're all laughing so hard, we don't see Eva walk up.

"Hey, Scottie. How are you?" They hug and the European kissing begins. Damn, does everybody he knows do that dumb shit?

"Hi, Eva. You look fabulous girl." If he snaps those fingers one more time, I swear to God!

"Thanks baby, you already know you do, too. Hello ladies, how are you all doing?"

Seem like we all speak at once. "Fine."

"So, have you guys decided on anything?"

We all give her our orders. All I get is three bottles of this spray that you use on your sheets. 'Posed to make your sheets feel silky and slippery or some shit like that. Smells good as hell too. Amber gets some aromatherapy oils and some motion lotion. Said she heard about it and wants to see what it's like. Scott gets his lil ring toy and Aaliyah...see I knew she was a freak. She gotta go all out and get the butterfly which ain't anything but a plastic dick that moves on its own and that damn heartbeat bullshit. We finish with our paperwork when Scott interrupts.

"Alright ladies, it's been fun, but it's time to go."

I agree. Ain't no damn telling what's gonna happen next. I already done seen about ten people disappear, and the front door ain't open up once since we arrived. Amber extends her hand to Eva.

"Well it was nice meeting you Eva. When should we expect our orders?"

"Oh, I'll let Scott know when your orders are in. You remember the part of the order form that said write down who invited you? Well that's what that part was for. So we'll know who to notify."

See, this bitch lying. That was so they could know who brought in the most money. Ain't nobody stupid. That's why I put Scott's name in big ass letters on mine and only bought three little bottles of cheap ass spray. Four dollars a piece and three for ten. Bet they won't be inviting his ass to nothing else.

"Oh, okay then. Well you have a good night." Eva walks us to the front door when I see the French poodle lady. I decide to have another one for the road and so does Aaliyah and Amber. Scott is still talking with Eva.

"So Eva, why didn't Chyna come out with you? You two are normally joined at the hip."

"I know. But she had other plans tonight that couldn't be changed so I had to go it alone. So Scott, where are you guys headed after this?"

"Well first I have to drop them off in Newark. After that, who knows...the night's still young. Why, girl? Is there an after party nobody told me about?"

I immediately laugh to myself and think, *Hell yeah!* And they ain't tell yo' faggot ass 'cause you brought cheap ass people over here.

"Well it's nine-thirty now so Pam and I should be wrapping this up in about a half hour or so. After this, we'll be going to the city to hang out for a bit. Why don't you and your friends come with us?"

Scott turns around to look at us. I'm feeling so nice right now that I don't mind getting my groove on a dance floor right about now. "I'm down, Scott."

"Nobody asked you, Florida Evans. Amber? Aaliyah? You guys wanna go?" *I can't stand his punk-ass.*

"I don't mind Scott. In fact, that'll be perfect because I'm supposed to take Aaliyah home tonight anyway. And I've had much too much to drink to be getting behind any wheels tonight. Just let me touch base with Khalil."

"Aaliyah, what about you?"

"Are you kidding? I'd love to go. Anything beats sitting in that house."

Aaliyah
The Quiet Storm

The sex party was fabulous. The music. The people. Everything about it. I have gone to a lot of them back at home. Never any quite like that one. Back home, we were lucky if we received a can of Colt 45 and some wing-flings, and you had better not throw away your cup, if you got one.

Which reminds me. I think I lost count of how many drinks I had somewhere around number five. But at least I'm among friends. Something tells me I'll be okay around them if I were to pass out or something. Not at all like back at home. Hell, I got so drunk at a party once, that the next day I couldn't remember how I got home. Not only was all my money gone, but my car was too. My own family!

They did have the decency to take me home. My sister, along with my cousins, are known for dropping people off in the park. They don't care *who* you are. That's why I don't drink with them anymore. Really I don't do much of anything with my family anymore, aside from my sister.

I appreciate the way Shawn's friends have welcomed me into their lives, without knowing much about me. I know it's really on the strength of Shawn, but I still feel like I've been approved, if there is such a thing. I feel so relaxed right now. So at peace. The warm air coming in through Scott's sunroof really makes this ride that much better. I'm smiling because I know for a fact that Keisha doesn't share my enthusiasm regarding the sunroof. That girl is crazy with a capital C. I'm glad she fell asleep or else she'd probably be letting Scott have it at this moment.

But putting things in perspective, Shawn really does have nice friends. Khalil is cool enough, I guess. He seems to be a true friend to Shawn thus far. It amazes me though, how some men can have all their ducks in a row, but they still cannot take time out to do right by their children. It's almost as if he's so focused on being a good man, that he's forgotten he has an eight year old daughter. It's ironic. But who am I to judge?

Scott is cool, too, I guess. The way he and Keisha go at it is the best comedy I've witnessed in a long time. That is, outside of the Dave Chapelle show anyway. I haven't laughed as hard as I have tonight since that Rick James episode aired. *I'm Rick James, BITCH!* Those two should really think about taking their act on the road.

Scott does need to tone the drama-queen stuff down a bit. Other than that, he's tolerable. As far as I can tell, he's only looking out for Amber when he does get crazy.

And Amber...Amber is such a kind person. So nice, in fact, that her pureness is almost an aphrodisiac. And on top of that, she's gorgeous. I find myself thinking about her whether it be something she said or just her fragrance. For some reason, she invades my mental.

I remember Amber saying that she recently lost a lot of weight, but I'm sure the weight couldn't have made that much of a difference. She's a beautiful woman, but her inner beauty reigns supreme. Rarely do you find women who possess those qualities. Women who are *genuinely* kindhearted without having ulterior motives. *I should know.* A blind man can see that Amber is the epitome of such, which is why I find myself becoming so fond of her. I can't explain it really...I find that I can be myself around her and never once does she judge. No questions, no prying, no unsolicited advice, none of that. Any woman knows how stressful it can be when trying to fit in somewhere you don't belong. All the masks. All the fake smiles.

The mindless dribble of conversation, none of which I've had to endure around Amber. Amber is the God's honest truth, a beautiful person inside and out. I wish now that I'd met Shawn a long time ago and on different terms. Then maybe I wouldn't have to...

"Aaliyah, are you okay?" Amber interrupts my thoughts.

"I'm fine Amber, why do you ask?"

"Girl, you seemed like you were a thousand miles away."

"No, I'm here." I smile at her. "I was just thinking about how good I feel at this moment."

"You're in love, huh?"

"Honestly, Amber? I think I am." Look at the way she's smiling at me. So sincere. She doesn't even question me as to whom I'm in love with. Just me being in love is good enough for her.

"It's a beautiful thing, isn't it Aaliyah? Being in love and having it reciprocated. It sends chills through my body just thinking about it."

I take my eyes from Amber's smile and just happen to notice Scott's inquisitive stare in the rear view mirror. Oh boy, here he goes.

"No, bitch. Those chills you was just talkin' bout? They ain't coming from you being in love. Them bad boys was sent Federal Express by way of Courvoisier, okay?"

Sometimes I wonder if Scott believes that Amber and I are getting a little too close. Maybe he's even threatened by it. He always has a way of interrupting our one on one girl moments. He's funny, yes...but at the most inopportune times, he can be obnoxious. I feel like he needs to be put in his place.

"Leave Amber alone, Scott. How would you know where her chills are coming from? You know nothing about what a *woman* feels like when she's in love." Maybe that will shut him up.

"Oh, *hell* no! Hold up, wait a minute, back it up, and *re*-wind! Let me tell you something, *Miss Thang*! How many times have you told a man, *"Just because you have a dick, don't make you a man?"* And how many times have you told a man, *"I'm more man than you'll ever be?"* See...some of you women are fooled by the misconception that just because you got Sammy's Fish Box between yo' legs, that's all you need to be a woman. Well I have news for you, *Miss Thang*. I've got more estrogen in my left nut than you have in your entire body. You ain't fierce unless *I* say so!"

"Scott, calm down." Amber referees. "I'm sure Aaliyah didn't mean that in a bad way."

"How do you know that, Amber? You don't know anything about her *or* what she's capable of. All you know is that her name is Aaliyah and that she's fucking Shawn. Other than that, you're in the dark about this bitch right along with the rest of us."

Now he's gone too far.

"You know what, Scott? You're absolutely right. You *don't* know anything about me. Just like I *don't* know anything about you. I didn't know a resume was required in order to meet your approval. Allow me to make a mental note of that."

He's right, he doesn't know me. But if this shit continues, I may just have to give him a private screening.

"Ummm, Aaliyah is it?" Here he goes with his annoying snapping of the fingers.

"The only thing you need to know about me is...my name is Scott...and that I'm happy...I'm carefree...and I'm gay...and yes bitch, I was born this way!"

I glance over at Amber as she hides her smile with her hand. She's used to his antics and the fact that he can't hold his tongue. At this moment, it's not funny to me. Like he said, he doesn't know me. So what the hell makes him think that he's allowed to speak to me in this manner? I've had enough. I need to get out of this car before a major mishap occurs.

"Amber, I've changed my mind. I really don't feel much like going out tonight."

"C'mon Aaliyah, don't do that. Scott's just being Scott. Ignore him. I promise we'll have a nice time." She pleads.

"Uh, uh Amber. If she doesn't wanna go, let her ass stay home. All I wanna know is one thing. How the hell she gettin' there 'cause I ain't takin' her." Scott says.

That's it, that's the last straw and the look on my face confirms as much. "Well you know what, mutha fucka; you can pull over right here and let me the fuck out! I'll find my way home, trust!"

"Listen to that Amber. Bet you ain't never heard her talk like that before, have you?"

Before Amber can get a word in edgewise, Scott pulls over to a screeching halt and looks at me. "Bitch, you ain't said nothin' but a word! Get the fuck out!"

"Scott, no! That's enough!" Amber yells. "You two are trippin'! Nobody's getting out in the middle of nowhere. I can't believe this. Scott, just drop us off at my house. I'll take her home. Unbelievable!"

Through all the yelling and commotion, Keisha wakes up from her doze in the passenger seat. "What's going on? Why y'all screamin' n' shit?"

"Nothing, Keisha." Amber answers. "Everything's fine."

I feel bad that Amber had to see a glimpse of that side of me. But with Scott, there's no other way. He has this way of pushing and pushing until he gets a rise out of you. It's like he just has to have the last word.

No sooner do I finish my thoughts, he starts again. "Next stop...Society Hill...and don't forget to take *"FuBu"* up here with you."

For once, nobody laughs. I think we've all had enough of Scott for one night. Within minutes, we pull up in front of Amber's house. I can tell Scott is ready to get rid of me, but I don't think he wants Amber to go. He gets out of the car, and lets Amber out of the back. He has a frown-like smile on his face.

"You mad at me, baby girl?" He asks.

"No, Scott, I'm not mad. I'm just disappointed." She responds quietly.

"Okay look Amber, I'm sorry. Let me make it up to you. I'll pick you up tomorrow when you get off work, and I'll take you to City Island, your favorite spot. We can have lobster, filet mignon, whatever you want, it's on me. Just me and you, please?" He almost begs.

"It's not about me, Scott. It's about what you did to Aaliyah. She's the one you owe the apology to. Not me."

That's what I mean about Amber. Never concerned about herself. Always looking out for others. I love that about her. Too bad her persona doesn't have more of an impact on those around her. Scott looks *past* me and offers a lame apology. I *lamely* accept. To prove how sorry he is to Amber, he even offers to take Keisha home. He says it's the least he can do. I agree.

Scott and Amber say their goodbyes. I stand by idly, thinking to myself that I wish I had people in my life that cared for me as much. Amber gets so much love from so many people. I wonder how she could have ever made an enemy at all. Anyone who gets within ten feet of her can automatically see that she hasn't got a bad bone in her body.

Amber runs in the house to let Khalil know she's taking me home. While she's inside, I notice a flyer on Khalil's windshield so I take it off. It reads something about an open mic poetry night. I'll just give it to Amber when she comes out. I hate that she has to drive to the city like this, but what other choice do I have? I could call Shawn but I know he's probably just getting in from his proposal meetings. I really don't want to disturb his peace with my drama. I'll just have to make it up to Amber. She really does go out of her way for others, including me, and I know I don't deserve it. Most people would have you earn their love, their respect, their attention, but not Amber. It just comes naturally from her. Sort of radiates from her soul.

It is nice of Khalil to let Amber take his car for the ride. It's so spacious in here. Almost like being in your own living room. These Escalades have a way of floating over the open road.

The soft sounds of Vaughn Harper's *Quiet Storm* are playing subtly in the background, serving as a smooth back drop to a nice ride over to the city. Although Scott put a damper on things, it's still a lovely summer evening. The night is still rather young, but I know Amber has work in the morning.

I enjoyed getting out and having fun with the girls and Scott, but he really showed his behind tonight. It's funny to watch him and Keisha's interaction. Funny how they compete for Amber's attention, as if they don't know she already knows what they're doing. What they should know is that she loves them both dearly. If he had called her Kunta Kente' one more time, I think I would've peed on myself.

Traffic is not too bad on the New Jersey Turnpike this evening. The roads are clear. The stars are shining bright in the sky. A clear, beautiful summer night and a drive into the city with Amber. Perfect.

"Oh, Amber. This is my song." I lean in to turn up the volume on the radio. "Don't you just love this? It's a classic, right?"

She has to admit, *Between the Sheets* by the Isley Brothers is an all time classic. I turn to look at Amber. She seems to be really enjoying this song right now. She begins singing along with me. We finish the verse and laugh with one another. I've almost forgotten about how badly Scott worked my nerves.

"Amber, I just want you to know how sorry I am for the way things got out of hand tonight with Scott. I would never do anything to disrespect you; it's just that he..."

"It's alright, Aaliyah. Scott has a way of taking a person there. But to know him, I mean *really* know him, is to love him. I guess what I'm trying to say is...he's an acquired taste." Both of us laugh at her comment.

"I told you about his and Keisha's past confrontations. And you saw for yourself tonight, the way they interact. It's just the way he is, I guess. He's just...Scott."

"Okay, Amber. For you, I'll try to tolerate him. Anything for you."

"Thanks Aaliyah. Just give it some time. Pretty soon, you'll be yearning for a taste of his madness."

I wouldn't go that far.

"Oh, Amber. I forgot to give you this flyer that was on Khalil's windshield."

She takes the flyer from me and quickly glances at it.

"Amber, are you thinking what I'm thinking?"

"What Aaliyah?"

"Well, I was just thinking that this place on the flyer is not too far from me and it just started. You wanna go?"

"Oh Aaliyah, it sounds good, but I have to go to work tomorrow. Early morning for me."

The look of disappointment in my face must've resonated loudly as Amber quickly changes her tune.

"You know...why not? We can go. I love poetry and have been to so many readings and slams. Have you?"

"No, Amber. I've never been. It just seems like the coolest thing to do. I mean, the closest I've been to a poetry reading is the movie, *Love Jones*. But I've always wanted to go."

"Great, Aaliyah. Then it's settled, we'll go. I'm sure you'll love it."

I'm elated that Amber has agreed to take me to the poetry reading. I felt my heart race and my nerves get the best of me when she tried to decline. But then she changed her mind. It's strange. It is almost the same feeling you get when you think your man is about to break up with you. You get nervous and your brain automatically kicks into overdrive all on its own, searching for any sort of lifeline that will keep him near. It's crazy, I know. But at this point, I feel so good being around Amber. I'd be willing to create scenario after scenario just to get her to stay with me a little while longer.

Khalil's smooth ride, the few drinks I've had, the Quiet Storm and the fresh summer air blowing in the wind makes me feel so alive. I am actually happy. Just Amber and I. I look over at her behind the wheel. Amber looks so beautiful. I know I've been told that I'm gorgeous, a time or two, but shit, I'm a model. I get paid to be spectacular. But with Amber, it's different. She's beautiful for no reason at all. Her aura is fierce. And when she speaks, you get a majestic vibe of how beautiful she really is.

"So Amber, tell me. How does it feel to be married?" I lean and place my elbow on the armrest between us. I stare at her.

"Well Aaliyah, it's sort of hard to explain. I mean, I *feel* great. I really do. Khalil and I have been together for so long, that I feel like not much has changed aside from my last name. But officially being married...you know...being a wife, makes me feel proud. I love him dearly and am glad that we made it through. I'm sure Shawn has discussed with you some of the episodes from our past. I wouldn't dare try to cover them up. It happened. Shit happens. It was rough for me, but God has a way of speaking to us through trials. My momma always says, "If He takes you to it, He'll take you through it." Khalil and I are married now. I wasn't sure if we'd get to this place. I've gone through so much with him over the last several years but I believe that love, true love is about accepting that person unconditionally. Yes, some of the incidents in our past would make even the strongest woman head for the border, but I understand that long-lasting relationships have their ups and downs. My momma taught me that. She always said that nothing in life that's really worth something comes easy. You have to work for it. I also learned that from my man Notorious B.I.G. "Anything in life you gotta work hard for it." It was a hard pill to swallow to forgive Khalil, and I am a much better person for doing so. Khalil has changed tremendously over the years. He's a good man, and I'm more in love with him now than ever before."

If Amber only knew the truth. If she only knew that she was talking about my...

"But life is good right now, Aaliyah. And I give all my thanks to the Man upstairs for being in the place that I'm in. Now, all we have to do is get you ready to marry Shawn. I'm so happy for the both of you. I truly am. I've known and loved Shawn like a brother for years. He's one of my dearest friends. You have a good man in him."

I follow her lips as she speaks. The sight of those luscious lips makes my clit throb. Her voice is light, sexy. Her words sincere. Everything she's saying makes sense. She's such a good person. I lean in closer and place my hand on her thigh to let her know I agree with everything she's saying. It's so soft and supple. They're so thick and honey-coated that I would love to massage them. Then suck on them just a bit to see if they really do taste like honey. I've never felt this way about another woman before. She's reeling me in with her vernacular. I stare at her full breasts, and I tingle all over. I know this isn't right, but I can't seem to move my hand away. Amber looks at me confused, nervous.

"Is everything okay, Aaliyah?" She asks quietly.

"Uh...Yeah Amber, everything's fine. I'm sorry for touching your thigh like that. I just couldn't help but admire your dress. It's so soft and looks really good on you."

"Thank you, Aaliyah. I'm just glad I was able to fit into it. I love it too. Makes me feel sexy, girl. You know how hard it is to find something you actually like, then have it look sexy on you."

"Amber, you look *incredible* in it. You really are a very sexy woman." Amber smiles and looks at me.

"Thank you, Aaliyah. I'll take a compliment any place I can get it."

We pull up to the club much too soon for me, as I was enjoying our time alone. The valet takes the keys. We head inside. There's a table for two that seems to be waiting for us. Perfect.

"We found perfect seats Amber."

"Yes, Aaliyah, I know. Lucky us."

The short, heavy set waitress comes over to see if we'd like drinks.

"Hello ladies, what can I get you?"

"We'll have two apple martinis."

I order before Amber has a chance. I want this to be my treat. I smile at Amber hoping that it will pierce her soul. "This one's on me Amber. It's the least I can do."

She smiles that warm and endearing smile again. That smile that makes me want to forget about Shawn and crawl into her bed tonight.

"Thank you Aaliyah. I really appreciate that."

This entire experience is so mesmerizing. I'm feeling real nice right now from all the drinks. It's a good thing I've learned how to pace myself.

The rhythmic beats from the drums mixed with the slightest hint of jazz, sets off a bizarre vibe in this club. It's chilling really. The goose bumps running slowly through me tell me as much. I'm a hundred miles and running from my hometown, which is a damn good thing.

Amber taps me on my arm. She pulls me from my own world.

"Aaliyah, here comes the first poet."

I'm so excited. A petite, dark skinned, young woman comes to the mic. A Nubian princess graces the stage and commands all of our attention with her presence. She's pretty, but in no way any comparison to Amber. She speaks as the drums whisper in the background. The lights go dim.

"Peace, everyone. My name is Mother Earth, the Ebony one, the creator of all things," she proclaims. "Here to adorn your mind, and soul with some words to reach yours. I call this one, *Only In My Empire*."

Mother Earth seems to make love to the mic as she delivers a powerful poetic testimony. Her hands caress the large, metallic black mic. Her ruby lips frame the its bulbous head. Her voice is somewhat harmonic as her words ooze spiritually from her tongue.

"These Visions of Grandeur
Promote deep-seeded, uncultivated feelings
That sorrowfully soar throughout my soul …
Awaiting you …
Debating you …
Resisting you, yet missing you.
Is it wrong to love you?
Because damn … I do.
And my sweet Visions of Grandeur
Have me struggling in a world where....
Time and Space and Reason and Righteousness
Have No Place
It's just you and me and we …
For we are a set of free spirits yearning.
And My Love …
I want to lock you up in my Empire for days
To complete this fantasy … this craze
Nah … Hell No … It is truly beyond that.
To fulfill what is so unfulfilled
To both you and me and we.
Perhaps we should alter the rules,
Transform the Earth
To have it rotate on our axis
Because this world as we know it
Is not designed for what we believe …
You needing me and us needing we …
And You and me carouseling thru this galaxy,
Making eternal history,
Exploring the possibilities – infinitely
This mesmerizing infatuation is beyond my understanding.
It Will be next lifetime, sweet friend.
And my Visions of Grandeur …
With my wet-sticky-day-dreamin'

Envisions a time where
You will journey to a light at the end of my fantasy/fallacy
And penetrate so deep that you will caress my soul ...
And touch my spirit with the endowment that God has
blessed you with.
And I grab a hold of visions and refuse to release them,
Where vultures and rhyme and reason will devour them.
Cause it does hurt like hell ...
To not possess you the way that my entire being needs
to...
How every breadth I breathe needs you ...
So let me just hold on ...
And never let go
Knowing that if I step back into this harsh realty,
I will realize that I confused it with fantasy.
It was only after I looked into your eyes,
That I saw Paradise ...
And every woman wants that.
Suddenly I realized,
That you could be my Savior in disguise.
Is it wrong for me to love you?
Cause right here,
right now,
Damn baby....
I do."

She walks off the stage dramatically. I imagine her
saying "Sexual Chocolate" and drop the mic. Whoa, she was
really powerful! And through it all, I could only think of Amber.
What did the poet say? *Loving someone you're not supposed
to? That forbidden fruit? Struggling in a world?* Or whatever
she said about rhyme and reason, it was all so fierce! Amber
stands, along with everyone in the room, and gives her a
Standing-O. I can't help but join in. It was definitely a hot

performance. We finish our apple mars. Then Amber drops the bomb on me.

"Aaliyah, girl, I really have to get home. I'm having a ball, don't get me wrong, but I'm so tired right now."

I want to tell her that we could kick Shawn out. She could share my bed tonight and all the things that come with it.

"No problem Amber. I appreciate you spending the time with me." I tell her, but I wonder if she she's only here to make up for the drama Scott brought earlier. I really can't say.

I can't complain. I'm having a good time. Just being in her presence is enough for me. I feel a bit of nostalgia coming on as we exit the club. I really did enjoy myself tonight. I feel like I may have *even* enjoyed Scott. Hell, if it weren't for him, Amber and I would've never been afforded time alone. I'll have to remember to thank him when I see him again. *Yes, he'll probably love that.*

We pull up in front of my loft. I don't want to say goodnight. I don't want the night to end. I glance up at my bedroom window and see that the lights are out. I'm more than sure Shawn is sleeping by now. I turn to face Amber before getting out.

"Thank you, Amber for such a wonderful evening."

"Oh girl, anytime. I had fun." She tells me. She does look tired.

I intend to open the door and get out. Instead I find myself leaning in to give Amber a kiss on her cheek. The drinks combined with my attraction for her leads me to do something that I've wanted to do all evening. The apple mars give me some much needed confidence. I kiss her on her lips instead. All I can taste is the sugary sweetness of the martini on her soft and succulent lips. I unknowingly close my eyes and dream I could be in this spot forever. Amber pulls away and forces me from my fantasy. The look on her face tells me she's shocked. But so am I.

"Oh....uh....I'm so sorry Amber." I ramble. "I'm so embarrassed. Oh my goodness, I'm at a lost for words." Amber's look is one of concern.

"What was that about, Aaliyah?"

"I don't know what I was thinking. I've just had too much to drink, I'm not sure." I can tell by the look on her face that she doesn't believe me, but she is willing to accept my apology.

"Don't worry about it Aaliyah. It's been a long night. We're both tired. Just forget about it, okay? It was nothing." She smiles. I want to devour her, instead, I fall back.

"Okay, Amber, have a safe ride home." I step out of the truck and can't help but love the way she's smiling at me. Maybe the kiss did do something for her, because she looks as if she has something to say.

"Aaliyah?" Amber questions. Oh my God, I'm so nervous inside. Could she want to get down? I mean, I've never done this before, but I'm willing to be a quick study if given the opportunity to get between those thick thighs. Oooh, I'm feeling moist just thinking about it. *Please tell me what I want to hear. Please!* I'm almost too afraid to answer her.

"Yes, Amber?" She smiles again as if she knows I want to have my way with her. She smiles as if she knows I need some reassurance that it *will* eventually happen between us. She reaches toward the back seat and I can't help but wonder why.

"Khalil sent this sandwich for Shawn. Would you give it to him sweetie?"

Damn, damn, damn!

Scott
Must Be Nice

I can't believe that bitch broke fly with me. All up in Amber's face all the time. Amber may be naive to the fact, but I'm not. I can see through all that hand-me-down Chanel. She ain't foolin' nobody over this way.   Amber needs to wake her ass up and smell the "single white female" in that bitch. She wanna wear the same perfume. She wanna know where she got her dress. She like her earrings. What's next? Her man? Amber always befriending people she doesn't know. I told her about that shit before. Amber is the best friend I will ever have, and I refuse to see my baby girl ever hurt.

Now I'm stuck with Keisha's ass, riding through Newark this damn late. I know damn well I don't need to be over this way. I hope nobody decides to follow me and steal my damn headlights. That's the new thing over here now. Stealing headlights. And my Lexus RX330 is the truck they target the most. And it only takes these sorry ass bastards about thirty seconds to rip your lights off and leave your front bumper dangling. Fuckin' idiots! Is it that hard to get a job?

If you ask me, I'd say the manufacturers have something to do with it, because these people move like well-oiled professionals. Fully equipped with ski masks, gloves and the proper tools to guarantee a swift and rapid removal of your shit. Most of these guys from Newark know they some broke ass mutha fuckas. All they do is rob and steal. Now they into stealing headlights? What's next? Windshields? That'll be some fucked up shit to come outside, ready to leave for work and see that your fucking windshield is gone and not one piece of glass on the ground. And I wouldn't put it past anybody from around here. These fake ass gangstas out here are hungry and whatever they gotta do to eat, trust me, they gon' do it. I cannot believe my ass is out here like this. And look at this bitch, all slobbin' on my leather seats.

"Bitch! Wake your drunk ass up!" I pinch her arm to get her attention. "Wake up, Keisha! And close your mouth before I stick something in it!" She opens her eyes. She has a puzzled look as if she doesn't know where she is. She then notices that Amber and Aaliyah are not here. This bitch drunk as hell, yawning and shit, looking like Sarafina.

"Where's Amber and Aaliyah?" She asks me.

I could get smart with her ass but now is not the time. I need to fill her in on what happened a minute ago.

"Girl, Amber had to take her ass home. After I let her have it, she ain't wanna hang no more."

"Oh boy, Scott. What did you do this time?"

"I ain't do shit. I just told her ass to get the fuck out my car after she called herself getting fly with me. I'm not beat for her ass anyway. Yeah she cute, but all that smiling and being all nice and hostiditty 'n shit, is a front. I can smell a phony bitch a mile away. And trust me when I tell you, that bitch is up to something. I don't know what it is, but mark my words, you heard it here first."

"Whatever, Scott. You probably said the same thing about me when we first met. So save the drama for somebody who gives a fuck."

See, you can't win for being nice with bitches.

"You know what, Keisha? I had my suspicions about you, yeah. I'm just like that when new pussy comes around and doesn't leave. But you never came across as a snake bitch.

You never gave me that vibe. Yeah, I fuck with you and call you names, but we both know, at the end of the day, I ain't got nothin' but love for your black ass."

I stop at that. This bitch might take my kindness for weakness. Can't have that. She already looks like she's blushing. *Oh God.*

"Awww, Scotty. You love me, huh?"

Just as I'm about to say "psych," I notice high beams in back of me. I ain't got time to get car-jacked tonight. Maybe if I ignore them, they'll go away.

"You ain't gotta answer, Scotty. I love yo' punk ass, too. Come here and gimme a kiss." Keisha kisses my cheek.

I don't respond to Keisha kissing my cheek because the flashing lights distract me.

"Somebody's flashing their high beams at us Keisha." She turns around to see what I'm talking about.

"Well, pull over and see who it is."

"Bitch, are you crazy!? I'm not pulling over around here. Fuck around and have both of us gagged and tied up in a trunk!"

"Boy, pull your punk ass over and see who it is! If they was gonna jack you, they wouldn't be high beaming and asking for permission. You think they need an invitation around here?"

She does have a point. Usually they rear end you first, just to get you to pull over, then they do whatever. Maybe she's right. I pull over to the side. The car pulls along side of us. It's a cherry red Benz, big boy style, with tinted windows so I can't see who's inside. The passenger window begins to come down.

"Damn Scott. We didn't think you'd ever pull over. Didn't you see us flashing you?"

Oh, thank God. It's only Eva and Pam.

"Girl, y'all scared the shit outta me! Don't do that shit no more!"

They both laugh. Obviously they think I'm playing.

"No, I'm serious Pam. I don't fuck around in this neighborhood like that. People don't want you to have shit around here. So next time you see me late night around here, you betta call my cell to let me know you behind me or else your ass will be following me straight to the fifth precinct. No stop signs and no red lights."

Now they're really cracking up. When I think about it, it is funny, but hey, I'm too damn pretty to get knocked around by some broke ass thugs. Although now that I think about it, it could be an interesting experience.

"Alright Scott, no problem." Eva's still laughing, but she offers an apology.

"We didn't mean to scare you. We were just trying to find out if you were still going to the city tonight."

"Yeah I'm going, just have to drop Keisha off first. Why don't you..."

"Uh uh. Why I can't go?" Keisha jumps in.

I can't even finish talking because Keisha's black ass is all up in my business. Now what in the hell makes her think I want to hold her ass up all night?

"Keisha, you can't even stand up. What makes you think I want to baby sit your ass for the rest of the night?"

"C'mon Scott. I'm good. Just let me get myself together. By the time we get there, I'll be straight."

I give her my best "I know you are lying" look. But, what the hell. If I don't have a good time, I can always laugh at her.

"Okay Keisha, damn. But I'm telling' you now...if you embarrass me, you're a left ass."

"Alright y'all. We'll just follow you over." I tell Pam and Eva.

"That doesn't make sense Scott," Eva responds. "Why don't you and your friend get in the car with us? May as well save some money on gas and tolls. Besides, we'll have more fun that way."

These bitches must be crazy if I'm riding in anybody's backseat.

"I got a better idea, Eva. How 'bout we ride in *my* car? You know damn well I don't do backseats."

"Fine, Scott. But you really need to calm down with all the *I don't do* bullshit. Just follow us to my house, and we'll leave my car there. You think you can handle that? Or is following someone also against your rules?"

"Just go ahead Eva before I change my mind."

I would have snapped on her but I couldn't think of a thing to say. Damn! That ain't like me. I can always find *something* wrong with someone. But not Eva. The bitch is bad. Aside from the fact that she fucks for money, I can't find a damn thing wrong with her. I can't even honestly say that that's a bad thing. Everybody's got an angle nowadays. But at least with Eva, you already know she's reaching for your pockets.   That's why I respect Eva. She's a ho, but she's real with it. She advertises her shit, got business cards and everything. She ain't pretending to be nobody's wifey and using mutha fuckas. She lets both men and women know what time it is. You want it, you gotta pay for it. Point blank. And she got the bank account to prove it. We get to Eva's house and wait for them to park. Eva gets in the front and pops in a CD. I hate when people touch my shit without asking.

"Eva, what is that?" I ask, because anything I wanna listen to is already loaded in its proper place.

"Just listen to it, Scott. I wouldn't put anything corny in your ride. I know how you are."

I really don't have a choice, now do I? She's rubbing her hand over my cheek because she knows I'm real particular about my shit. She could've asked me first. I got all my CDs arranged just the way I like 'em. Got my e-q set up just the way I like it, all my radio stations preset, even got my air flow set up just the way I like that too. And now she wanna come up in here touching shit. I don't get down like that. I see now that I'm gonna have to start letting her ass have it too, just like everybody else. She fly, but she ain't special. Shit, she can get it, too.

"Look, Eva. You gon' have to get your ass in the back seat if you can't keep your hands to yourself. Don't be up in here touching shit, okay?"

"Alright Scott, damn." Eva replies.

"Just wanted to put some music in so we can chill."

Suddenly I hear the sounds of go-go music coming from my stereo. Aww, *hell* no!

"But this is not your ride, Eva, and I ain't listening to this shit!" I pop her CD out and give it to her.

"Just leave it on WBLS where I had it please...thank you." Must be crazy if she thinks I'm beat for that shit.

The sounds of Vaughn Harper play through my speakers. He's speaking to all the ladies now, telling them to find their comfort zones, their places of relaxation. Whether it be the bedroom, bathroom, or even the car, he wants them to unwind and chill as he takes them for a ride. Humph, with a voice like that, he can take me for a ride too. Hell, he might be talkin' to the ladies, but dammit, I'm all ears.

Lyfe Jennings, *Must Be Nice* replaces his voice and sets the mood. Eva seems to be taking Vaughn Harper's advice because she removes her shoes and reclines the passenger seat until it can't go any further. I hope she doesn't have an attitude with me about the CD. I give her a playful shove.

"What's wrong with you, Eva? Why you so quiet?"

"I'm okay, just listening to the music, that's all. I love this song."

Eva begins to sing along. Now, don't get me wrong, the song is bangin'. *But*, this bitch can't sing. What she needs to do is stick to what she does best…Fucking and poppin' outta cakes and demonstrating dildos or whatever the hell her and Chyna do. I begin to laugh out loud because Eva's killing me right now. I can tell she's really into it because she done closed her eyes while she's singing. This shit has to stop so I interrupt her.

"So Eva, what happened with Chyna tonight?" I ask trying to start conversation. Anything to get her to stop howling.

"Oh, I spoke to her a little while ago. Her grandmother got real sick and had to be rushed to the hospital."

"Damn, sorry to hear that. Is she alright?"

"Well, I don't know. That was the only thing she said when I spoke with her. Haven't heard from her since."

"But that's your peoples, Eva. You haven't followed up with her? I mean, normal people would be by their friend's side at a time like this."

"I tried." Eva continues. "I tried a couple of times, but her phone keeps going straight to voicemail so I left her a couple of messages. She'll call me back when she gets a chance to. I'm sure everything's okay."

"Oh, okay. I was gettin' ready to say you's a foul bitch for not touching base with her."

"Trust me Scott, I've tried. I think maybe it's the reception in the hospital. I can never get a signal when I'm in there."

"What hospital is she in?"

"She was rushed to University Hospital down on Bergen."

"Girl, I hate that filthy ass hospital. Them some dirty mutha fuckas down there. Good hospital as far as medical treatment is concerned, but filthy as hell. You will never catch Saint Barnabas looking the way University does."

And it's true. The only reason it's like that is because of where it is. Newark. I bet if they were to relocate University to a suburban area, you'd be able to see your reflection in the pavement. It is one of the largest hospitals in the city and employs thousands of people and you mean to tell me you can't keep the floor mopped? You can't keep a roll of toilet paper in the restroom? You can't sweep up the crack bottles in the parking lot? You can't clean the hardened blood from the lobby chairs? Gimme a fucking break!

I recently read an article involving certain employees from University Hospital. About how they were being overpaid and had all these perks that weren't authorized. One woman who worked there had her own personal driver that was paid for by the hospital. And this bitch was being chauffeured to and from Newark to Pennsylvania, every gotdamn day, and you mean to tell me nobody can take the time to wake this bum up in the emergency room lobby and ask him to leave? He's been sleeping there for two weeks! And he smells like a steak and cheese sandwich loaded with onions and rotten cheese. Somebody's gotta smell that mutha fucka, let alone see him. But it wouldn't happen anywhere, except Newark. Newark residents will never have peace of mind until all the drug dealing stops. Until all the shootings stop. Until all the gang violence stops. These good black people been living and dying here in Newark for years and they need to be treated better than this. Some of our most influential people still live here in Newark, like Amiri Baraka. Shit, even some of today's best came from Newark. They need to do better by their people, their legends, and their heroes. I don't care how many stadiums they build, or how many low-income houses they build, there's entirely too much crime in Newark.

I somehow find my way back to the moment. I notice Keisha and Pam are awfully quiet in the back seat. I adjust my rear view mirror to give me a better view. They appear to be whispering to each other.

"Pam, Keisha. What the hell y'all whispering about?"

Both of them look up at the same time, grinning and smiling. Pam offers an explanation.

"Nothing, Scott. I was just telling Keisha about Eva and Chyna's business. You know, the types of things they do for their customers."

Both Keisha and Eva laugh at her response. Eva turns around to face Pam.

"You're always telling our stories, Pam. You need to stop living vicariously through us and get some stories of your own to tell. Which one are you telling her anyway?"

"Whatever, girl." Pam continues. "I was just mentioning the party you did a few weeks ago."

"Well, which one? We do parties all week long. What did she tell you Keisha?"

I see Keisha in the rear view. She's smiling and seems speechless. I know damn well she ain't trying to act shy right now.

"I don't want to tell it, Pam. You tell it."

Oh, this bitch tryin' to act brand new. She repeat every damn thing else. But honestly, the look on Keisha's face says something ain't right. My curiosity gets the best of me.

"Look." I point to both of them in the back seat.

"One of you bitches back there needs to speak up. All this whisperin' and gigglin' goin' on. We wanna giggle, too."

"Okay, okay nosy ass." Pam speaks up. "I was telling her about the bachelor party Eva and Chyna did, and the show they put on for the bachelor." Now I really gotta know. Knowing Chyna and Eva, they showed their asses. Literally. The suspense is driving me crazy so I have to ask.

"C'mon Eva, spill it. Details, bitch. Details."

"Why, Scott?" Eva asks. "And why do you need details? You don't do pussies, remember?" They're all laughing at me. Won't be nothing to laugh about when I pull this bitch over and clean house.

"You're absolutely right, Eva, I don't do pussy. But where there's pussy, there's usually dick. Rock hard dicks to be exact. And I do believe I asked for details." Eva realizes this is a no win situation. She starts to tell the story.

"Alright," Eva replies. "Some guys booked us for a bachelor party and when we got there, they wanted extra."

What the fu...? "Well, what the hell is *extra*?" I ask.

"Well if you shut up and let me finish, Scott, I'll tell you. One of the guys at the party told us how his friend, the one who was getting married, always wanted to watch two women fuck each other. He asked us how much we would charge to do it, and we told him a grand a piece. We never thought he'd go for it, but he did. So....we put on a show. Chyna and I had sex in front of everyone in the room. And then..."

"Then what, bitch?!" I demand.

"And then we fucked the bachelor."

Oh, no this bitch didn't just say that. That's why she stuttered just now, 'cause she knows that's some foul shit. Eva continued. "I mean, it wasn't planned, it just happened.

One thing led to another and before we knew it, it was going down."

Everybody knows, fucking does not just happen. I hate when people say that. It's always planned. Always. How in the hell do you fuck by mistake? Whether it's consciously or *sub*consciously, a person knows when they're 'bout to get laid. I know I do 'cause I ain't never slipped and fell in nobody's ass.

"Damn, Eva. Kinda low, don't you think? Doing the man the night before he was to wed?" I'm asking because she gotta be thinkin' the same thing. "He ain't even try to resist?"

"Resist?" Eva laughs. "Resist who? Me and Chyna? There's no such thing as far as we're concerned. I mean, he said no a couple times, but his dick spoke a different language."

"That's 'cause his dick was busy talkin' to your tonsils." I interrupt. "That dude ain't stand a chance in hell against the two of y'all new millennium Del'rio bitches. That was dirty, even for you two. Damn shame that man had to walk down the aisle with you two bitches on his brain. And I mean that literally."

"Why?" Eva questions me with an attitude. "What's a shame? Because he was getting married? How many men have you fucked that were *already* married, Scott? So before you start pointing that fragile finger of yours, take a look in the mirror. I'm a professional, and what I do is business. Nothing more. You're the one with the personal attachments. I get paid to provide fantasies and that's exactly what I do. Our business happens to thrive because of word-of-mouth. If we weren't good at what we do, we wouldn't come so highly recommended. When was the last time you got paid to have an orgasm?"

I guess she got me on that point. Can I *really* cast this stone? I've been with two men that I actually knew were married. Both of them claimed to have never been with another man before. *Yeah right.* The best head I ever had was from a married man with two and a half kids, a mortgage and a 401K plan. He sucked dick like a *Dirt Devil* vacuum cleaner, but he'd never done it before? Yeah, okay, tell it to my swollen balls. It's amazing how many men are living double lives these days. Scared to admit what they really want because society says it's wrong. Well, they can stay in the closet all they want. But I'm out and in the words of my girl Jill, "Miss Scott" if you nasty, I'm living my life like it's golden.

"You do have a point, Eva. But all I'm trying to say is, how far are you and Chyna willing to go? Where does business end and personal begin?"

"It's always business, Scott. Always. Like I said, we're professionals. We never mix business with pleasure. If the price is right, we're willing to do whatever it takes to get to the top of our game. And the best part is that we enjoy doing it. Do you know anyone that doesn't like sex? I don't. Just so happens that we've made it our business. It's not always about sex because not everyone asks for that. Some men request a simple date for an occasion or even some women might request our services for a bachelorette party. It's whatever the client wants. We're willing to do what no one else will and what no one else has. That's what Selective Succulence is all about."

I glance quickly in the rear view to get Keisha's reaction. We go at each other all the time, but she's a realist like me. I know she's thinking the same thing I'm thinking. This bitch is not a ho, she's a Whore. I can't help but push the envelope so I ask.

"Keisha, why you so quiet?" I'm hoping she'll begin the process so I can finish it.

"I understand about Eva's business and all. But Eva, what do your actions say about your character? I'm the last person to judge anybody, but there's a thin line between what you do and prostitution, which is illegal in this state."

That's right, Keisha! And she just continues. "It sounds to me like you and your friend have crossed that line and don't even know it."

Okay, I can tell by the fire in her eyes that Eva's catching an attitude so let me jump in and take her focus from Keisha. Can't have Eva ripping Keisha, because that's my job.

"She's right, Eva. You and Chyna ain't doin' nuthin' that ain't been goin' on since the beginning of time. Y'all ain't doin' shit but runnin' a modern day brothel. Pretty soon, the two of you *whores* will start recruiting more ladies of the night to join your twisted ass *business,* if that's what you wanna call it."

I knew I'd eventually find something to say about this bitch. Ain't nobody perfect.

"Whatever, Scott." Eva retorts while rolling her eyes. "You think what you wanna think. You have that right. Just like I have the right to use what I got...to get what I want." Eva turns around to look at Keisha.

"And Keisha, you can judge me if you want. That's your right as well. But at the end of the day, all that matters is my clients' happiness, their satisfaction, and their referrals."

The rest of our ride is quiet. Probably because each of us was thinking about what Eva was saying. Sure, we all have skeletons in our closets. We've all done dirt a time or two. But at whose expense? How far does it go and when will it stop? What price is paid when your soul is sold to the devil? What price is paid when you don't even realize it's already gone?

Keisha breaks the silence. "Scott, on second thought, you can take me home."

Khalil
Please, Baby, Baby, Please!

Look at my girl. Laying here looking as good as she wanna look. Sleeping so peacefully. I creep up to her precious face and give her a peck on the lips. It's still dark outside, but I know I have to wake my baby up. She has to work today. She must've partied hard last night, because she is out…cold.

Oooh, she even has a lil dragon going on in that mouth of hers. But she's still sweet. Her hair is wild and all over the place. And she's only wearing panties, no nighty, no nothing. Damn, she must've really been tired to come to bed half naked like this. I wrap my arms around her and envelope her into me. She leans back and rests in my arms. I can tell she finds comfort here. I kiss her on her shoulder and whisper in her ear. "Baby, you have to get up."

She stretches and moans, and gives me the business about how she doesn't want to get out of bed.

"K, I'm tired. Can we do it later baby? Please?" She stretches some more and falls into my chest with even more comfort. I giggle.

"Baby, I'm not trying to get at you this morning, but don't give me any ideas. I'm talking about work honey. You have to work today, right? Do you wanna call out?" Amber opens her eyes and looks up at me. She's so cute when she's just waking up.

"What?," she says confusingly. "K, it's Saturday, right?"

I laugh and kiss her on her forehead. "No, baby, you have work today sugah. I'll get the shower started for you."

I get out of bed and head into our bathroom. Amber likes a hot shower, which is the reason why we don't take them together too often. She uses absolutely no cold water. I'm a man, but I can't handle that. Too damn hot for me. You can't see a thing in the bathroom when Amber's in the shower. Nothing but steam. I already told her....one day she's gonna fall or suffer from third degree burns, whichever comes first.

I start her super hot shower and put her Victoria Secret's shower gel where she can see it. I pull out her bath sponge and get her toothbrush and toothpaste ready. She likes to brush her teeth in the shower. To each his own. I need to look in the mirror while I'm brushing just to make sure I don't miss anything.

Amber even likes to finish off with that Skin-so-Soft oil, by Avon. I love how that makes her skin so silky smooth. My Momz used to put that on me when I was a kid. She said it kept the mosquitoes away. Go figure. I peep out of the bathroom door and see Amber stretched across the entire bed now. Damn, she's out! What did they do last night? My God.

"Amber! Are you going to work today?" I throw a towel at her and finally she sits straight up in the bed and stares. Hair wild as hell. Her thirty-eight double-d's in mid-air screaming, *"hello."* And lips poked out. It's a Kodak moment for sure. She stretches again.

"Alright, K. I'm coming." Amber crawls out of bed and slowly makes her way to the bathroom. This is a hilarious sight here. She staggers into the bathroom and nudges me in my cheek. She knows I'm laughing at her.

Amber sits on the toilet as if I'm not here. She's so open. I'm still laughing as she lets her panties slide to the floor. I can tell she's finished, but she's still sitting on the toilet with her head in her hands. I walk over to her and lift her head to face me.

"You okay baby? You wanna stay home today?" She looks back at me with her eyes half closed.

"Not so loud, K. My head is killing me. Just let me sit here for a minute. And could you turn out the light please, it's bothering my eyes." I smile. I know she's got a hangover. And Amber never has more than two or three drinks when she goes out. I didn't think she knew how to get drunk.

"Damn baby, what were you drinking last night? You know you can't handle alcohol like that. I bet you were following behind that damn Keisha. Let me see if we have something for that headache of yours." I reach in the medicine cabinet and pull out a bottle of Excedrin. I take two from the bottle and give them to her. "I'll be right back baby. Let me go get you some water so you can take those."

Amber reaches for me before I can leave the bathroom. "Wait K. Bring me some orange juice instead."

"Okay." I leave the bathroom and head downstairs to the kitchen.

I put on a pot of coffee. I know she's gonna need more than aspirin to wake her up. I also toast a bagel for her. Knowing Amber, she won't wanna take the aspirin on an empty stomach. She's a nurse. I get the orange juice and the bagel, and I head back upstairs.

When I get back into the bathroom, Amber is already in the shower. I pull the shower curtain back a little and give her the glass of orange juice. She takes a sip and points to the aspirin on the ledge. I hand them to her. Damn, it's hot in here already.

I know how Amber likes to listen to music when she's getting ready for work, so I turn on her clock radio that sits on the shelf behind the toilet. I can hear Steve Harvey's morning show as I'm leaving the bathroom. That man is funny as hell, and he knows he wears some bad ass suits. So fresh and so clean. My man Steve. I need to call his show and ask him to hook a brother up. I hear he has his own line now. Just for us

157

grown and sexy brothas. I walk out the bathroom and crack the door to give her some privacy. And because, in a minute, I won't be able to see my hand in front of my face in here.

I walk back into the bedroom and turn on *Eyewitness News*. Every morning, I try to watch the news. I like to know what's going on in the world. As I sit and listen to the death toll climb in Iraq, I can only wonder when they'll bring our troops home. So many young kids over there dying. It's sad. Not old enough to buy alcohol, but old enough to die in a war they don't understand. I understand there was a cause, but enough is enough. Haven't they proven their point?

The timer from the coffee pot beeps and takes my attention away from the news. I head back downstairs to make Amber a cup of coffee. Two spoonfuls of Cream-mate and three scoops of sugar, just the way she likes it. Light and sweet just like her. Sometimes I get it the perfect match for her skin.

I go back upstairs and sit the coffee on the dresser. I would take it in the bathroom, but I can already see the steam escaping under the door. If I go in there, I might pass out. Instead, I open up the bathroom door but I don't go in. I yell to her.

"Amber, you've been in there for fifteen minutes. You're gonna be late for work if you don't come on."

"Just a few more minutes baby. It feels too good to stop right now."

I laugh at her.

"You better come on before I come in there and flush the toilet."

She laughs and sticks her head out of the shower and yells back. "Would you please? It will only make it hotter." She sticks her tongue at me like a little kid.

Several minutes later, Amber emerges from the bathroom. She only has a towel wrapped around her. The aroma from her body gel fills the room. *Mmmm, I love that smell.*

I watch her as she places one of her legs on the ottoman and begins drying off. Look at those legs. So seductively sculpted. I can't help myself so I get up from the bed and take the towel from her. She looks at me questioningly.

"What are you doing, K?"

"Just thought I'd help you with that baby." I begin drying off her back. The smell of her body penetrates my senses. I gently kiss her neck. I move the towel slowly over her back, then down to her legs and can't help but kiss her calf. Once. Then twice.

"Uh, uh baby. I have to go to work. Don't start Khalil." I look up at her and smile.

"Aaiight, Ma. I'll be cool." I stand up and finish drying her off. When I'm done, I lay across the bed and follow her with my eyes as she puts on her underwear. *She's lucky as hell she gotta go to work or else I'd just have to take it this morning.* When she moves to the dresser, she notices the coffee and bagel. She looks at me and smiles.

"Thank you, K. I really needed this." She takes a bite of the bagel and sips on the coffee. "This coffee is really good baby. You sure know how to make it good to the last drop."

She smiles as she's being cute this morning.

"I know baby. That's what I'm here for. You sure we can't *get it in* before you leave?" I'm smiling at her hoping my charm will allow me to get my way. She smiles back and comes over to the bed. She climbs on top of me and straddles me. Amber softly kisses me. I wrap my arms around her and begin removing the bra she's just put on. Then she stops me.

"You want it bad, don't you baby?" She whispers and the anticipation makes me feel myself inside her already.

"Yes, I do. Please?" I whisper. Amber laughs and kisses me again. She begins to get up off me, and I grab her to hold her in place. I'm rock solid now and grinding slowing on her as I hold her tight. I know she feels me on her clit.

"Why you playin' like that Amber? Don't do that to me baby."

My begging falls on deaf ears. She wiggles herself free from my grip and continues getting dressed. I lay there on the bed and watch her with a pitiful look on my face. I'm hoping to make her feel sorry for me so she'll give in. She looks over at me.

"I promise baby, when I come home, I'm all yours. So stop trying to make me feel bad right now. You know I gotta get outta here."

I'm not really upset because I know she has to go. Just thought I'd play my trump card. My smile normally does the trick but I guess she really has to go. Just as I'm about to get up from the bed, the phone rings. I reach over and pick it up.

"Hello?"

"Hi. Khalil?"

"Yeah. Who's this?" I can't figure out the voice, and the caller ID registers as out of area.

"It's Aaliyah, good morning. I know it's early but I was hoping to catch Amber before she left for work." I am puzzled because she's calling so early. It's seven in the morning.

Aaliyah continues. "Is she still there?"

"Oh, wassup Aaliyah?! Yeah, she's still here but she's getting dressed. Hold on a sec."

I see Amber has gone back into the bathroom. I yell to her to let her know the phone is for her. She walks into the bedroom and I tell her it's Aaliyah. She takes the phone.

"Good morning Aaliyah. Everything okay?" Amber asks.

I can't imagine what that girl could want so early in the morning. I don't know about her. There's just something that ain't rubbing me right. That day at her and Shawn's house. I don't care what she says, that shit wasn't cool at all. Then she tried to make me think I was the nut. Like I said before, I know when a woman is throwing it at me. And she was throwing it hard. I could've fucked her that day, and I know it. Hell, John Wayne Bobbitt could've fucked her that day, and he ain't got no dick.

I watch Amber talking on the phone. I want to get a hint of what they are talking about. I can hear her making reference to this weekend. Something about hanging out. All of a sudden, Amber's facial expression changes. *What the hell are they talking about?* Now she's looking at me as if I just fucked her mother.

I can't help but ask. "What, Amber?"

She continues talking and shakes her head side to side as if Aaliyah can see her. Her face is turning red now and she's still looking at me. She looks as if she's about to cry. What the fuck is going on? I snatch the phone from her and tell Aaliyah she'll call her back.

"Aaliyah! Amber will talk to you later. Aaight?!"

I look at Amber and question her. "What's the matter? What happened baby?"

She walks away from me and into the bathroom without saying a word. I follow her and position myself in front of her. "Amber, I'm talking to you. What the hell is going on?"

She looks at me with rage in her eyes. It's a look I haven't seen on her in a long time, but one I'm very familiar with.

"You could've told me Khalil!," Amber screamed.

"Should I be concerned that you didn't tell me?"

What the? "Amber, what are you talking about?"

She's scaring me now because I'm clueless at this point. "What did Aaliyah say to you?"

"Aaliyah called to see if I wanted to hang out with her this weekend, because you and Shawn will be in Virginia. Is this how it's going to be, Khalil? I have to find out your itinerary from Shawn's girlfriend? I'm right here with you. We live together, sleep together, and eat together. You couldn't tell me you were going to Virginia for the weekend? You couldn't find the time to do that? Why, Khalil? Should I be worried? Is there something going on with you and Shayla again?"

I couldn't understand why Aaliyah would call this early just to tell Amber that. Of course I was going to tell her. I was just waiting for the right time. There's no way I would leave town and not tell her. I move close to Amber to get her to calm down. She seems furious at me right now.

"First of all, Amber...there's nothing, absolutely nothing going on with me and Shayla. I would never even think about putting you through that again. I...."

Amber interrupts me.

"Then why, Khalil? Why did I have to hear that from Aaliyah, huh? Why do you feel the need to hide shit from me?"

Now I know she's angry. Very rarely does Amber use profanity. I take her face into my hands and stare deep into her eyes.

"Baby, listen. Please listen to me. I was gonna tell you, I swear. I was just trying to wait for the appropriate time. I wouldn't disrespect you by leaving town and not letting you know. Believe me Amber, I wouldn't do no shit like that. Come on baby, as far as we've come? You think I would jeopardize our relationship? Our marriage? By doing some bullshit like that?"

"Well when, Khalil? When did you think *the right time* would be? Did it ever occur to you that all you had to do was be honest? That all you had to do was tell the truth?"

She does have a point. I never thought about it that way. The fact that Shayla was involved, clogged my senses.

"You're right, baby, and I'm sorry. But I swear I wasn't trying to hide anything from you. Lexis has a recital this weekend, and I told her I'd be there. I was just trying to figure out a way to tell you so that you wouldn't be concerned about Shayla. I didn't want you to worry. You have to believe me Amber. There's nothing going on with me and Shayla. I love *you*, not her. You know that. Please baby, believe me."

The way Amber's looking at me tells me she doesn't. *Dammit*, I should have just told her. The day I spoke to Lexis, I should have told her. What the fuck was I thinking about? And why the fuck did Aaliyah call and tell her that shit? That's it, I'm not going.

"Alright, Amber, fine. If this is gonna cause a problem for us, I won't go. I'll call Shayla and tell her I'm not coming."

"Why, Khalil?" Amber yells and questions. And it looks like tears are forming in her eyes.

"Why don't you wanna go now? Because I know? Now all of the thrill is gone?

"If this trip is for Lexis, why would you let me stop you from going? If this trip is for Lexis, why was it so hard for you to tell me? That doesn't make sense Khalil." She yells.

Now she's pissing me off. She can't possibly believe after all this time I'm still fucking with Shayla. I begin to yell.

"Dammit, Amber, I'm not fucking with that girl! I love you and I would not risk losing you! Ever! Now if you don't want me to go, I won't!" I walk away from her. I don't like to see her cry. It does something to me when she cries. It bothers me. But I know I can't leave the conversation this way. I can't let it end like that so I walk back into the bedroom. I see Amber sitting on the edge of the bed with a blank stare on her face. Tears are falling. She's trying to wipe them away before I can see them. I kneel down in front of her and take her hands in mine. She won't look at me but I speak anyway.

"You gotta trust me, Amber. You have to. I love you so much. And I would never, ever, do anything to hurt you. Please look at me, baby."

She wipes away her remaining tears and looks at me. I can see the hurt in her eyes. That same look I knew so well in college. I swore to her and to myself that look would be gone forever. Why didn't I just tell her? I move up and kiss her lips.

"Do you know how much I love you, Mrs. Devereaux? Do you know how much you mean to me? You're my wife now, Amber, and I would never disrespect you. You hear me, baby?"

"Yes, I hear you." Amber responds softly. "And I don't want you to cancel your trip. Go and see your daughter. If you promised Lexis you'd be there, you shouldn't break that promise. I'll just have to deal with it, that's all," she says and gets up from the bed. She finishes getting dressed and grabs her car keys.

I stop her.

"Wait a minute, baby. Please don't leave like this. I know you gotta go to work, but please...talk to me."

"There's nothing left to say, Khalil. I have to go." She grabs her jacket and walks down the stairs.

I sit back down on the bed when I hear the front door slam as she leaves. Damn!

Fly on the Wall
A Hood Rat in Rare Form

"I'm sick of this bullshit. Why the fuck ain't she answering the phone?" Shayla dialed and dialed. She could not get an answer. Frustrated, she finally hung up the phone. "I know what I gotta do," she spoke to herself.

Shayla is twenty-six years old and the epitome of ignorance. She stands five-feet-five inches and wears her one hundred seventy five pounds flawlessly. She morphed from her Halle Berry haircut to long, flowing braids that stopped at her mid back. Biscuit-brown skin compliments mesmerizing, dark brown eyes that had the ability to make any man who looked long enough forget their wives first names.

Shayla survives off her first impressions. She is stunning, and she knows it. Men are instantly attracted to her and women copied her style. Shayla knows she's a dime. It isn't until she speaks that her true colors shine through. The waving of the hands and the gutter-like neck movements make most people in her presence cringe with disgust. Her beauty could not outshine her hood-like aura, and Shayla did not care. For some reason she didn't understand that true beauty came from within. Shayla thinks this is something that ugly people tell themselves. If it weren't for her God-forsaken demeanor, she'd be the total package. Since she has no self respect and basement level morals, she's become the equivalent to man's best friend. Just too bad she couldn't hold onto a man like a dog can.

Shayla can count her friends on one hand. Reason being, she bedded any man in a five block radius and is actively working on expanding her influence. The last friend she did manage to establish was engaged to be married only to find

Shayla sitting on her fiancé's face two weeks before her wedding day. *"Well I can't help it if you can't satisfy yo' man,"* are the words Shayla spit at her friend when she got caught. Shayla is conniving and backstabbing.

She believes that all women have to be this way if they were ever going to get ahead in life. Shayla's attitude grew worse when she had to drop out of college because of an unplanned pregnancy. She loves her daughter fiercely but feels that she shouldn't be raising her alone.

Shayla had been pregnant twice by Khalil before she decided to keep Lexis. He'd told her he loved her and that he wanted to be with her. She knew he had a girlfriend but always thought he'd eventually leave her. He didn't. Khalil had begged her not to keep Lexis. Said he wanted to finish college and that it would ruin their lives.

Shayla believed differently. She figured a baby would ultimately make Khalil realize that his place was with her. A baby would somehow bring their relationship out of the darkness. A baby would keep him tied to her for the rest of his life. She had grown tired of having abortions. Two was enough. She wasn't looking for marriage, but she thought Khalil would at least be there for her. Help her raise their child. Be a father to Lexis.

Shayla has been sneaking around with him for over a year, but when he found out she was going to keep the baby this time, he grew angry. He wanted nothing to do with her. He felt she was trying to destroy him and his future. He'd stopped returning her calls and began avoiding her at all costs. But this didn't stop Shayla from having Lexis. The only thing it did was make her more unbearable. It made Shayla dangerous.

Shayla had an evil spirit and the only thing she had going for herself was her outer appearance. After being wronged by so many men, Shayla swore that she would always make them pay. A long list of enemies was all Shayla had in her life that was consistent. Men she'd date would eventually head for the hills. Nobody could stand her. Nobody understood her or the depths of her madness. Shayla didn't care. Her sole concern was making Shayla happy by doing what she felt was necessary, regardless of who her actions would hurt. She'd been hurt enough, and now it was her turn to smile. Caring about nothing but herself and her child, Shayla was on a mission. A mission to destroy anything and anyone who got in her way.

Shayla's own mother couldn't stand her. They hadn't spoken to her in years. After Shayla's father died years ago, her mother met someone and began dating again. Since Shayla was so close with her father, this infuriated her. No one was going to take her father's place. No one could. Her father loved her more than anyone else ever had, and she hadn't had that kind of love since he died. Rumor has it that dear old dad may have loved Shayla just a little too much. She figured she'd teach her mother a lesson. A lesson she'd never forget. And she never has.

Shayla knew Khalil had a girlfriend when she met him in college, but instead of backing off, she pursued him. She could tell Khalil was the kind of brother that would treat her like a queen. And on top of that, he was physically supreme. From his abs to his ass, the man was well put together. He was in college, which meant he had his head on right, and she'd heard he didn't have any kids. He had a job and he didn't live in his momma's basement. This was enough for Shayla.

"Puhlease, I can't wait to give dis nigga sample. Shit, back in da hood I ain't never let no bitch stop me from gettin' whut I want, fuck I'm gonna change now fo'."

A product of her environment is what Shayla was, but the saddest realization was that she didn't know it. Although she was scholastically intelligent, Shayla was your typical hood rat. She jumped into bed with any guy who looked good and was willing to pay for her chicken wings and shrimp fried rice. She lived by the credo...*Use what you got to get what you want*, which was tolerated as a teenager, but as an adult in a world laden with HIV, and all types of diseases that a shot in the arm could not cure, this was the wrong attitude to possess. Shayla knew that one day she'd have no choice but to grow up, but obviously, today was not the day.

Shayla has been trying to get in touch with her sister for over a week. Her sister is the only person who tolerated her madness, because they were so much alike. Both are beautiful and determined to get what each of them wanted.

Same mother but different fathers. While they had the same attitude, they looked nothing alike, except for the fact that they held their mother's eyes. Deep and sensual dark brown eyes. Although her sister wore contacts most of the time, Shayla did not. Shayla also opted to be a natural diamond. She was thick in the hips and had ass for days. Her sister was a lot thinner, taller. The model type.

Shayla used to envy her sister when they were younger but grew out of it as the years passed. She'd grown to believe they were equally beautiful. And they were.

While squeezing into her size twelve Baby Phat jeans, knowing damn well she's a fourteen, her cell rang. Opening the flip, Shayla spoke out of breath, "Wassup."

A female's voice responded, "Why don't you tell me. You've been blowing my phone up all day."

"Did you get my message?"

"You mean your three messages? Yes I did."

"Well?"

"Well? What Shayla?" The voice responds in an aggravated tone.

"You don't understand that this is going to take some time. Shit like this cannot be done overnight. You're going to have to be patient."

"I'm sick of being fucking patient. I been patient for eight muthafuckin' years, and now it's my time to shine."

"Listen girl, I didn't call you back to listen to this bullshit."

"Oh, it's bullshit now? It wasn't bullshit when we thought this shit up a year ago, was it?"

"I'll talk to you later, Shayla."

"What the fuck do you mean you'll talk to me later? Fuck that, I'm lis'nin right now!"

"Goodbye Shayla."

"Bitch you better not hang...Hello?...Hello?"

"Oh I gotta trick for this bitch," Shayla says nastily as she closes her flip.

"She musta' fuh'got who she fuckin' wit."

Shayla paces through her one bedroom apartment thinking of her next steps. She is mad as hell right now and only going to get more upset if her plans aren't executed properly. She knows her daughter had Shawn's number, but she was in school at the moment.

Shayla walks into her daughter's bedroom and begins looking through her phonebook. She knows Lexis had to have Shawn's phone number, somewhere. After all, he was her Godfather. She leaves her daughter's room after having no luck. She began looking through the kitchen drawers.

She suddenly thought to herself that her apartment is way too small. Cute, but much too small for her and her daughter. Shayla had to turn the living room into her bedroom while giving Lexis the only bedroom for herself. But this wouldn't do much longer, as Shayla needs her own space. But this was all Shayla could afford.

Shayla never did get her degree after she dropped out of college. And she only worked part time jobs through temp agencies that only called her for bullshit that never lasted more than a month. Her sister, however, got her the job that she'd been working at for almost a year.

Shayla knows it is time for her to make moves and get herself and her daughter out of this one bedroom apartment. She's waited for Khalil for far too long now. It is obvious that he wants nothing to do with her. And since he got married, it seems as if he'd also forgotten he had a daughter.

Suddenly Shayla finds an old picture of herself and Khalil that one of her dorm mates had taken back in college in the kitchen drawer. Shayla was sitting on her bed while Khalil lay his head on her lap. She had on his alma mater baseball cap, and he had the prettiest smile on his face. They looked happy, she thought to herself.

Shayla is disgusted. Disgusted with herself and the predicament she'd allowed herself to be in. She falls to the floor and covers her face with her hands. Tears well up and fall from her beautiful face. Everything from the past surfaces as she's on her kitchen floor crying. Crying for herself and for Lexis. It isn't supposed to be like this, she thought. She isn't supposed to be alone. Coming to her senses and wiping the tears away, Shayla gets up and reached for the phone. She couldn't take it any longer. Her sister obviously has plans of her own, so Shayla would just have to handle things herself. She dials the number. The phone is answered after only ringing once.

"Hi, Khalil. It's me Shayla."

"What do you want Shayla? I already told you I'd be there this weekend." Suddenly Shayla thought to herself that her big news could wait. It would be even better in person.

"Oh, okay Khalil. Just making sure you didn't forget. Lexis will be happy to see you."

"Aaight Shayla, goodbye."

Khalil

Hustlin'

Of all the times I've lied to her. Of all the times I've gone off and just "*did me.*" Of all the times she'd chosen to ignore what was obvious, she waits until now to not trust me. I married Amber. I chose *her* to be my wife. That has to count for something. I know I fucked up in the past. I know I did her dirty. All the while, she stood by me hoping that one day I'd grow up and become a man. She has to know that she is the reason I am who I am. She has to know that it was her love and her faith in me that made me the man I am today.

I reach for my cell to call Amber, but she doesn't answer. Me, Shawn and Jamal have been on the road for about six hours, and I've been trying to talk to Amber since I left. I know I shouldn't have left for Virginia without straightening things out with her first. But I don't wanna disappoint Lexis either. I'm more than sure that Shayla fills Lexis' head with all kinds of shit about me, which is why I have to go. If I don't, it'll only give Shayla more ammunition against me. I would love to be around Lexis more. I would love to give her the kind of love that only a father can give her. But Shayla makes that impossible. I haven't seen my daughter in more than two years, maybe even longer than that.

I take my wallet from the glove box and open it to Lexis' picture. I smile. She must've been about five or six in this picture. I know she's gotten big. She is eight years old, and I don't even know what her favorite color is. Lexis Diamante' McNeil. I smile. I remember how Shawn always tells me she looks so much like me. I wish Lexis and I were closer. I wish we had a normal father-daughter relationship. Then she could be daddy's little girl. Can't wait to see her.

The sound of Rick Ross's *Hustlin'* pulls me from my daydream. Jamal has turned up the volume to its maximum. I can feel the vibrations from the bass in my seat. He's all excited and throwing his hands up. I can barely hear what he's saying.

"Yo, dawg. This that shit right here." Jamal begins to sing along.

I reach for the volume and turn it down.

"C'mon, Jamal. It's too loud."

He gives me a look like I just shot his mother or something.

"Damn, K. Why you do that? That's my shit."

I point to Shawn in the back seat.

"You see Shawn back there sleeping, man. He drove most of the way here so have some respect."

No sooner than I finish my sentence, I glance back in my rear view again and see Shawn stretching. "You alright back there?" I ask.

"I'm good, baby." Shawn sits up, yawns, and looks around. "Where we at?"

"We're about a half hour away." I look at Shawn and laugh. "Damn, man. You was snoring your ass off back there."

"For real, dawg." Jamal laughs. "Shit was serious."

"Well, if y'all didn't have that music so damn loud, I'd still be snoring."

"I know." Jamal responds. "Why the fuck you think I turned it up?"

We all laugh.

A couple of minutes pass, and we decide to stop and get something to eat before reaching Shayla's house. We spot a McDonald's, and I pull up in the drive-thru.

"Naaah, K." Jamal continues. "Park the car, man. I need to use the bathroom bad."

Now that he mentions it, so do I. I park the car, and we all decide to head inside. Damn it's nice out here. It's gotta be about eighty degrees and only ten in the morning.

Once inside, Shawn yells to me to order him a number one and Jamal asks for a number three as they both run in the restroom. I guess these two clowns don't know I have to go too. I order our food, then head to the restroom. *Dayum,* what is that smell? Shawn's laughing while running out.

I hear Jamal's voice coming from one of the stalls. "Yo. Whoever that is? You *don't* wanna be in here right now." *Dayum!* Jamal stinks. Jamal got this bathroom smelling like wet monkey ass. I would leave out, but I can't hold it any longer. I grab my nose with one hand and undo my zipper with the other. I handle my business as fast as I can. I hear Jamal straining and making all kinds of noises, then he calls my name.

"K, you out there?" I don't answer so he calls again. "Yo, Khalil, stop playin' man. I know you hear me."

Still I don't respond. One of the stall doors is opening and Jamal peeks his head out. He spots me at the sink washing my hands and laughing. He yells to me again. "Why you playin, Khalil? For real man, ain't no tissue in here. See if it's some in that stall over there."

I laugh harder. Everybody knows to check for toilet paper before they use a public bathroom. Damn. I can't help but fuck with him right now.

"Why didn't you do that before you sat down, Jamal?" I ask with my hand still covering my nose.

"Man, I ain't have time for all that shit! Stop playin' and gimme some tissue." I laugh at him and throw the tissue to him. I leave the bathroom. I meet up with Shawn who's already gotten our food and begun eating.

"Damn, Shawn. Couldn't wait?" I ask while taking a bite of my sandwich.

"I tried, man," Shawn says with his mouth full. "But y'all were taking too long in there. I'm hungry as hell."

We finish our food but decide to order more. Hell, we've been on the road for six hours and aside from getting gas, this is the first time we stopped.

Jamal finally comes out of the bathroom smiling at us. "I'm tellin' you, yo. I think I lost some weight in there."

We laugh at him and continue eating. Suddenly, Shawn's facial expression changes. He's looking in my direction, across the booth, but past me. Kinda looks like he's seen a ghost. I turn around, and look behind me but I don't see anything except a few people in line.

"Shawn, wassup? Why you lookin' like that?"

"Look Khalil." He points to something behind me.

"Hold up a sec, I thought..." He seems confused and doesn't finish what he was about to say. I turn around again, but I still don't know what the hell he's pointing at.

"Shawn, man. You trippin'." I laugh at him and get up to throw my trash away.

"I think you inhaled too much of Jamal's fumes in that bathroom, yo."

We sit and chill before heading to Shayla's house. Jamal's cell rings, and he takes his conversation outside. Shawn and I bullshit and reminisce about Virginia and our college days.

All of a sudden Shawn has that look on his face again but this time he stands up. I can't help but to turn to see for myself what his problem is. Walking through the door is a man with a little girl about three feet tall with corn-rows in her hair. Light skin with deep pitted dimples and a contagious smile. She has on a yellow dress that stops at her knees. My baby girl, Lexis.

She looks so happy. I smile and follow her with my eyes. She looks at me, skips right past me and gets in line. She doesn't even know who I am.

Shawn was right, aside from her complexion, she does look just like me. I feel a lump the size of Manhattan forming in my throat. I suddenly need air. I turn my attention to the man she's with. His pants are hanging almost below his ass and his underwear is showing. Who the fuck is he? My fists clench and my mind fills with rage. Shawn must be reading my mind, because he puts his hand on my shoulder.

"Breathe easy, K." I turn to face him. I don't say a word. The words are there. But they won't come out. I turn to look at Lexis.

She's smiling and talking to the man she's with. Her tiny voice hypnotizes me. "Hey Malik, can I have ice cream too?" She asks sweetly.

He looks down at her and puts his hand on top of her head and smiles. "You can have whatever you want, Lex."

She leans on the counter and stands on the tips of her toes. She tells *Malik* she wants strawberry. She says it's her favorite. My blood is boiling, and I don't know why. I wonder if I even have the right to be angry. All I know is...This man has his hands on my baby girl. This man just told my baby girl she can have whatever she wants. My baby girl is smiling at him. She seems happy with him. Suddenly I realize...My baby girl doesn't even know who I am.

I walk over to them, with Shawn right behind me. I stare at *Malik* with a *fuck you wanna do?* look, then shift focus to Lexis. She looks up at me with the brightest eyes and smiles.

"Hi," she says with so much energy. I kneel down so I'm eye level with her and smile back.

"Hello Lexis." I say with a trembling voice.

"Do you know who I am?" She looks at me puzzled and confused.

"No." She replies. "But how you know my name?" She backs away from me and into *Malik's* arms. Her smile disappears and is replaced with fear. He wraps his arms around her and stares at me.

"Wassup man? Can I help you with something?" The look on my face says, *Hell no muthafucka! And get you're fuckin' hands off my daughter!*

Shawn senses as much and quickly steps from behind me to extend his hand.

"How you doin', man. I'm Shawn, Lexis' uncle."

The stranger reciprocates and acknowledges Shawn. He introduces himself as Malik, Shayla's friend. He explains that Shayla had some business to take care of. He would be babysitting for about an hour.

Lexis finally notices Shawn and her smile returns. She's not afraid anymore. She bolts from the stranger's arms and throws herself at Shawn almost knocking him down. He stumbles backward but catches her embrace. They hug.

"Hi, Uncle Shawn!" She says while hugging his neck. "Mommy told me you was comin'. What took you so long?"

"Hey, Lexis!" Shawn smiles and picks Lexis up. He's almost as excited as she is. "Dang girl, you gettin' big! What are you now, about thirteen?" Lexis laughs and hits him playfully on the chest.

"You know I'm only eight, Uncle Shawn. I just turned eight not that long ago silly." He puts Lexis down and kneels in front of her. She continues with excitement.

"Did you bring my daddy with you? He said he was comin' too." Shawn takes her by the hands and looks up at me.

"Lexis. There's someone I want you to say Hi to." Lexis looks up at me, then back at Shawn.

"But I already said 'Hi' to him Uncle Shawn."

"Yeah…But you didn't say his name. His name is Khalil."
She looks up at me with questioning eyes. She smiles at me.
"Hi, Khalil." She reaches out to shake my hand. "My
daddy name Khalil, too."

What I feel at this moment is darkness. An indescribable
array of emotions swallow me whole. Hurt. Shame. Guilt.
Betrayal. Disgust. Regret. Disgrace. Sorrow. I feel pain. A
deep, infested in my soul, kind of pain. My body goes numb. I
fall to my knees in front of Lexis. I wrap my arms around her
as I feel tears swelling in my eyes. I fight them back, because
I don't want to scare her. One of them escapes. I quickly wipe
it away. I release her from my embrace but remain face to
face. I want to say to her so badly, "*C'mon Lexis, you know
me, it's me, daddy, remember?*" Instead, I simply give her my
hand and I smile. "Hello again, Lexis. Nice to meet you."

I notice Shawn has pulled Malik to the side. I'm assuming
he's explaining to him exactly who I am and why I came off
the way I did. Or maybe he's just giving me a few moments
alone with Lexis. To maybe explain to her who I am. It's only
been a few years. How could she forget who I am? I talk to
her at least…at least…Damn, I gotta get my shit together. I
stand and watch Lexis as she turns her strawberry ice cream
into a memory. I laugh to myself as she licks the remains running
down her wrist.

"Is it good, Lexis?"

"Mmm Hmm." She responds with a smile. "Strawberry's
my favorite."

"Come sit down so I can talk to you for a minute."

I don't know why, but I feel so nervous. The butterflies
in my stomach have taken over. She looks hesitant, but she
sits with me anyway. I continue. "Lexis, you really don't
remember me? Not even a little bit?"

"Nope, but you got the same name as my daddy."

Every muscle in my body tightens. This is my own fault. I can't be mad at her. It wasn't her that kept me away. It wasn't even Shayla that kept me away. I chose to stay away. For my own selfish reasons. I chose not to deal with my responsibilities. I chose to focus on myself rather than her. I can't blame anyone but me.

"Lexis?" I hold my breath and continue cautiously so as not to frighten her.

"I am your daddy."

I remove her picture from my wallet and show it to her, hoping that she'll believe me. "See this picture of you? You gave it to me the last time I came to see you."

Lexis takes the picture from me and looks at it. Her facial expression changes from inquisitive to sorrow. She folds her arms and pouts, and with all the sassiness she can muster, says, "How come you ain't call me back the other night? Mommy let me stay up and wait but you didn't call."

I can't possibly tell her that I was busy having dinner with my in-laws or that I was just coming off my honeymoon and was too busy to call her back. But I don't wanna lie to her either.

"I'm sorry Lexis." I take her hands in mine and continue. "I promise it won't ever happen again."

As the words part from my lips, I know this is not just another empty promise. I never realized how much I love this little girl until right now. My little girl. I intend to make good on my promise to her. All of a sudden her smile returns along with those bright eyes. She puts her hands on her hips, which reminds me of Penny from *Good Times*.

"I still love you Daddy, even if Mommy calls you a no good bastard."

I hug her and kiss her cheek. She hugs me back and this time, I allow my tears to fall.

Aaliyah
Baby Girl

Thank goodness Shawn went to Virginia this weekend. Gives me some time to just chill, clean the loft, sip on some wine, and of course, handle my business. Speaking of which, I see Amber now pulling up. Amber seemed upset when I called her, like she didn't know that Khalil and Shawn were going down to Virginia. Do they talk? I don't know, and I don't care. All's I care about is getting me some "me" time this weekend. For sure.

Funny how I don't care to go back there. It's my hometown and all, but full of memories that I wish would vanish. Full of shit that I can't even bring myself to talk about or deal with. There, I made a pact with the devil. But hey, you have to do what you have to do, to get ahead in life. That's what my mother always taught me. So, I follow suit.

I run to the full length mirror in the bedroom just to make sure my gray shorts fit to perfection. And they do. They come just slightly under my ass, which is good. Not too revealing, but just enough to show off the fabulous legs. My black tank top looks good too. I have on my Escada perfume, which is really sweet and erotic. And, of course, my furry slippers with a fresh pedicure. I got the curly look going today with the hair. It's sort of wild, but fresh to death. It's going to be a girl's night in and I want to be comfortable and slightly sexy for Miss Amber. It's so wrong, but that woman has piqued my curiosity so that I forget why I'm here.

There's plenty of champagne and wine in the fridge. We have wings, chips and dips, sandwiches and anything else in here that she may want. Shawn put me on to this new beer called Presidente'. I think it's Domenican. It's good as hell. Very light and will get you tipsy quickly which is just what I want. I take a sip of my chilled Presidente' and head for the CD player. This damn CD Shawn's been blasting for awhile is hot, so I put on the track, *Baby Girl*. I sing along as I walk out the door.

There she is. Amber. Looking as scrumptious as a bacon, egg and cheese sandwich. She smiles at me and waves. I keep my eyes on her hoping that she'll take the hint. I meet her halfway on the stairs and help her with her bags.

"Hi, Aaliyah. It's good to see you again. Seems like we've been seeing a lot of each other lately, right?"

"Yes, Amber, we have been. But I don't mind. You're a great person to be around." She looks at me with that look. I see what Khalil sees in her.

I allow her to go ahead of me up the stairs and into the loft. I follow those shapely hips and plump ass all the way, like I'm their guardian or something. I never knew I had these feelings until now. She is the bomb. She has to know this. I think she knows that I'm watching, because she turns her head as we reach the top of the stairs.

"Aaliyah, I told Keisha and Shawn not to come since you said you wanted to talk. They understood. I hope everything is okay." She smiles.

Amber has to know that I'm diggin' her, unless she's the ultimate tease, or worse, I am truly delusional. I return her smile.

"Thanks Amber. I really just wanted to talk to you more, to get to know you, without interruption. Sorry if that seems selfish of me, but that's how I feel. Your friends are lovely, but they are a bit overbearing."

We get into the loft and put the groceries on the kitchen table. She really didn't have to bring anything over, but I guess that's Amber. She responds, "I understand. Scott can be a handful and Keisha, well Keisha, that's just my girl." We both laugh.

We unpack her groceries. How nice. She has strawberries, champagne, some good books, a few DVDs and some chocolates. There are definitely two bitches in this loft tonight.

"Amber, you didn't have to bring all of these goodies."

"Girl, it's no problem. Really."

"Oh Aaliyah, I love this song." Amber sings along.

Amber's rocking and singing. I notice her breasts bouncing, swaying to the music. I love how the buttons are screaming for help with those tits. I wouldn't know where to start, but I swear, I could undo that bra with the quickness. I lean in towards her. Damn, she smells sweet. "Whatcha got here for us to watch Amber? Any good movies?"

"Yes, Aaliyah, definitely some good ones. I have *Mo Betta Blues*, *Imitation of Life* and *Madea's Family Reunion*. I'm cool with whatever you want to watch girl. I've seen them all about a hundred times!"

I wish I could tell her to forget about the movies, let's bring the champagne into the bedroom. "I haven't seen Madea. I like Tyler Perry. Can you stand to watch it once more Amber?"

"Sure Aaliyah."

"Before we get into our movie Amber, do you want some food? I have so much stuff in the fridge, and you brought so many goodies. Can I make you a plate?"

I can't help but to be nice to Amber. She is so fucking sweet. I giggle inside when I think about Scott's ass making reference to Amber's genuineness. I can hear him saying it now all over again, "Amber, you're so damn good, I'm still waiting for you to tell me that you died for my sins." Oh he is too funny. Pain in the ass. But Funny.

"Aaliyah, I don't want to eat too much. I'm trying to keep my figure intact. Took me a long time to get here."

I move in closer to Amber, keeping my eyes on her all the way there.

"Amber, you are gorgeous just the way you are." I want to devour her.

She blushes.

"Aaliyah, you are too kind. I guess one night of splurging won't hurt a thing, right?"

"Amber, if it ain't broke, don't try to fix it!"

We both laugh. We make our plates of chips and finger sandwiches and both grab a beer to wash it all down. We head over to the sofa and I get the DVD ready to play. I can't wait to see Tyler Perry.

"So, how's married life so far, Amber?" I turn around to look at Amber as I prepare to push play. Sometimes I feel like I am in the movie theater with this huge plasma and surround sound in here.

"It's good, so far Aaliyah. It really is."

The phone interrupts. I run into the kitchen, where I left the phone on the counter. It's probably just Shawn calling to check in.

"Hello?" I answer.

A familiar, nasty voice greets me.

"Lee Lee, what's going on? Shawn and Khalil are down here and all. Khalil actin' all stuck up and shit. He ain't even tryin' to fuck me or nothing. What happened?"

Oh my goodness. I excuse myself and take the conversation into the other room. Amber really can not hear this, and I can not afford to give anything away.

"Excuse me, Amber. I have to take this call. I'll be right back."

"No problem Aaliyah."

The sounds of an ignorant skank blast through my receiver.

"Lee Lee! I know that fat bitch ain't over there with you! What the fuck is going on? I sent your retarded ass up there to break that shit up. Now, I hear that bitch in your fucking house? You crazy, bitch?"

I had to interrupt her. This is getting out of control.

"Listen, Shayla. I tried to get through to Khalil. He's not trying to hear it. He is in love with his wife. Just leave them alone. Amber is a beautiful person. I don't see why you really have to ruin their marriage. If he ain't want you then, he damn sure don't want you now."

I felt bad telling her this. I only agreed to play my stupid ass part, because I know how hard Shayla worked to get me those covers. I don't know how she did it, but she did. I am grateful. Besides, no one wants to ever be bothered with Shayla. No one. Not even momma.

"Listen Lee Lee. Do you know what I had to do to get you those fucking covers? Do you know the humiliation I had to go through? All the dicks I had to suck for you? For my half-sister? You said it would be a breeze. After you got Shawn wide open, you said it would be a breeze Lee Lee. Khalil belongs to me."

I can hear Shayla crying. She's bawling hard.

Damn, my sister has issues. Our mother abandoned her after she caught her in bed with my father. She basically had to grow up on her own and fend for herself. I always got the best of everything. The height, the so called good hair, the good men. Granted, I've had my share of ups and downs growing up too as our mother has a truck load of issues too numerous to mention.

"Listen, Shayla. I'm so sorry I ever got involved in this. I'm so thankful to you for getting those covers for me. I'm sorry you had to go through all of that for me. I hope I can make it up to you. But honestly Shayla, you need to get a grip. These people, including Shawn are too good to me and each other. I am loving the way I'm feeling right now. Amber is fabulous. I know you don't want to hear that, but she is. We're getting ready to watch a movie right now. I'm sorry Shayla, I have to go."

She yells. "Uh uh bitch! What you mean she lovely? That bitch has my man. Lee Lee! You s'posed to be helping me! Lee Lee, I need Khalil in my life! Bitch! You better make something happen or else." I didn't take Shayla's threat lightly. She has a lot of issues and will stoop to anything; she's a bottom of the totem pole bitch. Besides, she's sounding a little *Fatal Attraction-ish* at the moment.

"Or what Shayla? Look, like I told you, I'm going to chill with Amber now. Curl up and watch a movie and have some drinks. You'll be alright. Just find another man." Shayla starts laughing like she was just possessed by Vincent Price. She sounds like him in that Michael Jackson video *Thriller*.

"Oh Lee Lee. You curlin' up with Amber? Is that it? I always knew you was a freak, you stupid bitch! That's why you ain't get Khalil to fuck up. Cause you wanna fuck Amber, don't you? You stupid ass bitch! You really dumb, you know that? Ditzy bitch! What the fuck does everybody see in Amber!"

I can't take her anymore. "Bye Shayla. You'll be alright, like I said. I'm not ruining this good life I have up here. See ya."

I hang up and walk back into the living room to watch the movie with Amber. Shayla is such a mess. I love her dearly and witnessed her go through so much pain during her entire self-proclaimed 'crisis.' The phone is ringing off the hook now, but I ain't picking that shit up.

I've always come in and out of Shayla's life throughout adulthood. I love her dearly, but mostly feel some sort of sadness and sympathy in my heart for her. For all she's been through. Like I said, growing up for me was no set of roses, but I definitely came out less scarred. One thing I will say is that she damn sure takes good care of Lexis.

"Everything alright, Aaliyah?" Amber asks as I walk back into the room.

"Yep, Amber. Everything is good." I played it off really well, very nonchalant.

I hope Amber never finds out anything about this madness. I want like hell to leave my past behind me and continue with my new found life and freedom. I wish I'd met Shawn under different circumstances. I'll keep this secret. I will take it with me to the grave.

I get on the couch with Amber and curl up under the throw she has on. She didn't seem to mind it. Although it's summer, the air conditioning is blasting heavy in here, and I am a bit chilly. I move in just a little closer to warm up. Amber looks at me and smiles. I have no choice but to try once more. I lean in and rest my head on Amber's shoulder, just like a best friend would. Maybe that's what is attracting me to her? The best friend relationship I never shared with anyone.

If that's the case, I feel more normal about the whole attraction thing. Self-diagnosis is not a good thing. Maybe I am a freak, just like Shayla said. Or maybe I'm just curious…Bi-curious.

Amber seems a little stiff now that I've placed my head on her shoulder, which prompts me to think about what it is that I am doing. Let me retrace my steps. I'm sort of in love with the perfect man, Shawn. He is to die for, the bomb in the bedroom, an entrepreneur, college educated, and a hell of a good man. What is even better is that he adores me. I have a wonderful career as a rising model. My sister gets me two national covers that will propel my career to new heights. Yet, I agree to risk my pending marriage and possibly break up a marriage on the strength of family. Whose family would ask someone to do some shit like that? Being around these *decent* people has rubbed off on me. I'm starting to have a conscience.

As bad as it sounds, the real tragedy is that now I want to experiment with Amber and that means that I want to fuck another man's wife. It sounds twisted just to think of it. That's the nature of the beast.....Lust. They say there are three things in this world that can break up friendships, cause wars and all types of drama. Those three things are religion, money and sex. It's the truth. What other things in life do you know of that make people crazy? As crazy as I am sounding right now? Sex. Having said all of that, I still can't help myself, my curiosity is at an all time high. I have to make this happen.

Shawn calls. Amber and I both speak to him. For a minute there, I thought he caught on to this organized chaos. I do love him, but like I said, wished I had met him at a different time, a different place. My own selfishness at this point doesn't make any sense, but it's so real.

Fuck it. I'm going to do my thing and take a chance. If she won't tell, I won't tell, and we can go on about our lives as usual.

"Amber?" I hit the pause button on the DVD player.

Amber looks at me. "Yes, Aaliyah?"

I creep into her closer, and I again place my lips on hers, allowing my tongue to roam freely in her mouth, my panties are wet, my nipples rise, damn this shit is so erotic. My eyes are closed, and I envision what will happen next. My fantasy comes to a screeching halt. Amber pushes me away.

"Aaliyah! What's wrong with you? I didn't acknowledge it the first time because I knew you had a lot to drink, but you're sober now. Why are you doing this?"

Damn, Amber is upset with me. I try to explain. "Amber, it's just that I find you so sexy and appealing, I can't help myself really, you just turn me on, I guess."

She leans back, grins, and replies, "Aaliyah, Blair Underwood turns me on, but because he's married, even if given the opportunity, I wouldn't touch him. Shit, people are attractive, doesn't mean you have to kiss them. Besides, you know I just got married, and you are marrying one of my best friends. I won't tell Shawn about this, but really think about what you're doing Aaliyah." I knew all along I was dead wrong. Amber continues. "I'm going to go home now, before this gets out of hand. Aaliyah, you are a beautiful woman, but in the words of my main man Scott, *I don't do pussies.* This will be our little secret, to protect Shawn, but don't let this happen again. Feel me?"

I didn't know Amber had it in her to tell someone off. She's even sexier now, but I got the point.

"Amber, I'm really sorry."

She grabs her keys and heads out the front door.

Shawn
The Godfather

I can hear Khalil and Lexis talking from the back seat. It's a good thing I was able to reach Shayla on her cell and convince her to let Lexis ride with us. Surprisingly, she didn't even put up a fight. Khalil seems to be in his glory, but deep down inside, I know he feels fucked up. And it's his own fault.

Yeah, he's my boy, but he needs to understand that play time is over. Shit, it ended when Lexis was born. Every time I try to intervene and put him up on something, it's always, "Shawn, not now" or "I don't wanna hear it, Shawn" or "I heard this all before Shawn." Now look at him, sitting back trying to figure out how to rekindle a relationship with his own daughter. A relationship that's been nonexistent since her conception. I get so tired of being the "sound" one in this group. The one that always keeps the peace. The one that always says *"No, don't"* or *"Be careful"* or *"Do this"* or *"Not now."* I swear, being the voice of reason has become so redundant.

Don't get me wrong, Khalil is one of the most intelligent brothers in my cipher, but his actions have a way of contradicting his beliefs. His lack of prioritizing has become his downfall.

I was raised to believe that family always came first. Even though it was always just me and my momz, she instilled that in me. I guess because she didn't want me to follow in my father's footsteps. And so that I'd know what it is to be a man when the time came to put away childish things. I think it's funny when I watch TV sometimes and hear women tell their husbands or their boyfriends to step up. They say shit like,

"Teach your son how to be a man because I can't do that, only you can." Shit, my momz was, and is, my father. And I honestly don't believe he could've done a better job at raising me than she did.

Finally we reach Shayla's house. I don't think I'll be doing any driving on the way back because right now, I'm tired as hell of driving. And Jamal's ass didn't come in handy at all. Aside from the fact that he's lazy as hell, Khalil and I were too scared to let him drive, thinking that we'd fall asleep and wake up in West Bubblefuck somewhere. I swear Jamal knows women in almost every city and state, and I'm almost certain we would've stopped to see a few of his chicken heads along the way, which means, we wouldn't have gotten here until some time next week.

I park the car and get out to stretch my legs. Khalil and Lexis emerge from the backseat. Jamal opts to stay in the truck because it seems another one of *his* songs is playing, and he feels compelled to let the entire neighborhood listen in. Don't get me wrong, I'm an avid fan of hip-hop, but these nondescript characters can't rap to save their lives. Their only advantage in the rap game is being lucky enough to have hot beats. If it weren't for that, they'd be ass. I gotta make a mental note to myself to be sure and break the volume button on the way home. The way he plays his music, mark my words, Jamal will be deaf in two to five years.

The scenery around here is sickening. Shayla lives in one of the more fucked up areas in the city. I knew she moved recently, but I hadn't had the pleasure of seeing the new spot. This is what we call, *da hood.* Back in college, this was the part of town me and a couple of frat buddies bounced to when we wanted to get our swerve on. Tricks, weed, whatever it was, we could always find it here. Honestly, I never thought

Shayla would end up in this neck of the woods. I mean, I've seen worse, but this is not the kind of area to raise children.

I guess this is all she can afford being that she only works part-time, dead-end jobs. Nothing but run down tenements up and down the block. Brothas hanging on the corner, broken glass in the streets, zombie-like fiends out looking for their next hit. This shit is definitely *not* wassup. I quickly tap on the passenger side window to get Jamal's attention. I tell him to make sure he locks the truck up when he gets out. And to be safe, put the club on, too. Never can be too careful.

Shayla comes out of the house and greets us. She must've been looking for us. Either that, or she heard the sickening sound coming from the truck. Still looking good, I must say. I see she has braids in her hair now, and I can't help but think that even though I've known her for a while, she seems strangely familiar to me. She walks over to me and gives me a hug without even acknowledging Khalil, who seems to be staring at her just like he used to do in college. *Oh, hell no.*

"Hey Shawnny, wassup." Shayla gives me a peck on the cheek, then lights her Newport, takes a pull and blows the smoke out seductively. I can see Khalil following the smoke from her lips.

"How are you Shayla?" I hug her back and take in the effects of what she's wearing. Still obsessed with the tightest jeans and skimpiest tops. Even though she has the body for it, she really should learn to save something for a brother's imagination. She does have a daughter now. A very impressionable daughter at that.

"Damn, girl...Can you breathe in those jeans?" I ask her playfully.

"Whatever, Shawn." Shayla responds jokingly while hitting my arm.

The music still pumps from the truck. She points toward the truck.

"Whose truck is dat? And who dat inside?"

"It's my truck Shayla," Khalil replies, walking closer.

"And that's my man Jamal from back home. Don't you remember him?"

"Remember him from where, Khalil?" Shayla rolls her eyes along with her neck.

"I ain't never been home with you. I ain't never met yo' family or yo' friends, 'cept for Shawn. Shit, the only place you ever took me was to bed. Do you 'member dat shit, bitch?"

Here we go again. And, as always, here's my cue to intervene and stop the madness before it begins.

"Come on Shayla." I take her by the arm.

"Come inside and show me where the bathroom is."

Once inside her apartment, I take her to the side and speak in a low tone.

"Shayla, what's wrong with you? If you feel you gotta let Khalil have it, make sure Lexis is not listening in. She doesn't need to hear the negativity from you two."

I can see she understands me, but she isn't trying to hear it.

"Aaiight, Shawn, you right. But why he gotta be all smug 'n shit like he ain't done shit wrong? Here I am, strugglin' to make ends meet and he drivin' 'round in fifty-thousand-dollar cars 'n shit. Then he got da nerve to ask me if I remember some nigga he ain't never introduced me to? What, he got me confused with Amber or sumthin?"

Damn, I think to myself. For someone with a lil' college under her belt, Shayla definitely needs to invest in some sort of speech therapy. She's worse than Jamal. The streets definitely have a hold of her tongue.

"All that may be true Shayla, but now is not the time to focus on the past. Lexis hears everything you say. What's important is that he's here right now. He came for Lexis. And from what I can tell, he's really trying. You need to meet him half way."

"There you go again, Shawn," Shayla responds. "Takin' up for him. Just like you always do. How come you never talk this same bullshit to him, huh? How come you don't see the foul shit that he be doin', huh? Because he's yo' boy, right?"

If only she knew.

"How the hell do you know what I say to Khalil, Shayla?" I respond in a pissed tone. "You have no idea of the lengths I've gone to. You have no clue as to what Khalil and I talk about. I just told you that he's trying. He's really trying, that much I can vouch for. And what you need to do is empty your heart of all that bitterness and recognize. Khalil has changed a lot. And you probably don't wanna hear this, but most of his change is because of Amber. Yes Shayla, his wife, Amber. He's really trying to do the right thing. I understand you're angry because he didn't stay with you after you got pregnant. He probably even made promises to you that he never kept. But you're just as guilty as Khalil is, Shayla. You're just as much to blame as him. You knew he had a girlfriend, and you knew he was in love with her. You chose to pursue him despite the obvious. You made this bed for yourself. and you're mad at Khalil, because he doesn't sleep in it with you? I'm gonna tell you the same thing I tell Khalil day in and day out…Grow the fuck up, Shayla! It's not about either of you anymore. It's about Lexis. And the sooner you realize that, the sooner you can go on with your life and stop worrying about what the fuck Khalil is doing."

I can tell I got her attention. The look on her face confirms as much. Good! Now is not the time to sugarcoat anything with these two grown-ass individuals. And now that I think about it, maybe she should stay angry with Khalil. I saw the way he was checkin' her out a few moments ago. And if I know Shayla at all, she saw it too. And she will definitely feed off of anything he throws at her. Even his weakness for a fat ass. Good damn thing I came along. Looks like that monkey wrench I just threw at her about Amber came right on time. I'm not trying to be privy to any fucking between these two.

Looking around Shayla's one bedroom apartment, I can honestly say she has a legitimate beef. I couldn't live in here by myself, let alone with a child. Her living room has been converted into her bedroom, that much is obvious, being that her full sized bed takes up most of the space in here. A slightly ripped folding door separates her self-made bedroom from the rest of the apartment. Mirrored headboard, matching dresser and two night stands, offset by a dingy area rug that doesn't really go with anything but itself.

No wonder she's so bitter. I mean, it could be a cute spot for a single person with no kids, but not at all fit to raise a family. I've never been one to judge, but I see Khalil isn't the only one with dyslexic priorities. Looking in Shayla's closet, one would never be able to tell she's struggling in any way. Prada, Versace, Gucci, and every other designer seems to be renting space. I've added up about two-thousand dollars in merchandise, and that's only on one hanger. Oh well, I think to myself. At least the central air works.

I hear Khalil and Lexis' voices as they make their way through the front door. Lexis is telling Khalil to come on so she can show him her room.

"This way daddy!" Lexis speaks with so much enthusiasm. I approach them and make my presence known. I'm smiling from ear to ear because Lexis is so hyped right now. And she has every right to be, considering Khalil's absence in her life.

"Uncle Shawn, you can come too!" Lexis spots me as I come from the bathroom.

"I'm 'bout to show daddy my room. Malik bought me a Playstation, and I got all these new games to play on it." She begins naming all of her games, one after the other without pausing for air. Damn, no more ice cream for this girl. I don't even think she stopped to take a breath.

"Whoa, Lex, slow down," I say with a smile on my face.

"We're gonna be here for a while so take your time." Lexis really is excited. Damn. I hope Khalil understands the kind of impact he has on her. He really is blessed, and I hope he sees that. I think maybe he does because he's grinning harder than she is.

"Come on Lexis," Khalil responds taking Lexis by the hand.

"Let's go see that room of yours."

The three of us begin walking to Lexis' room when Shayla stops us.

"Khalil, can I speak to you for a minute?" Shayla asks but in an almost demanding tone. "In private?"

I can't help but think this isn't such a good idea.

"Wassup Shayla?" Khalil replies, letting go of Lexis' hand and walking toward Shayla. "What's on your mind?"

Lexis and I continue to her room while Khalil and Shayla remain in the living room, or should I say her bedroom, to talk. Lexis shows me her new Playstation that the stranger from McDonalds bought for her. Shayla must really be *puttin' in work* with this cat for him to buy her daughter such an expensive gift. Though she always did have a gift for getting whatever she wanted. It's just a shame she picked the wrong brother when she set her sights on Khalil.

After Lexis finishes showing me around her room and all the games she has, she starts showing me pictures. Each one she pulls from her scrapbook, she explains when and where the photo was taken. This girl should be in commercials, I think to myself while going through the pics. Lexis is truly a natural beauty. She's been blessed with her mother's beauty, and her daddy's charm, sprinkled with a whole lot of adorable. Shayla better be careful or she's definitely gonna have a problem keeping the boys away. I skim through the various photos until one in particular catches my eye. I stop Lexis before she can go any further.

"Wait a sec, Lex," I say with slight concern. "Let me see that one again." I point to the photo in question and stare at it in disbelief. It's a picture of Lexis, but she's with a woman. This woman who looks so familiar to me. Maybe my eyes are playing tricks on me so I wipe them and look at the picture once more. *What the fuck!* Lexis notices my interest in this particular picture and begins explaining.

"I graduated from kindergarten that day, Uncle Shawn. That's me and my Auntie right there." *Auntie? What the hell?* "Mommy says I take after her because I'm so tall. She says I can be a model someday just like her sister." There's no way in hell, I think to myself, that this shit is possible. I pretend, in front of Lexis, that the photo is just another photo.

"Your Auntie is very pretty, Lexis." I reply smiling and holding the pic in my hand. "What's your Auntie's name?"

"Her name is Auntie Lee-Lee."

Those last few words from Lexis' mouth made the pit of my stomach turn inside out. I feel nauseous. Did Lexis just say her Aunt's name is Lee-Lee? *My* Lee-Lee? Naaah, there must be some sort of mistake. I quickly dispel the notion that Aaliyah and Shayla are sisters…but just to be sure…

"So, Lexis." I get her attention before continuing my inquiry.

"Your Auntie's name is Lee-Lee?" Please God let her say no!

"Yup." Lexis responds uninterested.

"Her whole name is Aaliyah, but she says I'm the only one allowed to call her Lee-Lee. She my mommy sister."

I slip the picture into my pocket without Lexis seeing me and without even knowing why. Maybe it's because I'm going to need proof when I confront Aaliyah about it. Maybe it's because I need to look at it a few more times myself, so that I'll believe what's right in front of me. Or maybe because I don't want anybody else to see it.

I feel like I need to keep this under wraps until I can confirm its depth. My mental has already begun to take on an imagination of its own. Yeah, I met Aaliyah through Shayla, that much is true. They worked together but that was it. They didn't even know each other except in passing. Right? Her Aunt? Her sister? All this time? What the fuck is going on?

I quickly think of an excuse to leave Lexis' room and go see what Shayla is up to with Khalil. She definitely has more information about this shit. I walk toward the front of the apartment and I hear their voices. Khalil and Shayla, that is.

"I've told you a thousand times that I'm sorry Shayla." Khalil's voice seems sincere.

"I'm sorry for everything I did to you. I was young and I wasn't thinking about the long run."

"You say dat shit like it means sumthin' to me, Khalil." Shayla responds sarcastically.

"Why should I believe anything you say now? I believed you back then when you told me you loved me but that was obviously a lie, wasn't it, Khalil?"

Something tells me that once again, my presence is needed, but because of the picture I've just seen, I can't seem to focus on their drama. For once in my life, I have drama of my own. The voices continue despite my obvious lack of interest.

"Shayla, listen to me." Khalil pleads.

"At that time, at that moment, I did love you. I didn't lie about that. It wasn't all bad, Shayla. We did have some fun. But that's all it was supposed to be. Fun. You were something different for me. Something I didn't have at home. We both knew it wasn't supposed to go anywhere. But you, all of a sudden, changed everything. What did you expect me to do?"

"No, Khalil. What did you expect *me* to do? How many fuckin' abortions was I supposed to have, huh? How many times was I supposed to go under the knife? Knowin' fuckin' well that as soon as I was able to fuck again, you was gonna be cummin' in me every chance you got."

I'm not sure but I think Shayla is crying. Her tone of voice has elevated and sounds weepy.

"Why, Khalil? I never thought you would do what you did. We didn't deserve what you did. You don't even see her, Khalil. She needs you. My baby needs a father."

Suddenly, all is quiet, aside from the sobs coming from Shayla. She continuously asks Khalil why, over and over again. I do believe I've heard this all before. Same lines, different characters.

Then Khalil speaks. "I'm sorry Shayla. I didn't know. I didn't know it would turn out like this. I love Lexis, and I promise to make things right. I really am sorry for everything. It wasn't my intention to hurt anyone, especially Lexis. It'll get better, Shayla, I promise. Trust me, things will be different from now on."

Okay, enough is enough. Sounds to me like Shayla is playing on him, and he's feeling too guilty to notice. I walk in the room and I see Khalil has his arms around Shayla, consoling her. *Oh, this girl is good.* Of course, this is my cue.

"Yo, K." I speak with a serious amount of added bass in my voice. "Let me holla at you for a minute."

I know I must sound a little too concerned at this point. It has nothing to do with the two of them. As I said earlier, my own drama is having its way with me. And to be honest, I'm ready to bounce and confront my own fears at home.

Khalil turns to look at me. "Aaiight, Shawn, gimme a sec." Khalil responds, gesturing with one hand and still holding Shayla with the other.

"Let me talk to Shayla, and I'll be right out."

I notice how the two of them are clinging to each other, and I want to alert Khalil to what it looks like from the outside looking in. But, I don't. I'm sick and tired of reeling Khalil out of his madness. He seems to create drama at a moment's notice. Funny how some people constantly block their blessings. But like my momz always says, "*I gots my own fish to fry.*"

And it's time I realized that what Khalil eats, can't possibly make me shit!

Since Khalil is in his own world with Shayla at the moment, I go into the bathroom for privacy. I pull out my cell to dial Aaliyah. I feel an urgent desire to deal with my own new found concerns. I'd like nothing more than to tell her about my discovery, to tell her that I found out about her hidden secret, to let her know that she hasn't gotten the last laugh.

The phone rings. This shit is really fucking with me, even more so than when Lexis first showed me the picture. Everything is running through my head right now. I'm more than sure that Shayla's had a hand in all of this. She's bitter and vindictive and everybody knows, there isn't anything worse than a woman scorned. Aaliyah's voice pulls me from my anguish.

"Hey baby!" Aaliyah answers in a surprised, but happy tone. "It's about time you called me. I was beginning to get nervous."

Nervous? Funny she should say that, I think to myself. Why would she be nervous? All of my aforementioned thoughts evaporate into thin air as I can't bring myself to accuse Aaliyah of the obvious. Just hearing her voice has made me realize that I don't want any of it to be true. It can't be true. This woman whom I've grown to love cannot possibly be the same woman in the photograph. Aaliyah and betrayal cannot possibly fit in the same world. Not my world anyway. I readjust my thoughts and continue with conversation.

"Hey baby." I continue with small talk.

"I was just thinking about you and wanted to hear your voice. Everything okay?"

"Yes, everything's fine, Shawn, except for the fact that I'm missing you."

The words coming through the receiver, along with the sound of her voice is enough to make tears swell up in my eyes. I clear my throat.

"I miss you too baby." I speak in a sort of melancholy tone. "We should be back on the road early tomorrow morning. I'll call you when we're leaving."

"Okay Shawn." Aaliyah responds.

"Are you alright? You sound strange."

I'd like to say, "Hell no I'm not alright!" But I need to maintain my composure so I don't. "I'm good, baby. Just missing you, that's all."

I pull the picture from my pocket again and stare at it. I know this woman in the picture, but I don't know her at all.

Her hair is pulled back in a long, flowing ponytail, and those eyes…The eyes staring back at me, I would kill for.

I wonder what the hell is going on? Why would she keep this from me? Why wouldn't she tell me she was Shayla's sister? What the fuck is her agenda? A whirlwind of emotions envelope me as my attitude shifts yet again, from sadness to rage. I can't deal with her right now. Not until I know for sure what the fuck is going on. If I don't hang up this phone, all hell will break loose! I can feel it in my bones. Anger consumes me as I speak into the receiver.

"Listen, Aaliyah." I say with a sternness she's probably never heard from me before.

"We're about to head to Lexis' recital. I'll call you tomorrow." Just as I'm about to hang up, I hear her call out.

"Wait a minute, Shawn!" Aaliyah responds with concern. "What's wrong with you?"

You know damn well what's wrong with me! "I told you Aaliyah!" I snapped back. "I'm fine and I'll talk to you later!"

She obviously gets the message that I'm not fucking around right now because she falls back. "Okay....well...." She stutters. "Amber is here and just wanted to say hello."

The sound of Amber's voice reinvents my sanity.

"Hello." Amber speaks. "Shawn? Everything okay?"

"Hey baby girl." I respond sincerely.

"Yeah, everything's fine. Just a lil tired, that's all. It's been a long day."

"Oh, alright then." Amber continues. "From the way Aaliyah sounded, I thought something was wrong. Where's Khalil?"

"He's talking with Shayla right now, Amber." I continue cautiously. "But trust me, baby girl, you've got nothing to worry about, okay?"

"I do trust you Shawn. And I trust Khalil, too. I have to. He's my husband. Be sure to tell him to call me when he's done, okay?"

"No problem, baby girl, I will. Do me a favor and put Aaliyah back on."

Hearing Amber's voice has calmed me down a bit. For a minute there, I'd allowed my emotions to get the best of me. Amber has a way of soothing one's soul without even knowing it. Her love for Khalil even inspires me. Maybe this is all just a misunderstanding.

"Hello?" Aaliyah sounds unsure of which one of my personalities she's about to encounter.

"Sorry about before, Aaliyah." I explain slowly. "I don't know what came over me. I didn't mean to snap at you like that, okay?"

"Apology accepted Shawn. Just hurry home."

"I will baby."

"But I was just thinking. Why don't you take my Amex card from the nightstand and go treat yourself. I feel kinda bad for the way I just spoke to you."

"Treat myself?" Aaliyah asks.

"What are you talking about Shawn?"

"I was thinking about this day spa I came across a couple of days ago. Take my card and go there. I think the name of it is, *Serene Scene*, and the address is on the card. If you look in my glove compartment, you'll see the flyer. Take my car and make it an all day thing. Get your nails, your feet, and your hair done. You know, pamper yourself. Just be nice and ripe for Daddy when he gets home. Make sure those toes serve well as my appetizer."

"You're crazy, Shawn." Aaliyah laughs softly.

"But Amber and I are already settled for the day. I mean, watching movies and all."

"I'm not talking about today, Aaliyah. Do it in the morning so by the time I get home, you'll be nice and relaxed, okay? I just want you to realize how much I appreciate you. You mean the world to me girl."

What I'm really thinking is that I'll need some time alone when I get back. Enough time to prepare my attempt at interrogation. I can't approach her with botched facts and fictitious accusations. I'll have to be on point, which means my mind has to be right.

"Okay, Mr. Fontaine." Aaliyah jokes. "If you're sure."

"I'm sure, Ms. Mc...." I stutter and hesitate. "Ms...." *Oh my God!*

"What's the matter baby?" Aaliyah laughs and interrupts my dumbfoundness. "You forgot my name?"

I'm at a loss for words. All this time. All this fucking time. The same last name! Shayla McNeil. *Mc...Fucking...Neil!* We went to college together. How the fuck did I miss that? Aaliyah McNeil! Shayla McNeil! Both names implant themselves in my head. My blood boils to the point of eruption. There's no way I can conceal my blatant anger. *Breathe, Shawn. Breathe. Stay focused baby. The ball is in your court now. Handle it!* Thinking quickly, I adjust my tone and respond as if the epitome of truth did not just bitch slap me.

"Of course not, Ms. McNeil." I assure her.

"I just wasn't sure if I should say Ms. McNeil or *Mrs. Fontaine.*"

It dawns on me that this is the first time I've lied to her. Something I said I'd never do, and never have until now. I end the phone call with Aaliyah and step from the bathroom. I didn't realize I'd begun to sweat. A lump forms in my throat as I try like hell to piece all this info together. Aaliyah is Shayla's sister? Why wouldn't she have told me that when we met? What was she thinking about? Why didn't Shayla tell me? Did the two of them think no one would ever find out? I just don't get it.

It hits me that Khalil was right all along. He said Aaliyah looked familiar, but he couldn't figure out where he knew her from. Could they have met before? Did Aaliyah know Khalil before I introduced them? This is too much for one man to consume. *Damn, it's hot in here.*

I fan myself and grab at my collar. I remove my shirt and use it to wipe the sweat from my forehead and realize my hands are shaking. I take deep breaths to calm my nerves. My mouth goes dry so I walk into the kitchen to get some water. It's becoming more difficult to breathe. I splash water on my face and brace myself against the sink. I think I'm going to be sick.

I tell myself out loud, *"Pull yourself together Shawn. Whatever doesn't kill you will only make you stronger."* I place my head in my hands and don't even notice Jamal coming up behind me.

"Yo, dawg." Jamal says with concern. "You aaiight?"

I can't possibly let Jamal in on what's going down. Knowing him, he'll think it's funny and blow up the spot. Regardless of how serious a situation is, he'll somehow find humor in it. I use every ounce of strength in my body to answer him and I lie. Again.

"Yeah, man." I respond while gasping for air. "It just got real hot in here all of a sudden. But I'm good."

"Hot?" Jamal continues with laughter. "Man, you must be goin' through menopause or some shit, 'cause this central air is bumpin'!"

Funny he should mention air because I don't feel shit right now. What I need is a few moments to gather my thoughts, and for Jamal to get the fuck out my face!

"I don't know, man." I continue with more untruths. "Maybe it was something I ate." Hopefully, that will curb his appetite. I drink some water and leave from the kitchen with Jamal on my heels. I don't know why but his presence is bugging the shit outta me. I turn around to face him.

"Jamal, why don't you take the truck and go get something to drink. We may as well chill a lil' bit while we're down here." If anything will get his aggravating ass out of my face, it's alcohol.

"I'm down wit' dat." Jamal responds. "But I don't know my way 'round here. Fuck is da store at?"

"Go three lights down and make a right. You can't miss it."

"Aaiight, I'll be right back. What you drinkin', yo?"

"Get some Henny, man." I reply thinking I could use a drink right now. "And get some Coronas, too. I need something to chase that Henny with. And make sure you bring enough for Khalil."

Jamal leaves and I have room to breathe. I walk past Shayla's room and hear faint whispers from what I assume is her and Khalil. I wonder what the hell they're talking about all this time. I proceed further to Lexis' room and see that she's into her Playstation. She's playing *Knockout Kings,* and she's whipping the computer's butt. I don't disturb her, but instead head back toward Shayla's room.

My nightmare resurfaces. I can't take this shit anymore. I'm angry all over again, and my intentions are to bust in Shayla's room and confront her about the picture. I reach her door and stop in my tracks. The noises coming from the other side keep me from going in. I'm not sure but I think they're kissing. Fuck this shit, Shayla's got some explaining to do!

Just as I'm about to be rude and interrupt, I hear Khalil's voice. "Shayla, no, wait a minute." I stand by quietly and listen in.

"Please Khalil." Shayla begs. "Wait for what? I've been waiting for eight years now. Don't you think that's long enough?"

"Stop it, Shayla." Khalil insists. "I can't."

"Khalil, please." Shayla continues with no shame. "Baby, look. I got this new red teddy and these red stilettos, the kind you used to like to fuck me in. I promise Khalil, I can be a good woman to you if you jus' gimme a chance. Please, Khalil. I ain't do nuthin' wrong, I just wanna family, too. Is that so bad?"

"No, Shayla, it's not bad." Khalil speaks with pity. "But you can't have that with me."

"Why you doin' this to me, K?" Shayla's crying becomes more obvious.

"Lex deserves better than this. She deserves a family too. Please K, stay a few days so we can be a family."

"Get off of me, Shayla." Khalil demands. "I won't do this again. Not now. I'm married, and I love Amber too much to destroy what I have with her."

"You love Amber?!" Shayla screams. "I can't tell mutha fucka! You just had yo' tongue down my fuckin' throat, but you love Amber?! And look at you! Yo' mouth says one thang but yo' dick speakin' a whole nutha' language, nigga!

"Look me in my eyes 'n tell me you don't want none of dis ass! Look me in my eyes 'n tell me you love her."

"Yes, Shayla, I do love Amber." Khalil reiterates with promise. "Me kissing you just now was nothing more than lust, but it's cool. And the fact that my Jimmy's on swole is because I've always found you to be extremely attractive. I've never denied that. And you know you are, Shayla. I've always had a weakness for you. Lex is living proof. But I have much more discipline within myself than I did in college. I can turn it off, just as fast as you turned it on. I stopped it all on my own, before anything happened. I grew up Shayla and it's time you followed my lead. I'm sorry you can't handle that, but it is what it is. Amber's my wife now. And anything you have to offer, I already get from her. I'm sorry for ever hurting you, Shayla. I didn't mean to lead you on just now, but I had to see if I could withstand your advances. I had to know if your presence was a threat to my marriage, and I can honestly say, it's not. Now I can go home with my head held high and love my wife the way she deserves to be loved. She's all the woman that I need. As far as Lexis is concerned, I was sincere about what I said earlier. I plan on being in her life much more than I have been. I hope you can find it in your heart, for Lexis' sake, to forgive me for taking so long to be a part of her life. Please don't keep her from me. All I can offer you is support when it comes to our daughter. Shawn has helped me realize Lexis needs much more from me than a check. And I need her just as much as she needs me. It's funny I didn't know that until today. Look, I have five-thousand dollars in my pocket. Take this and use it for Lex, for whatever, I don't care. And before I leave here, I'll use my debit card, and we'll go food shopping and clothes shopping for Lex. Get my baby girl whatever she wants. Later on, we'll work on getting you and my daughter out of this hell hole and into something better. Something that compliments the two of you. Something inhabitable. My daughter deserves better than this, and I promise you that she will have the best. And when you're more comfortable, Shayla, you need to let Lex come and stay with me and Amber sometimes. Sooner or later, we're gonna have to deal with this. It's inevitable."

That's what I'm talking about, Khalil! I mean, he didn't

have to kiss her, but what he just said to her is a start. Especially for him. I knew, sooner or later he'd grow up. Maybe I didn't have to be here after all. Maybe he actually listens when I'm talking. I guess my man…is finally just that…a man. It's about fucking time because something tells me the tables are about to turn. For once in my life, something tells me I'll be the battered soul and Khalil will be the voice of reason. I only pray to God that I'm strong enough to accept his counsel when that time comes.

Khalil
Smoke Screen

Finally we get to the Sheraton. I'm glad as hell Shawn thought to reserve a room for us ahead of time. I guess he knew we wouldn't be too welcomed at Shayla's house after the recital. Especially if she wasn't getting her way, with me, that is.

I remove my digital camera from its case and review the photos I took of Lexis. She was the star of the recital! I smile as I observe how gorgeous my little girl is, but I know I can't take full credit for that. Shayla is a beautiful woman too, at least when her mouth is closed.

I place my camera back in its bag and stretch out across the queen size bed and close my eyes. I feel like partyin' right now. I'm healthy, I'm financially stable, my little girl loves me, my marriage is secure, and I love my wife to death. What more could any man ask for?

I take a sip of the Henny that Jamal brought back from the store and immediately my head swirls. I must be tired from the long drive down. Either that or Shayla just left me drained. It can't be the Henny, because I've been known to drink muthafuckas under the table.

Images of Amber dance around in my head. Shawn said he spoke to her while I was in the room talking to Shayla. He said she didn't seem angry. I hope she knows how much I love her…that I would do anything for her.

I still don't know why I was so afraid to tell her I was coming here. I've been asking myself that question since she stormed out of the house the day I left. Maybe I was afraid that there was still something between me and Shayla. Maybe I thought she still had a hold on me somehow.

I've done some stupid things in my life. Real stupid. Renee, Tonya, Michelle, Peaches, Shontay…and Cookie, damn. That's just to name a few. All of which Amber found out about and still chose to forgive me. But I was younger then, with nothing to lose, except her. There comes a time in every man's life when he must step up and choose which path to take. When that time came for me, all signs pointed in one direction…Amber.

"Yo, K!" Jamal yells at me from across the room. "Pass that shit over here, dawg."

I assume he's talking about the bottle of Henny I'm holding in my hand so I pass it to him. He takes the bottle from me and holds it in mid-air, staring at it.

"Damn, fam. I don't 'member you puttin' five in on dis shit."

"Yeah, well." I respond jokingly. "I don't remember you putting any gas in my truck, nor do I remember you paying any tolls on the way here. Nor did you pay for the McDonald's you savagely devoured. Do I really need to go any further?"

"Aaiight, K, damn!" Jamal rescinds. "I was jus' fuckin' wit you, fam."

I laugh to myself because I know damn well Jamal's not playing. I don't think he takes anything more seriously than money. His money.

"Where's Shawn?" I ask Jamal.

"I don't know." Jamal responds, finishing the last of the Henny and opening a beer. "He said he was goin' downstairs to get some air or some shit. Sup wit' yo' boy, yo?"

"What are you talking about?" I ask, uninterested in Jamal's bullshit.

I'm sayin',", Jamal replies shaking his head. "When we was at yo' baby momma's house, I peeped him in the kitchen, all bent over the sink and sweatin' n' shit. Dude had to take his shirt off, said he was hot and couldn't breathe. I'm tellin' you, dawg, if I ain't know no better, I'd swear yo' boy was trippin' off sumthin'."

"Something like what, Jamal?" I reply agitated. "Shawn is the most level headed brother I know."

"I ain't sayin' he a fiend or nuthin' like that..." Jamal continues. "But dude was actin' like he was high or sumthin'. Sweatin' n' shit, holdin' his head, fannin' hisself. I ain't no genius but it don't take rocket science to figure out when a mufukka got a hold of some bad shit."

"Shut the fuck up, Jamal!" I respond blatantly. "Shawn does not get high. I don't think he's ever done any drugs except for weed, and he hasn't done that shit since we left college. Did it ever occur to you that maybe he *was* hot?"

"What!?" Jamal laughs at me and downs his Heineken. "Mufukka, you stupid! Yo' baby momz had the air bumpin' up in there. If dude was hot, it was 'cause of the shit he was on."

"Whatever, man." I respond laughing. "You always blowin' shit out of proportion. I know my boy, aaiight? And if I said he wasn't high, then he wasn't high. Is that the only solution your small ass mind could come up with? Of all the things that could've been wrong with him, that's the best you could do?"

"Believe dat shit if you want to, yo." Jamal replies while reaching into his pants pocket. "But I bet you this bag of haze that Shawn is…"

The door to our hotel room opens. Shawn walks in with his shirt draped over his shoulder. He glances at me and then Jamal and notices the bag of weed in his hand.

"Are you talking about me, Jamal?" Shawn questions. I must admit that Shawn does appear to be out of it a little.

"Naww, man." Jamal lies and continues. "I was jus' askin' my man if he wanted to smoke a lil sumthin' tonight. I figure we may as well turn this trip into a vacation for us since we miles away from home. You game?"

Again, I laugh to myself because I know Shawn isn't about to smoke any weed. Jamal really should know Shawn by now. Now maybe if me and Jamal were alone, I'd be able to indulge. But I know for a fact, ain't shit happenin' with Shawn in the building.

"Why not?" Shawn responds, sitting down on the sofa next to Jamal.

"What are you rolling with, white owls or dutches?"

Ain't this a bitch? Shawn? Weed? In the same sentence? Naww, no way…something is definitely up.

"Word up, Shawn?" I ask in a puzzled manner. "You really about to smoke?"

"Why not, K?" Shawn continues with explanation. "I'm a grown ass man who stands on his own two. If I wanna smoke, why the hell shouldn't I? Besides, I've got some things on my mind that I'd rather not think about right now. And this weed is exactly the kind of escape I need at the moment. You gotta problem with that, Khalil?"

Okay, now I know something's wrong. Normally, I'm the one on the defensive end of things.

"Shawn, wassup brother?"

I question, hoping he'll appease me with some sort of account as to why his sanity has gone astray.

"I mean, if something's on your mind, we can talk about it. Whatever it is, weed is not the answer."

Damn, I sound just like Shawn. I wonder if we've somehow switched places. Almost seems like we're role playing right now.

"Nothing's up, Khalil." Shawn responds, not the least bit moved by what I've just said. "Just feel like having a good time tonight, that's all. I know I'm entitled, so let me live."

Shawn takes the weed and the two white owls from Jamal. He splits it down the side with his nails, one after the other. He dumps the remains from the cigar onto the nightstand and pours the weed evenly inside both owls. He rolls them up, then licks the sides to ensure the weed stays in tact. *Oh well, I guess we smokin' tonight.*

After drinking, smoking, laughing, talking and listening to music, Jamal decides he wants to go out. The hotel room is filled with so much smoke at this point, that I'm surprised the smoke detectors haven't gone off. If anyone walks in here right now, I swear they'd receive an instant contact.

"Come on, y'all." Jamal insists. "Let's go do sumthin'. I know it gotta be some clubs or sumthin' 'round here. Let's go out, meet some honeys, you know, get our freak on."

"I'm tired as hell Jamal." I respond while opening the last bottle of beer. "All I wanna do is lay here and enjoy this buzz I got. Shit, I haven't felt this good in a long ass time. And besides, all the honey I need is back in Jersey waiting for me."

"What about you, Shawn?" Jamal asks, still searching for someone to cater to his madness. "You wanna bounce?"

"Naaah, man." Shawn replies. "I'm with K on this one. I'm feeling real nice right now. Real mellow, and I'm not trying to fuck that up by taking in the sights of VA. I've seen too much of what it has to offer and there isn't anything down here for me."

"Whateva', man." Jamal continues while walking to the door. "You two fake ass executives stay here and jerk each other off. But I'm goin' to get me some pussy!"

Shawn and I laugh at this clown. I almost wanna yell to Jamal to call Shayla. I'm sure she'll give him what he wants. I know it's the weed, but the thought of their two ghetto asses bumping pelvises makes me laugh so hard that I fall off the bed.

A few hours pass with more talking between Shawn and I. Although he hasn't said anything, I can sense that something's bothering him. I can't remember the last time he acted so recklessly. I mean, it's only weed and we are grown, but this is not normal behavior for Shawn. Something happened between the time we got here and now. I just wish he'd fill a brother in. He's normally the voice of logic, but right now he's out of control, for him, anyway.

"Alright, man." I persist with questioning. "What's going on with you?"

"Already told you, K. Just chillin' right now."

"Naah, man, something's up. Just the fact that you've been high and shirtless for the last few hours tells me something's wrong. Fess up, Shawn. What's on your mind?"

"How did you know Amber was the one?" Shawn's question throws me for a loop. It has absolutely nothing to do with what I just asked him. I'm puzzled.

"Huh?" I respond.

"How did you know Amber was the woman you wanted to spend the rest of your life with? I mean, when you think about it, you didn't just promise her, you promised God. You stood up in that place, on holy ground, in front of a minister and you said, "*I do*." How did you know she was the one?"

See, I knew we shouldn't have smoked no damn weed. Shawn done lost his fucking mind. "Come on, Shawn." I laugh.

214

"That weed got you buggin'. Where the fuck did that come from anyway?"

"Just answer the fucking question, Khalil!" Shawn insists and seems more focused. "Just tell me how you knew!"

"Aaiight, yo, calm down." I continue laughing, thinking that Shawn is definitely not himself right now. If anyone knows the history between Amber and I, it's him. So why on Earth is he asking me this shit right now? The only way I'll find out is to entertain him, so I do.

"I just knew, Shawn. I mean, when I lost her back in college, it was the worst time of my life. I wanted to die. Nothing else mattered, but her. You were there, you should know. You saw what happened and what I went through. It wasn't pretty at all."

"I know I was there, Khalil, but I want to hear from you exactly how *you* knew. We never discussed that."

"Is there something going on with you and Aaliyah, man?" This is the only thing I can think of that would make him question me in this manner. What else could it be?

"Damn, Khalil!" Shawn responds with intensity. "Is it that hard for you to discuss your *wife* without shifting focus? I asked you a simple question about the woman you love. What's the fucking problem?!"

"The problem is your question came outta left field. You already know everything about me and Amber, from the beginning to now, so your question doesn't make any sense. You were there when I met her, there while I dated her, there when I lost her, hell, you helped me get her back! What the fuck *don't* you know about us? You know that she's my soul mate, Shawn. You know she's the wind beneath my wings. You know that she completes me. She's my woman, Shawn, and has been for as long as I can remember. And yeah I fucked around, and been with other women, but Amber's pussy is the

215

only pussy for me. It's that damn good. I know this now. I know when her clit throbs before she does. I can make her cum without being in the same room. I can finish her sentences without knowing what's on her mind. She has made my life whole. Our bond is unbreakable. She's my air, Shawn, and without air, I can't breathe. If I stop breathing, I die. That's how the fuck I knew!"

"Now was that so hard?" Shawn asks calmly as if he hadn't just demanded a response from me.

"I just wanted to hear you confess all that. Sometimes people need to be reminded of how lucky they are. How blessed they are. Sometimes we're so blinded by covers, that we lose sight of what's important. Our peripherals vanish, and we only see what's right in front of us. Sometimes you have to dig deep just to get to the surface of things."

That's it! No more drugs for his ass!

"What is it that you're trying to say, Shawn?"

"I'm not *trying* to say anything, Khalil. I'm saying it. You have a good woman in Amber. You know everything about her. Her friends, her family, her likes, her dislikes. Nothing is camouflaged with her. You don't have to guess about anything. Her life is your life, and vice-versa. You don't ever have to feel like she's somehow covering something up. Because if she were, you'd know because you know her so well. There's never any need for you to question her motives because you automatically know she's on the up and up. She has no reason to lie to you about anything because the two of you have been through so much together. You two communicate and that's what a lot of relationships lack these days. Communication."

Shawn's going on and on about me and Amber's relationship. He's not really preaching but more so co-signing the fact that I have a good woman. Usually, the only time he goes on like this is when I have somehow fucked up. Maybe he thinks something went on between me and Shayla. I *was* in the room with her for a while, and he did walk in and see me with my arms around her. That's got to be it. That's why he's acting so strange.

"Shawn, if you're wondering, nothing happened with me and Shayla today." I interrupt his soliloquy and continue, "Is that what's bothering you? You think I fucked Shayla today?"

"Naah, Khalil." Shawn continues with an exhausted look on his face. "I know you didn't fuck her. As a matter of fact, I heard some of the conversation you two had. I wasn't eavesdropping but I was on my way in to talk to you about something. I couldn't help but stand there when I heard you putting Shayla in her place. I was proud of you, man. It's been a real long time comin', but you got here, nonetheless."

"Well what is it then, Shawn?" I ask, still not convinced of his sanity. "Why the sudden interest in how well I know my wife? Where did all that come from?"

"I don't know, K. Maybe your relationship with Amber has me thinking of my relationship with Aaliyah. I mean, how well do I really know her? You know Amber's entire family, and I know nothing about Aaliyah's. She's always talking about how her past was *not so fortunate*. She puts the brakes on whenever I bring it up. She never mentions her parents, or if she has sisters and brothers. What kind of grades did she get in school? Was she a tomboy when she was little? And did you know that sometimes she doesn't want me to touch her? Sometimes I catch her on the phone, and she'll say it was the wrong number? What is all that about, Khalil? Sometimes, I'll notice how her speech pattern changes from articulate to plain ghetto. I pretend like I don't, but I do. Just simple questions, Khalil. Questions that can easily be answered if she'd only let me in. What is she hiding, K? Why doesn't she talk to me

217

about any of these things? Your relationship with Amber has made me realize that I've asked a total stranger to be my wife. To spend the rest of my life with her. How can I go through with it, K? I can't marry her because I don't know who she is. All I know is a shell and until I can see what's inside, I have to assume it's no good for me."

At this moment, I want to tell Shawn about the little escapade I had with Aaliyah. About how she paraded around in front of me wearing only a towel. About how she invited me into his home and offered me drinks while he wasn't there. But I can't say anything now because I should've told him when it happened. If I tell him now, it'll only add fuel to the fire. A week ago, he was in love with her, and now he doesn't know *who* he's in love with…literally.

"Shawn, man." I play it off. "You're just high right now. Aaliyah hasn't given you any reason to question her depth. Far as I can tell, she loves you. You're not thinking clearly and maybe it has something to do with all this smoke up in here."

I try to add a little laughter, hoping that it will ease his mind. I do believe Aaliyah loves him, but I also believe she has a story behind her. Just can't figure it out. But honestly, I've never heard Shawn speak about Aaliyah this way. Weed always did have a way of bringing shit to the forefront.

"You know what, K?" Shawn continues with seriousness. "Everything happens for a reason. Everything. I haven't smoked weed in years, but I probably would have never seen things this clearly if it weren't for this smoke filled room. How's that for irony?"

Amber
Good to the Last Drop

So glad I'm off today. I don't think I could've dealt with any patients in my current frame of mind. Between Khalil in Virginia and Miss Beverly in the hospital, I'm a mess. Right after I explained everything to Keisha about Khalil's Virginia escapade, she gave me the bad news about Miss Beverly.

Miss Beverly suffered a stroke and had to be rushed to the hospital. When something this significant happens at the nursing home, it's normal procedure to have them transferred to an outside facility, preferably one with a trauma unit. It sort of eases my tension, just a tad, to know that Miss Beverly was brought to UMDNJ. It's one of the best hospitals in the country when it comes to patient care. I just hate the fact that it has such a stigma attached.

The news, however, left me devastated, and it took me a day or two to get enough courage to come and see her. I know this is what I have to do. Miss Beverly is a fighter, so I pray that she will get through this. She's been through so much over the years like losing her husband, suffering from dementia, and even winning her battle against breast cancer. She is a survivor. But even more so, she's blessed. My eyes fill with tears as I remember the pleasant times I've had with her.

As I now walk through the revolving doors of University Hospital, I grab Keisha's hand and come to a complete halt. I turn to face her.

"Keisha, what if she doesn't make it?" I scare myself as I ask this question. Miss Beverly and I have become so close. She's sort of my unofficial grandmother. I don't know what I'll do if I lose her.

"Don't think like that, Amber." Keisha hugs me and jokes. "Miss Beverly is a stubborn 'ole mule and ain't nuthin' 'bout to stop her flow."

Keisha continues with her reassurance that Miss Beverly will be okay. She says I'm being paranoid for no reason at all. "Listen Amber," Keisha tells me. "I know you're afraid for Miss Beverly, but I think you're more afraid of what Khalil is doing in Virginia. If you're gonna be with him, you gotta trust him, feel me? Ain't no way around that, Amber. And besides, you really think he gon' risk everything for a chicken head broad? Some hood rat chick who named her child after some shit she ain't never gon' be able to afford?"

I laugh, maybe Keisha's right. It's just that from my past experiences, I've learned to expect the worst so that when it actually does happen, I'm already mentally prepared. *Please God, let Miss Beverly be alright.* We walk across the hospital lobby, which seems to take forever and finally reach the visitors desk. A large woman with a burgundy finger weave and a gold tooth greets us with a smile.

"Good morning, Ladies." The stranger nods. "May I help you?"

"Yes." Keisha responds, obviously sensing that I'm much too nervous to focus at the moment. "We're here to see a Ms. Beverly Wilson."

The large woman begins toying with her desktop. I think to myself, while standing here, that Beverly Wilson is only two words. Why on Earth does it seem as if this woman is typing up the entire script for the movie, *Roots*? When she's done, she hands us two passes and points toward the elevators.

"Here you go, Ladies." The receptionist continues with a smile and point towards the elevators. "Take those elevators up to the fifth floor and this patient is in Room 517B."

"Thank you." I respond solemnly while taking the pass.

"You're welcome."

Before we proceed to the elevators, Keisha and I decide to stop in the gift shop. We figure we'll get some flowers and liven up Miss Beverly's room a bit. I buy a dozen roses and the prettiest card that reads "Get Well Soon." Keisha gets her a few helium balloons and a can of peanut brittle. Miss Beverly loves herself some peanut brittle. How she eats this stuff when her teeth aren't in, I'll never know. It really is a sight to see.

Keisha and I finish in the gift shop and move to the elevators. We wait. Everything seems to happen in slow motion. Somehow, the thought of seeing Miss Beverly makes me very impatient. I don't want to see her, but can't wait to see her at the same time.

I think of all the things I want to say to her. Things I should've said but never got the chance to. I think of all the things I said I'd do for her, like take her to a matinee and an early dinner. Take her for a stroll in the park on a nice summer day. I always said I'd do those things on one of my days off but never got around to it.

As a nurse, I've grown accustomed to sickness, illness and even death. It's part of the job. Part of my medical training is to be able to stomach anything from stroke victims to Alzheimer's patients. There's something, however, about going to see Miss Beverly that has me shook.

Management frowns on undue familiarity between employees and patients, but Miss Beverly is more than a patient to me. She's family, and I love her. She's the type of caring spirit I want to become when I reach that age, Lord willing, I'll make it there. I've really grown to love her. I've looked to her over the years, for advice on love, marriage, commitment, sex, and all things in between. My relationship with Miss Beverly extends far beyond professional. It is an extremely special relationship that I am not yet ready to end.

I reach into my tote bag and quickly scan the items I brought for her. A few nightgowns because I know Miss Beverly wouldn't be caught dead in hospital garb. She's probably having a fit right now. A pair of slippers, some underwear, a comb and brush set, a few bottles of Keri lotion and her favorite Dove soap. I'm laughing because Miss Beverly always says she can't use anything else on her skin except Dove. She says if she doesn't, someone may mistake her for an alligator and turn her into a purse. That woman is a nut.

I ramble through the care package and find what I'm looking for. I remove the eight-by-ten wedding photo of me and Khalil. I smile and think that Miss Beverly's going to love this. I bet she thought I forgot. Studying the picture, I notice how Khalil and I are both facing the camera with me leaning into his chest. He has his arms partially wrapped around me. I trace my fingers across Khalil's face. I remember how gorgeous he looked that day. His goatee is outlined perfectly and his rich, dark skin seems almost life-like. In the picture, I stand next to him. I remember how beautiful I was as well. My train appears to be endless, as it only disappears when there's no more picture left to view. This photo is so exquisite, and it captures every detail of that day. I must remember to send the photo studio a well-versed letter of appreciation for taking such beautiful pictures. Their services were worth every penny.

Miss Beverly will love this photo, I think to myself while placing it back in the tote. Khalil and I really do fit, if that makes sense at all. I hope she approves. Because of the nursing home's bureaucratic red tape regarding patient familiarity, Miss Beverly wasn't able to come to my wedding. Well that, and her God-awful granddaughter, Loreatha, who backed the nursing home one hundred percent.

I push the elevator button for the "umpteenth" time as anxiousness overwhelms me. Keisha slaps my hand away.

"Amber, pushing that button will not make the elevator come any faster. Just relax, okay?"

"Come on Keisha." I respond impatiently, pointing to the stairway. "Let's take the stairs. We've been standing here too long."

"Stairs?!" "I ain't walkin' up no damn stairs. These four inch heels won't let me."

I look down at her feet and realize she's right. A simple hospital visit and Keisha has managed to turn it into *Rip the Runway.* A beige, strapless halter jumpsuit that stops at mid-calf, offset by strappy heels to match. I'm sure it's all some sort of name brand, but I can't tell which, being that I'm not into that much designer clothing. Her make-up is flawless as usual, and her hair hangs to a point where it covers her right eye. Her dark shades give her that mysterious, jaded look. Honestly, Keisha can wear a Path mark bag and make it look appealing. I, myself, have settled on my white linen capris, a pink form-fitting blouse, and my silver, pink and white Skechers. I'm a simple girl, subtle and not one for attracting unwanted attention.

Before I'm done sizing the both of us up, the elevator doors open. I quickly step inside for fear that the doors may close and never open again. I press the button for the fifth floor, when I hear footsteps running and voices yelling to hold the elevator. I quickly press the button that reads open, but it's too late. The elevator has already begun its ascent.

The elevator reaches our floor and stops. Keisha and I emerge and make our way down the hallway. I think to myself that I've been in this hospital a thousand times, so why do all these foyers seem so long and endless today? One by one, I read the numbers on each door. Five-0-nine. Five-eleven. Five-thirteen. Five-fifteen.

"Right here, Keisha." I say as I point to Miss Beverly's name tag on the door. "She's in here."

I exhale and gently push the door open. I immediately hear the sound of oxygen being administered. You know, the sound like air is being let out of a balloon over and over again. My heart drops. I stop before going all the way inside.

Keisha leads me by the hand. "Come on Amber." Keisha whispers. "It's gonna be okay."

Tears fall from my eyes before I even see Miss Beverly's room. The thought that she's worse off than I previously imagined upsets my natural balance. Keisha forces me further into the room, when I see a sight that allows me to breathe easy. It's not Miss Beverly who's in need of the oxygen, but her roommate. It never even dawned on me that she could possibly have a roommate. Although I feel sort of silly, I wonder where Miss Beverly is. The other bed is empty.

Just as my imagination is about to run yet another marathon, I hear the sound of a toilet flushing. My heart begins to beat fast, not because of fear, but because of excitement. I can't wait to see her. I know she'll be happy to see me, too.

The bathroom door opens slowly, and out comes Miss Beverly aided by a walker and with the help of a registered nurse. I smile because she doesn't realize I'm in the room. I'm happy that she's up, and with some help, she's slightly able to walk.

Miss Beverly doesn't look too bad upon first glance. Her once gorgeous, caramel coated face, however, is a bit distorted and her left eye has a slant. But I'm a nurse, and I know for a fact that these things can change in time. The older woman helping Miss Beverly from the bathroom notices me and Keisha.

"Hello girls." She speaks softly with a foreign accent. "Are you here to see Mrs. Wilson?"

"Yes, we are," I respond quietly.

"Would you like some help with her?" I barely finish offering my services before Miss Beverly looks up and tries to focus on the sound of my voice. She squints her eyes and looks in my direction. My heart melts. She's recognized my voice. Despite everything she's gone through, Miss Beverly has not forgotten me.

"Amba?" Miss Beverly asks slowly with slurred speech. "Amba, baby…Daa you?" She turns to her nurse before sitting down and continues.

"Puh-lee han me mah ga-lasses baby. Ah ca'an see too good."

The nurse can barely understand what Miss Beverly's saying between her Southern accent and the effects of the stroke. But I understand her just fine. I explain to the nurse what Miss Beverly wants. I point to her eyeglasses on the side table, while moving closer to help her onto the bed.

The nurse tells us all the details of Miss Beverly's stroke. She explains that most of the damage is to Miss Beverly's left side, that the next forty-eight hours are critical. She says she's never seen someone as old as Miss Beverly bounce back so quickly. She also says Miss Beverly's been calling out my name since she got here, but no one could understand what she was saying. I look at Miss Beverly.

"Come on Miss Beverly." I whisper and take over for the nurse. "Sit down first, then put your glasses on."

The nurse retrieves the eyeglasses and then excuses herself. I help Miss Beverly put them on.

"That better, Miss Beverly?" I ask, still smiling. She's finally able to focus and realizes she's correct in her assumptions. She smiles now. The grandest smile I've ever seen on her warms my heart. Crooked, but grand nonetheless.

225

I sit down on the bed next to her, and she hugs me for what seems like an eternity.

"Oh, Amba!" Miss Beverly cries. "Whaa tuk' you...so lon' ta' geh' heer?....I dawt....I's nevah....gon' see you....no mo'."

Tears fall from Miss Beverly eyes as she tries so hard to speak. I notice how difficult it is for her so I interrupt.

"Hey, Miss Beverly." I hug her back and kiss her on her cheek. I rub away evidence of my Mac lip glass. Then I take a napkin from her side table and blot away the tears still running down her face. I can't remember the last time I saw Miss Beverly cry. It makes my tears fall, too.

"I'm so glad you're okay, Miss Beverly. Don't ever scare me like that again, you here me?" I wipe my own tears and pick up her left hand that appears to be laying lifeless on her lap. I began rubbing and massaging it, hoping maybe I can get her blood circulating on that side.

"Mmmm, Amba." Miss Beverly moans and lays her head back, against her pillow. "Daat feel....good....Mmmmm."

"You can feel that Miss Beverly?" I ask excitedly while squeezing up her arm a little harder.

"This right here? You can feel this?"

"Yeah." Miss Beverly continues. "Buh noh so hawd Amba."

I ease up with the pressure and Miss Beverly continues. "Yeah, Amba. Ly' dat. Keep 'awn, jus'....ly'....dat."

I continue with the massage and take in the effects of Miss Beverly. She's aged since the last time I saw her, which was only a few days ago. I reach for my tote and show her all the things I brought for her, including the wedding photo. I'm hoping it will make her feel better. She tries to take it from me, but the frame is too heavy for her to hold. I hold one side while she holds the other. She stares at it, then looks at me.

"Mah gooh'ness, Amba. Dis fuh' me?" Miss Beverly sounds a little clearer. "You look so pur'ty. An' dis ya' huz'bin? Amba, he gaw'jus'!"

She's struggling to hold her end of the picture so I take it from her.

"Thank you, Miss Beverly." I sit the picture next to the flowers. "I'll sit it right here so you can see it whenever you want."

Keisha makes a noise as she gets up from the chair she's sitting in. Miss Beverly looks over in her direction.

"Hi, Miss Beverly." Keisha speaks softly, extending her hand to touch Miss Beverly. "You feeling okay?"

"Moov way from me chile." Miss Beverly draws away from her and frowns. "I look okay ta' you?"

Miss Beverly turns her attention back to me. "Amba, why come you ain' tell me you had 'dis wuh'sum chile wit' you?"

I cover my mouth with my hand to hide my laughter. Keisha returns to her chair and looks at Miss Beverly with a smile on her face.

"Yo' ole' ass lucky you layin' in that bed." Keisha responds sarcastically. "What you should be doin' is prayin' yo' ass off right now." Surprisingly, not much has changed between the two of them. I can't believe Miss Beverly is actually trying to get out of this bed.

"You wa'wn sum uh' me, bish?!" Miss Beverly slurs with fervor as she tries to reach Keisha. "Cum' awn 'n geh' sum, heffa!"

It doesn't take much force for me to keep Miss Beverly on the bed. But I must say, for someone who just had a stroke, there's nothing weak about her.

I conceal my laughter while restraining Miss Beverly. These two can never be in the same room for more than five minutes without squaring off. I look deeper into Keisha's eyes.

227

She had been crying too. Her eyes have that glassy look and the remnants from her tears on her cheek. I smile inside because I know Keisha loves Miss Beverly just as much as I do, but she'll never admit it.

I remember when one of our other patients, Mrs. Lily, died some years back. Mrs. Annie Mae Lily was a petite, elderly white woman of seventy-two, about five feet tall with long, snow white hair. False teeth and cratered skin, but still held the bluest of eyes. You could tell she was probably the shit in her day, but that day had come and gone. She had all kinds of old furs and vintage jewelry that she'd dress up in and go absolutely nowhere. She'd insisted on having the finest china in her room that only she could use. The hospital submitted to her requests against their better judgment, especially since she'd be paying for it out of pocket. She'd sit in her room and drink tea all by herself. No one ever came to see her, aside from her attorney, which made us all believe she had some sort of fortune. Either that, or an heiress to one, which meant, either way, she had money.

Her and Keisha went at it every day for the entire five years she was with us. Let Mrs. Lily tell it, Keisha was every black hooker bitch in the book. And to Keisha, Mrs. Lily was "Mother Grand Wizard" for the Ku Klux Klan. They spit venom at each other all day, every day. It was almost like they became codependent on one another. Mrs. Lily somehow needed to cuss Keisha out at least once a day. And Keisha wasn't herself if she didn't do the same.

For Mrs. Lily's birthday one year, Keisha brought in a framed picture of Malcolm X and hung it in Mrs. Lily's room without her knowing. When Mrs. Lily finally noticed it, she came out to our station with fire in her eyes and hurled it at Keisha, who had managed to escape under the desk before the picture could hit the floor. Nobody had told Mrs. Lily that Keisha hung the picture, she automatically knew.

We laughed so hard that day. Even Mrs. Lily was caught with a smile on her face. It was the talk of the nursing home for weeks. But Mrs. Lily was a slick old biddy, and she swore to get Keisha back.

For the next several days, Keisha was on the defensive, knowing that Mrs. Lily was up to something and she wasn't about to sleep on her. Mrs. Lily, being the crafty little devil that she was, knew Keisha was being cautious. She knew it wouldn't be easy paying Keisha back, but she found a way.

One day, while me, Keisha, and Rhonda were working the floor, the distress signal sounded and our panel showed that it was Mrs. Lily's room. On our floor, we have the oldest, sickest patients. All are hooked up to some sort of machine. Whether it be life support, oxygen, or a simple heart monitor, all the patients on our floor are attached to something.

Whenever a distress signal goes off, it means the patient has taken a turn for the worse. They've either flat-lined or are about to. On this particular day, it was Mrs. Lily's room, and being that Mrs. Lily was Keisha's patient, she jumped up and took off down the hall without thinking twice. Rhonda and I stayed on post, which is procedure, and summoned for the on-call physician.

A few seconds later, we heard Keisha scream. I ran down the hall and opened Mrs. Lily's door. It was a sight I'll never forget. Keisha was on the floor, flat on her back, with some sort of grease all over her. I looked at Mrs. Lily who was calmly in her bed watching her favorite show, *All in the Family* with her favorite character, *Archie Bunker*, and drinking tea from her china. Mrs. Lily acted as if nothing happened and didn't even acknowledge Keisha laying on the floor.

We later found that Mrs. Lily had poured olive oil all over her floor. She had unhooked herself from her heart monitor, which made it send the distress signal. She knew this would make Keisha run in her room. Keisha ended up with a sprained ankle as a result and had to take a couple of days off. Even while Keisha was sprawled on Mrs. Lily's floor, Keisha, herself, erupted into laughter.

When Mrs. Lily died, a part of Keisha died too. Although they didn't get along, they'd become a part of each other's lives, more so than the rest of us. Mrs. Lily fed off of Keisha's energy. I think that's probably how she managed to stay with us for as long as she did.

We didn't laugh too much after Mrs. Lily passed away. I guess we hadn't noticed she was the spirit of our floor. Keisha didn't go to Mrs. Lily's funeral. Instead, she took the following two weeks off from work. She never admitted it to this day, but I know Mrs. Lily was the reason for her sudden vacation. Everybody knew it, including management, which is why they never bothered her about the time off.

I think that's probably why Keisha has never gotten personally involved with another patient since. She makes her rounds and that's it. I think Miss Beverly is the closest she's gotten to a patient since Mrs. Lily, and that's only because of me.

I wonder if Miss Beverly reminds Keisha of Mrs. Lily. She has to, now that I think about it. Keisha gets a kick out of it when Miss Beverly lets her have it. I know because it was the first thing Keisha couldn't wait to tell me when I came back from my honeymoon. It's funny how I never picked up on that until now. Sometimes, when you're on the outside looking in, your view may be distorted just a tad. People tend to see what they want, when in all actuality, the people you're looking at may see something totally different altogether.

"Amber!" Keisha's voice snaps me out of my daze. I look up and see Loreatha hovering over me and Miss Beverly. My mood changes as I switch to the defensive, because she's scowling at me. If it weren't for her beauty, I'd swear she was Satan. *Lord, here we go again.*

"Why you all up on my grandma like that?" Loreatha exclaims with pure hatred toward me. "Can I puhlease have some time alone with her?"

I want to tell her that she's my grandmother, not yours. Miss Beverly loves me, not you. She called my name, not yours. Instead, I get up from the Miss Beverly's bed. The last thing I want to do is upset *my* grandmother. Keisha observes my uneasiness and stands up. Somehow, she manages to create space between me and Loreatha.

"Come on, Amber." Keisha speaks to me but looks at Loreatha with fierceness. "Let's go down to the coffee shop. We can come back up in a few."

I know what Keisha is doing, but I'm not ready to leave just yet.

"I'm not going anywhere Keisha." I respond blatantly.

"I'm sure Miss Beverly doesn't want me to go." Hell, Loreatha must've mistaken my past kindness for weakness. She obviously doesn't realize that I'm not at work right now. She can get it real easy. There's only a small level of professionalism I need to maintain at this moment. I hope she understands that I'm off the clock. The look on my face lets Loreatha know that it's only space and opportunity between the two of us. And I am about to clean her clock.

I hear the loud tapping of heels coming down the corridor, the footsteps stop at Miss Beverly's door. The door opens slightly, and we all turn to see who it is. I look at Keisha and we both realize it's Scott's friend from the other night at the sex party. I immediately think that maybe she's visiting Miss Beverly's roommate. She looks at us and smiles.

"Hi, umm….ummm...." She hesitates because she can't remember my name. "Amber, right?"

"Yes, it's Amber." I respond with a smile.

"And you're Eva." I think to myself that she's just as stunning as she was at the sex party. I continue and point at Keisha. "You remember my friend Keisha, right?"

She acknowledges Keisha and turns to face Loreatha.

"Chyna, I'll be downstairs in the gift shop." Eva explains while looking at Loreatha. "I'm going to see if they'll let me hang one of our flyers in there."

I am confused. *Why she's calling Loreatha, Chyna?* That isn't her name. Keisha looks at me. She too is dumbfounded. We both turn from Eva to Loreatha.

"You're Chyna?" Keisha asks with a smirk on her face and pointing at Loreatha. "You're the one who Eva was talkin' 'bout the other night?"

I wonder why Keisha's laughing. Loreatha must be wondering the same thing.

"*Chyna* is my stage name, thank you very much!" Loreatha continues with attitude. "I don't see why it's so damn funny!"

Despite Loreatha's apparent hostility, Keisha continues to find it strangely amusing that Loreatha's alter ego is Chyna.

Loreatha turns her focus to Eva and stops her before she can leave the room. "You know these two?"

"Yes." Eva replies. "Scott introduced us the other night at our gig you couldn't make it to. You know, the night your grandmother was rushed to the hospital."

Eva says her goodbyes and leaves the room. Now it all makes more sense. Eva did say that she had a partner who couldn't make it that night. And Scott did go on and on about how gorgeous this infamous *Chyna* was. All this time, he's been talking about Loreatha. Yes, she's pretty, but gimme a break. *She's got nothing on Eva.* Not to me anyway. Shit, her nappy weave wearing ass ain't got nothing on me either.

Keisha is not going to let this *name* thing go. She's still giggling and says out loud, "So....Tell me, *Chyna.*" Keisha teases. "Exactly what kinda *stage* you talkin' 'bout?"

"What!?" Loreatha snaps and turns to face Keisha.

"Well....you said Chyna was your *stage* name." Keisha laughs and continues to tease. "So I was just wonderin' what kinda *stage* you was talkin' 'bout."

Not that it matters, but I realize that I'd like to know the same thing.

"My *business* is my stage!" Loreatha advises adamantly. "Wherever my business happens to take me, that's my stage. It could be a bedroom, an office desk, even a fucking cake! But wherever I'm standing, wherever I happen to be when I'm makin' my paper....That's my stage! Any more questions?"

Please, Keisha please! Ask her some more questions and get her to talk. I wanna know exactly what it is that she does. I have a feeling, but I want to hear her say it. Keisha must be reading my mind.

"So....*Chyna.*" Keisha's still laughing despite Loreatha's anger. "When you're on this *stage*, what is it that you're doing?"

Yeah, I think to myself. What is it that you're doing?

"First of all...." Loreatha points at Keisha. "That's none of your fucking business! And second of all, just the fact that you're asking me that, tells me you already know. And if you don't...well....you look like a smart woman, use your fucking imagination!"

Keisha looks at me with an evil grin on her face. She looks like she has more in store for this conversation. I interrupt her before she can get another word in. I don't like the way Loreatha is talking around Miss Beverly. I have to let her know. "Loreatha, do you mind?" I ask, pointing at Miss Beverly. "Don't talk like that around Miss Beverly. Have some respect for her even if you don't have any for yourself!"

"Who the fuck do you think you talkin' to!?" Loreatha raises her voice at me. "Don't tell me how to talk around my grandmother! If you got a problem with it, then get the fuck out!"

It takes everything in me not to bitch slap her. I don't think I've ever wanted to hurt anyone the way I want to hurt Loreatha at this very moment. But because of Miss Beverly, I keep a level head. I look at Keisha. We both know it's time to leave. Before doing so, I go back over to Miss Beverly's bed. "Miss Beverly?" I smile to her and give her a kiss on the cheek. "I'm leaving because I don't want to upset you. I know you need your rest. Don't forget about the things I brought for you. They're folded up right here, okay?"

I point to the nightgowns and the other items from the care package that are folded neatly on her side-table next to the flowers and the picture I brought for her. Loreatha turns to see what I'm talking about. She bypasses everything and picks up my wedding photo. She seems to stare at it longer than the average person would, then she looks at me with a devilish grin on her face. I ignore her and make sure Miss Beverly is comfortable before I head out.

"You need me to get you anything before I leave, Miss Beverly?" I know she doesn't want me to go.

"Naw, Amba...." Miss Beverly tries to reach out to me. "Don' go. Ain' you even gon' brush mah hair fo' you go?"

I look up at Loreatha who still has an evil look on her face. I want to tell Miss Beverly that I can't stay because *Satan* is in the room. I want to tell her that I hate her granddaughter and wish she'd die of bone cancer, catch syphillis, go blind and watch in front of a tractor trailer, then go straight to hell with gasoline drawers on. Instead I smooth Miss Beverly's hair from her face and kiss her forehead.

"Not today, Miss Beverly. I want you to get some rest right now. I promise I'll be back and I'll brush your hair, okay?"

"Okay, baby." Miss Beverly sulks, then looks at Loreatha and snaps. "It's awl yo' fawt, fool!"

I retrieve my purse from the table. Keisha and I make our way to the door. Loreatha, however, stops us.

"Amber." Loreatha calls while holding the wedding photo in her hand. The smirk on her face is unnerving.

"This is your husband? This is the wedding you wanted my grandmother to go to?"

She has a sudden interest in me? In *my* wedding? In *my* husband? I notice Keisha is gathering her things. She seems anxious to leave all of a sudden, like a light bulb has gone off in her head or something. It's weird.

"Yes, Loreatha." I respond not at all interested. "That's my husband."

I open the door to leave. Loreatha says something that moves the Earth beneath me.

"His name is Khalil, right?" Loreatha asks simply.

Her question unnerves me. She beams with evil. Keisha and I stop dead in our tracks. We look at each other. Then turn to face Loreatha. *How in the hell does she know my husband?*

Keisha suddenly grabs my arm and pulls me toward the door.

"Amber, let's go now!" Keisha yells and demands. Her eyes are wide and nervous. She seems to know something I don't. Almost as if she's just seen a ghost. She's frantic. I manage to break free of her hold on my arm. She's making me nervous, scared.

"Keisha, stop it!" I yell. "What's wrong with you? Why are you acting this way?"

The way she's looking at Loreatha is scaring me. Has me frightened. Something's going on but I don't know what it is.

"Keisha, say something! What the hell is going on?"

I shift my concerns from Keisha to Loreatha. The way she's standing there staring at me, staring at us....*It's evil!* My heart stops as I confront my fears.

"How do you know my husband?" I ask, almost afraid of what I'm going to hear. "And *where* do you know him from?"

Again, Keisha pulls me, demands that we leave. But I can't move. I'm glued to the spot I'm standing in. Loreatha has my full, undivided attention. Nothing but death can force me from this room.

"Know him?" Loreatha continues with even more of a smirk. "I know Mr. *Get Your Swallow On* very well! You see, Amber...." Loreatha moves closer to me invading all my space. "The night before he walked you down the aisle, he was on *stage* with me and Eva! And it was definitely good to the last drop!"

Shawn
His Wife, My Right

Amber's phone call left me real disturbed. She called me hysterical, and I could barely make out what she was saying. I'm nervous. I haven't heard her bawl like in a long time. Not since college.

"Oh my God!" I say out loud. "Amber found out about the bachelor party!"

That's got to be it. I pick up the phone to call Khalil. But no answer. *What the hell is going on over there?* My nerves are bad, because I'm jumping to all sorts of conclusions. Nobody's answering the house phone or the cell. I pick up my jacket and my keys to head on over there but the bell rings. I don't even answer. I'm on my way out anyway, so I'll just see who it is when I get downstairs. Again, the doorbell rings but this time, whoever it is, is laying on it.

"I'm coming!" I yell as I make my way to the door. I open the door. It's Amber. Amber's face is swollen and red from crying. As soon as she sees me, the waterworks resurface. She's trying to talk, but I can't make out a word she's saying.

"Amber, stop. What's wrong?" I lead her into the house and sit down on the sofa. She's crying so bad that all I can do is hold her. I feel so bad at this moment. My heart hurts for her. I'm frantic and my nerves are shot. I pull her deeper into my arms and allow her to get it all out. I don't say a word or ask her any questions. *It is deja vu, all over again.*

"Why, Shawn?" She managed to get out between sobs. "Why did he do that to me Shawn? What did I do? I didn't do anything wrong, Shawn. Why?"

I don't have an answer for her now, just like I didn't

have an answer for her then. "I don't know Amber." Tears fall from my eyes as I hold Amber close. All I can do is let her know that I'm here for her. She doesn't deserve this. Sometimes I wish that I'd met Amber first. There was no way in hell I would have ever put her through this kind of turmoil again and again. *Not to mention, more than once. How can you love someone and hurt them this way?*

We are both crying now. She doesn't even have to tell me why she is crying. I already know. I feel Amber's pain as if is my own. And the guilt is killing me. The guilt of setting up the bachelor party. The guilt of setting up that performance. The guilt of knowing what Khalil had done as a result. I had nothing to do with him fucking those tricks. Yet I feel partly responsible. I'd already planned to tell her the truth in case she asks me if I knew. I've never lied to her before. I'm not going to start now.

"Amber, listen to me." I try to get her to stop crying, but there's no use. I get up from the couch and come back with a damp washcloth. I lift her face and begin to wipe away her tears. She looks so hurt, so desperate for an explanation. An explanation I can't give.

Suddenly Amber begins punching me and screams, "Why, Shawn? I hate you! I hate you! Mutha fucka, Why! Why didn't you tell me?!"

She's screaming at the top of her lungs and crying uncontrollably. Her punches don't hurt me. Not as much as her words. I grab her by both her arms to get her to stop. I don't want her to hurt herself. She's scaring me. I've never seen her act this way before. This is worse than college.

"Amber, stop!" I yell at her hoping she'll calm down. She's out of control.

"Don't do this Amber, please! I'm sorry. I'm so sorry, Amber. I never meant to hurt you. Oh God, Amber, it wasn't supposed to happen."

I fall to my knees as the tears roll down my face. I wrap my arms around her legs. I repeat over and over again as I continuously tell her how sorry I am. I beg for her forgiveness. She falls to the floor along with me and wraps her arms around my back.

"Tell me this isn't happening Shawn. Please tell me I'm dreaming. What did I do Shawn? God, please tell me what I did." Her sorrow-filled voice makes my insides cringe with guilt. I need to reassure her it wasn't her fault. I take her face in my hands and wipe some more of her tears away.

"Listen to me Amber. You did nothing wrong, okay? You did everything right. Don't ever blame yourself for what went down. It's not your fault. Amber, listen to me."

I still have her face in my hands. She's so beautiful, so angelic, and so full of love. All she wanted in return was the same kind of love she'd given to him. I smooth her hair away from her eyes. She's still crying. Her eyes, that are normally so full of life, now look dark and empty. My heart is so heavy. There's nothing I can do or say that will make her pain go away. I grab the washcloth again and begin to blot away her tears, only to have them return within moments of me taking my hand away. As I look into her eyes trying to find some sign of life, Amber returns my gaze.

"I love you, Shawn. You've always been here for me."

"I love you too, Amber. Don't worry, we'll get through this. I'm here for you."

I find myself rubbing and caressing her face. Her beautiful, buttersoft face is warm and inviting. It is mere inches from mine, when my lips suddenly end up on hers. Our lips touch and greet for the first time. It's a gentle kiss, just to let her know that she does have a friend.

Amber looks at me confused, but she doesn't move from my arms. I lean in towards her gorgeous face. I'm so nervous inside. The butterflies in my stomach feel as if they're trying to emerge from a cocoon. I inch in slowly toward her mouth just to feel her soft lips against mine once more. I kiss her again. I can't help myself. This time it is long and endearing. A kiss not shared between friends but between lovers.

I lay on the floor with Amber, my best friend's wife. I'm kissing her passionately as if she were mine.

"Amber, this is wrong but I don't want to stop."

"Then don't."

I'm here staring into her eyes. It wasn't until this moment that I realized I've loved her all along. My heart is beating so fast; it's hard to breathe.

All those years in college up until now, she hadn't changed a bit. Although she'd lost some weight, she is still the same Amber—warm, caring, and a beautiful spirit within. I think, for a moment, before I continue with what my heart and my head are telling me to do.

"Amber, are you sure?"

I didn't want to ask in fear she wasn't. She never answers. She simply places her hand behind my head and pulls me into what is one of the most sensational kisses I've ever had in my entire life. Slow, long, sweet kisses. I stare at her as she continues to kiss me gently. I, in turn, caress her face while giving her sweet kisses on her lips, her cheeks, her forehead. *Oh God, she's killing me softly.*

I've known Amber for years but never in this manner. I feel my nature rising. In one sweeping motion, I pick her up from the floor and carry her up the stairs into the bedroom.

My eyes in sync with hers all the way there. The aroma from her supple skin makes me anxious. I gently place Amber on the bed.

I ask once more. "I would never do anything to hurt you, Amber, you know that don't you?"

Again, she doesn't speak, but she begins removing my shirt. I stop her and kneel down at the side of the bed. I stare at her. She stares back at me with tears still rolling down her face. Despite the tears, she is so beautiful at this moment.

I know she's extremely vulnerable right now. I begin kissing her tears when I notice I've begun crying again as well.

I can't do this. I can't take advantage of her. The thought of me taking advantage of her suddenly hits me. It becomes clear to me that I can't do this. Not now. I love her too much. Our friendship is too important to me, and I don't want to do anything which might jeopardize our bond.

"Amber, I need you to answer me. I need you to tell me it's alright."

Her only response is more tears. I know she's hurting, and I wish like hell I could make it go away. The bond we share is so special, and it's killing me inside to see her this way. My own tears have started to get the best of me so I get up. I walk into the master bathroom and close the door.

I stand in front of the sink and stare at myself in the mirror. I reminisce about the good times I've shared with Amber, laughing at some of our better days and choking up as some of the rough times and wondering if there were any signs. Any signs that will tell me that I've always been in love with her. *Wow, I've always been in love with Amber.*

I think about my own betrayal from Aaliyah. I think…That's my friend out there, my man's wife. And she's laying in *my* bed. I know I can't let this go down this way, but

I can't help the way I'm feeling right now. Maybe if I talk to her, we can make each other understand this is wrong. Yes, that's what I'll do.

I can hear Amber moving around on the other side of the door. She must have realized this is a mistake and getting ready to leave. I wash my face and get myself together before I go back in the room.

Think clearly, be easy. I slowly open the door to my master bathroom and nervously find Amber standing right there about to come in. She wraps her arms around my neck as she pulls me in closer to her, places her head on my shoulder as tears are still falling from her eyes. Amber plants gentle kisses on my neck and then whispers in my ear.

"I'm sure, Shawn." She takes me by my hand and leads me back into the bedroom.

My heart races. I hear Usher's *Can You Handle It*, playing softly in the background. Not only has Amber put on music, but she's lit candles too. That's what she was doing when I heard her moving around in here.

She stops at the side of the bed and turns to face me. Her mouth devours mine and our tongues become entangled. The passion, the heat, the connection…it's all so surreal. All of a sudden I realize I've never felt this way about any woman in my life! I want her so badly, but it's not just sexually. I want her wholeheartedly, her mind, her body, and her soul. I want Amber to be mine, to be *my* wife, to be the one *I* would love, honor and cherish all of *my* days. I pick her up and lay her on the bed.

For a while, I lay there with her while my hands hesitantly roam all over her body. I need to have her. She quivers and gyrates as my hands discover and become aquainted with all that is good and precious and dear. I take her face into my hands and my tongue ends up lost, deep in the abyss of her soul. She's no longer crying, and she seems as if she's at peace.

My hands somehow find their way to her blouse. I begin unbuttoning when she reaches to help me, all the while staring into my eyes. Her skin feels flawless and silky smooth, her body, beautiful. She's absolutely perfect.

I get up from the bed and begin taking off my own clothes, still holding Amber in my gaze, while she tugs at me, trying to pull me closer to her, grabbing my hands, sucking my fingers, slowly caressing my chest with her fingertips, kissing my navel, licking my nipples. I'm afraid if I lose eye contact with her, I'll wake up and this will all be just a dream. I lay back beside her. *Damn, she's sexy.* My lips find her mouth as I lick her lips again and again and her neck, and finally her breast where I playfully tease her nipples with my tongue, gently bite them, suck them, kiss them, love them. *Damn, she smells so good.* I feel myself ready to bust wide open. My hand caresses her body and move between her legs where the heat from her sweetness begins to rise. I hear her let out the most tantalizing moan I've ever heard. *Damn!* I'm ready for her, but I also want to take my time. The thought that I'll probably never get this chance again makes me want to do this right. I need to stroke her pain away.

I want Amber to feel safe with me. I want to be her protector. I want to be the one who washes away her pain, her doubts, and her fears. I want to take her heart under my wing and be its guardian.

The light flicking from the candles dance in her eyes. Another tear rolls down her cheek. I kiss it away. I look deep into her eyes and place her hand on my heart.

"Look at me Amber." I need her to not only hear what I have to say, but feel it as well.

She faintly responds, "Yes?"

"You don't ever have to cry again Amber, and I mean that shit from the bottom of my heart." More tears fall from her eyes. I, in turn, begin crying all over again.

I kiss her all over her body and find my way down to her navel. She smells so good; I want to smell her for the rest of my life. She trembles underneath me and lets out all kinds of moans as if I'm already inside her.

I was born a patient lover, so I begin with her feet. Lifting her leg and placing her foot up to my face, I gently lick around her perfectly painted red toes. I kiss her feet, suck her toes, and travel down her thigh with my tongue. Small baby kisses take me closer and closer to her magic. Becoming nearer to her wonderment has me in a state of bliss, a state of pure ecstasy. Finally I get to where I want to be. She's so wet, drenched, tender and inviting, so soft, supple, moist, succulent and smells so sweet. I taste her. I've eaten pussy before, but there is something different about this time. I want to be here. I need to be here. I don't tease her or play with it as I'd done in the past with other women.

I suck Amber with my soul, like if I suck her long enough, maybe her pain will dissipate. My tongue dancing around inside her goodness in a way it never had before with anyone. I hold onto her thighs and love her with my spirit. In and out, out and in, my tongue finds every inch of her and has the audacity to introduce itself as her new comforter. Kissing her pussy lips, licking them slowly, admiring the juices that flow uncontrollably makes everything inside me emerge to the surface. My heart, vulnerable and naked, is now on my sleeve. This woman, this woman laying here with me…my best friend's wife…was all the woman I've ever needed.

Her juices flowing, her legs trembling and her continuous sultry moans cause me to slow my pace. Somehow I've managed to escape into my own world, because I can no longer hear her sounds, her moans, her pleasure. I slowly move up to face her. She welcomes me back into her arms and kisses me softly.

"I love you, Shawn. Promise me that whatever happens, you'll never hurt me?"

I don't have to think twice before answering her.

"I already told you Amber. I promise you, for as long as I live....I got you baby." Her tears start again right along with mine. We cry in unison as our emotions get the best of us. This is deep and we both are fully aware of the magnitude of our encounter. All I can think of at this moment is keeping her safe. Keeping her with me.

Breathing has become so heavy and so erratic. The kissing so carnal and passionate. Our tongues dance with the devil as we can't hold on any longer. I slowly lay on top of her and part her legs with mine. The anticipation of what is yet to come has made me solid as a rock.

"Shawn?"

I know what she's about to ask me. Protection. I reach over and open the nightstand drawer without even answering her.

"No, Shawn. I want to feel you."

"Amber, baby, I need to feel you too."

I hesitate for a moment and then kiss her softly. I notice that more tears are formed in her eyes. They have not yet fallen. I maneuver my manhood directly atop her warmth. I grind on her, teasing her until she moans, and I lose my tongue in her mouth once again. Her lips are so sweet. She kisses me back with such dedication, so much passion.

I can't take it any longer. With one thrust, I'm inside her. I cry out. She cries out. She's so tight, so wet, and so hot. I can't believe that I am inside of Amber. I can see her nipples getting harder right before my eyes. Her body shudders.

An unfamiliar feeling runs through my being. It's not just the sex but the totality of all that is inside of me. I hold her tight as I somehow climb higher. Somehow dig deeper. She's so wet and so soft that I feel her walls of comfort give way to each of my blows. Our solaced spirits emiss Earth-shaking harmony as I rise to depths unbeknownst to mankind. I've had sex plenty of times but I realize now this is the first time I've ever truly made love.

"Amber, I love you." I manage to say those four little words before our historical encounter almost ends. I feel the spasms begin, but I don't want this to end. Not yet. *Oh God, this feeling.* This spiritual magic that has been absent from my life for so long. Suddenly I hear her calling out to me.

"Shawn, I'm cummin'!"

Her warmth turns to heat. Her wetness drowns me so good. She has her legs wrapped around me so tight pulling me in deeper and deeper. I take her mouth into mine as if on cue and with so much determination.

Unfeigned love empowers me as I stroke her with every inch of my body. Powerful, blunt force impacts take me to deeper plains. Making love to her face-to–face, mouth-to-mouth, soul-to-soul becomes too much for me.

Amber's so sexy and sweet that I feel myself spiraling into a cosmic free-fall of intoxication. My head spins, and the air in the room seems thin. Sweat runs down my head and I'm dizzy. My body jerks. I try to pull out. I can't. I won't.

I slow down with my thrusts and my strokes. I just wanna rest in all this deliciousness. I would love for this to go on for hours. I need to be inside of Amber for as long as I can. Nothing else in my life makes sense anymore, aside from me loving her, *making love* to her and giving her all the love that she's deserved for so long. I pull out slowly so that I won't explode. She grabs me.

"Shawn, please. It's okay."

I place a single finger over her lips as I get up from the bed.

"Shhhhh, It's not over baby, I promise."

I move from the bed while holding Amber in my gaze. Her eyes follow my every move. She's so sweet and looks so fragile. I want to take my time with her. Go slow, be gentle.

I tell her to turn to her side; instead, she crawls on her knees to the edge of the bed where I'm standing. She takes me into her hand and places me into her mouth. She takes me all in with those full, wet lips and goes down the shaft with her tongue. This feels so good, but she's going to make me cum with quickness, and I can't let it end like this. I try to tell her to stop, but I can't get it out. I run my fingers through her hair. I admire her body—those full breasts and fat ass as she sucks me down so good.

I can't take this anymore, not now; I need to be inside of her again.

"Amber, turn to your side."

I slowly pull out of her mouth, wishing like hell, I could hold on longer. She obliges. Her silhouette wavers in the background, overshadowed by the flames from the candles. The sight of her from the rear makes my heart race faster. I get back into the bed with her. I spoon her from behind and hold her as tight as I can.

Her warm body, her soft skin, her smell even makes me feel like I've died and gone to Heaven. This is the shit I've been missing out on all my life. True love in its most deep and purest form. I lean in and gently nibble on her ear, licking it softly. The urge to reassure her I love her compels me.

"Amber, I love you." My tongue slides down her neck. "Are you okay?"

She turns her head slightly and responds, "Yes baby."

Her body trembles in my arms, and my manhood swells as I massage it against her ass. I know she wants me, and I want to give it to her with all that I have. Still behind her, I lift her voluptuous leg with one arm. She leans back and rests her head on my shoulder.

I insert deeply with conviction and her drenched core grabs a hold of me. We both cry out in unison as our bodies combine once more. I feel how soaked she is and I know it's going to be hard for me to hold on, but I can't let this go.

My hands take on a mind of their own as I caress her body, her breasts, her thighs. With one hand, I reach around her and teasingly fondle her clit as I deliver even more powerful thrusts. I'm loving her as if I'd been loving her for years.

Amber moans and quivers as I move in and out of her. I pull all the way out and go back in, over and over again. The sensation her pussy leaves on my shaft is indescribable, it's so good. Her drenched core has a hold of me, and I can't hold on any longer. With desperation, I whisper in her ear.

"Tell me you love me, Amber."

"Oh God Shawn…I think I've always loved you."

I go deeper and deeper as we both make noises that could awaken the dead. She reaches back and grabs my ass to pull me further into her righteousness. I'm in love with this woman. Wholeheartedly. Concretely. And at this very moment, I call out her name as I empty myself inside of her. And I know, from now on…Amber is mine.

Amber

Revelations

I can't believe it. I simply can not believe what just happened. As I'm in bed with one of my dearest friends, reflections of what just took place won't leave my head. The event plays over and over again in my mind. I am, without a doubt, frozen in time.

We're both under the sheets, naked. I'm on my back, and Shawn, my husband's best friend, has his head on my breasts. His massive hold of me seems serene. I can feel his heart beating against mine; his breathing is slow.

Shawn seems to be at peace. I wonder if he's thinking what I'm thinking. We've been friends for so long that I hope our friendship is not ruined now. If it's not shot to Hell after this episode, I know it's definitely changed. I love my husband dearly, but right now, I'm loving his best friend.

Neither of us have spoken a word since the *"I love you's"* that poured from our lips in the midst of our adulterated acts of pure ecstasy.

I don't know what to feel, other than confusion. Way too much to consume. The heat. The passion. The groundbreaking love making. The pain. The lies. The betrayal. The tears. The need to make sense of it all, when all of it is really so senseless.

What I do know at this moment is that Shawn and I need to face reality. We've been through so much together. I pray we'll get through this. I'm almost afraid to speak. When I finally do summon the courage, my cell phone rings again. It's playing *Big Pimpin'*...Jay Z. My favorite ring tone breaks the silence.

It can only be one person, Khalil. His special dial tone. He's been blowing up my phone since he left for Virginia. I have spoken to him a few times. On the last phone call, I was crying so hard, trying to get the words out. I'm sure, however, he barely understood what I tried to say. I'm sure he managed to hear the words, *bachelor party*, amidst my sobs.

I've forgiven Khalil for his indiscretions so many times before. This time should be no different, but it is. The humiliation was actually in my face. All too real. This time, I was familiar with Khalil's drug of choice. I was afforded the opportunity of, not only knowing his *sexcapades*, but actually hanging out with one, and seeing the other at my place of employment from time to time. Of course I found out about his betrayals many times over in the past, but this time is different.

In the past I'd never had the pleasure of putting a face to any of the names....except for Shayla. I didn't have to face the reality of knowing who my man was attracted to, who my man would give himself to, who my man would lie to me for, who my man would love in addition to me. Never got to put a face to the betrayal. Until now.

It hurts bad. And just to think, I actually knew these two bitches! And Loreatha of all people! Or should I say, *Chyna*? Once she found out Khalil was my husband, nothing but death could've kept her from gloating.

I will never understand why Black women hate each other so much, but we do. Anything to keep the next woman down. Whether it's a mental, emotional, or a physical put-down, we somehow find a way to rip the soul from one another. It's a small world after fucking all. I still can't believe it really. Did he really sleep with the two of them at once the day before he married me?

I'm nuts, hurt, torn, angry, confused. So many thoughts are going through my head. I'm trying to be calm about it all, but I'm mad as hell! I want a divorce! I don't. I do. I don't know. I love him. I hate him. I despise him. I feel sorry for him. I love him again. I hate him even more. He makes me sick. He can go to Hell!

But wait, No! I still want him. He's still my husband. Why did I marry him? My heart. My life. My soul mate. The one I dream for. Bastard! Liar! Muthafucka! Stupid ass! But I need him! If forgiving him this time buys my ticket into Heaven, then I'd rather go to Hell! Asshole! But he needs me! Damn! That dick! Shit! Dumb ass! How could he?

Damn, I slept with Shawn. He felt so good, but Shawn? Oh God, too much! I need a drink! I want my Mommy!

Jay Z's still *Big Pimpin'* on the floor attached to my jeans. The cell phone is ringing again. Tears fall from my eyes.

Amazingly, I don't feel like I've committed incest. Shawn is the closest to a real-life brother that I've ever had. Yet I don't feel disgusted for sharing myself with him. I've never betrayed Khalil before. But making love to Shawn somehow felt right, comforting, and real. I belonged in his arms. I feel so safe with him, so warm, so protected; he made me feel so good, so loved, wanted and needed. And yes....I love him for that.

"Baby?" Shawn speaks. His head still on my chest listening to my heartbeat. I'm almost afraid to answer, but I need to.

"Yes, Shawn?"

Shawn turns his head to face me, still using my breasts as his pillows. I prop myself up so that I can look down at him. He's gorgeous, but I never looked at him this way until now. Shawn smiles at me and kisses my breast.

"What do we do now, Amber?"

251

Something inside of me wants him to continue to kiss me, caress me.

"I don't know Shawn. Nothing makes sense to me anymore."

I rub his head and gently glide my fingers over his temple, down the profile of his handsome face, trace his lips with my fingertips. He can see that I'm starting to well up again. He gets up and hugs me. I'm resting in his arms as he wipes my tears away and bends down to kiss my lips. I look up at him.

"Shawn, I'm so hurt."

He runs his hands through my hair then embraces me steadily.

"I'm hurt too Amber. I found out some things in Virginia, well at least, I suspect some serious things, and I didn't want to bother you with them earlier. I need to talk to you Baby Girl."

I'm prepared to listen to everything Shawn has to tell me, but I'm distracted. I can't help but to replay the session in my mind. Shawn is such a different lover than Khalil. He's gentle, and his strokes come with a different history behind them. His kisses, carnal. His passion, intense. His moans, even his language in bed....the way he talked to me, held me, caressed me, licked, kissed, sucked, how he dug so deep....it's inappropriate to think of it, really, but it makes me want to know him better in this way. I love Khalil, but Shawn has my heart right now.

How does one explain this? How is it even possible? As I lay here in his arms, my head now rests on his chest, and I want like hell to make love to him once more, no matter how wrong it is. I imagine I'm just in some sort of weird natural state.

Shawn must be reading my mind as he looks deep into my eyes. All reason leaves him as he kisses me fervently once more. I straddle him as if I'm going to ride him. Both of our breathing becomes heavy and hectic as he licks my lips, my neck, cups both my breasts into his hands, and sucks on my nipples.

I'm ready to cum all over again, but I can't. Oh God, he's fine! I'm confused. Should I stop? Why should I? He felt so good! What about Khalil? Fuck That! *Khalil who?* Damn! I'm supposed to be here. This is *my* time. No more pain, hurt, agony, betrayal. From now on, I look out for number one....Me!

This man with me...Shawn, my husband's best friend, his right hand man, his dawg, his brother, his homey, his partner, his side-kick, his boy, his road-dog, his ace, his peeps...I know he loves Khalil, but right now, he's lovin' me more.

Shawn's dick is getting hard again. I can't do this again, but I want to. Need to. It's the easiest thing to do. Can't confront reality. He's so sweet, I love him. I don't. I do. I don't know. Shawn's phone rings.

"Are you going to get that, Shawn?" The constant ringing of Shawn's loft phone disturbs our peace in the storm and brings us closer to our inevitable reality.

"No, Amber. I don't feel much like talking to anyone right now. All I wanna do is be here. With you." Shawn kisses my lips once more. I get up from the bed and wrap myself in his sheet, head to the window, and peak through the blinds. The answering machine comes on, and an all too familiar voice resonates loudly.

"Yo Shawn, man, listen. I don't know where Amber is, man. I'm going crazy Shawn. I came home, she's not here. I called her mother, she's not there. Talked to Keisha, and she hasn't heard from her all day. Keisha had a stink attitude with me on the phone, I think she knows something too. I even called Scott's punk-ass, and he hasn't talked to her either. Shawn, man, I'm real scared. When she called me, she was crying hard as hell. I think she found out about the bachelor party, man! How could I be so fucking stupid, man? What the fuck was I thinkin' about? Oh God Shawn, if I lose her again, I don't know what I'll do, yo. Call me back, man. Please. If she calls you, man, tell her I love her. You gotta help me Shawn. You gotta fix this for me, man. I'm goin' crazy, yo. Call me when you get this message."

Beeeeeep.

Once again, I'm frozen at the window. I'm wrapped in nothing but Shawn's sheet, naked in Shawn's bedroom, and the tears fall again. Shawn walks over to me, hugs me from behind, moves my hair to one side, and rests his chin on my shoulder. He kisses me on my cheek, like the old Shawn used to. It no longer feels like a brother kissing his sister.

"Amber, we'll get through this. But, I'm afraid that at this moment, I'm not the voice of reason. Amber, what we shared today made me realize that I've always loved you." Shawn stops speaking and turns me to face him.

"Amber, look at me. I'm torn. I feel real fucked up but happy at the same time. I've realized that I know you better than any woman in my life and you know me, too. We've connected over the years without even knowing it. Please, Amber, tell me you feel the same way."

Oh God, this is too much. Shawn's not thinking clearly. Yes, he's been my shoulder, my confidant, my rock even, but I've never looked at Shawn quite like this before. Making love to him has made me feel like I've been missing out on something my entire life. Yes, Khalil is a great lover, but Shawn's love making was spiritual, almost God-fearing.

"Amber, say something, please. Do dreams come true? Because I dream of you!" He begs.

"I don't know what to say Shawn. Right now, nothing makes sense to me anymore." I understand this is not what

Shawn wants to hear. But I refuse to lie to him. There have been too many lies.

I do love him, but I can't love him the way he deserves. *Does that make any sense at all?* I love my husband, but I hate him, too. Torn is an understatement at this point.

"We need to talk, Amber." Shawn continues. "There are some things that I need to share with you."

My tears are still falling, because I feel that Shawn does love me. *How did I get in this mess?* I can't begin to address this right now.

"Shawn, we can't deal with that right now." I play with the blinds, peeking out again to see the pedestrians walking the streets of Manhattan. I pretend as if I'm sincerely interested in what's going on down below.

"I know Amber, but please listen. I think Aaliyah is Shayla's sister." Shawn hands me a photograph and continues. "I know that sounds strange, but Lexis showed me this picture of her and her '*Auntie Lee Lee*.' This is the reason I had Aaliyah go to the spa today. I needed to be alone when I came home. I needed time to sort all of this out in my mind, make sense of it all. I never got into it with you about how Aaliyah and I met, because I never wanted you to think less of me. I never wanted you to pass judgment on Aaliyah without getting to know her. But I met Aaliyah one day at the modeling agency Shayla was working at part time. Neither of them said anything about being related in any shape, form or fashion. I still can't understand either one of their agendas. Maybe it's totally innocent, but since Shayla is involved, I doubt it. I just need some time to get this straight in my head."

I listen to the words that are coming from Shawn's lips and stare at the picture in my hand. I still can't fully comprehend what he's just said. Aaliyah and Shayla? No way! Shayla is a vindictive, shiesty bitch, but that's Shayla. Khalil is such a stupid ass. But why Aaliyah? I try to give her the benefit of the doubt.

"Maybe Aaliyah couldn't find a way to tell you, Shawn? Maybe she was scared or something?" I'm trying to make Shawn feel better, but that bitch definitely has something up her sleeve. Aaliyah doesn't know the wonderful man she has in Shawn with her stupid ass.

"No, Amber. Aaliyah knows she can talk to me about anything. When I felt like I wanted to marry her, I made that clear. I told her in the beginning....no secrets, no lies, we're in this together. Something's up Amber, and I can't figure it out. In addition to this, I need to figure out how to talk to Khalil. What do I say to my best friend? That I'm in love with his wife? That he should've done right by her? Do we keep this a secret, Amber?"

"I don't know what to think, say or do Shawn. I just don't know if I can go through this again with Khalil. I love him so much Shawn, but, but..."

My tears overwhelm me and I am no longer able to speak.

"But what, Amber?" Shawn grabs me tighter. I try to respond to tell him that....*I do love him too.*

"What were you going to say Amber? That you still want to be with Khalil? Go ahead and say it Amber. I know you do. You've loved that man so hard for so long. He doesn't know how fucking lucky he is to have you. I try to tell him that all the time, Amber, that he's blessed to have you. So go ahead and say it. No since in holding anything back, not now....we've already crossed the line, been past the point of no return. Talk to me, Amber. Don't shut down on me now. You've never had a problem confiding in me before."

"Shawn jus'....jus'....just forget about it." I try like hell to rid my face of the tears, but it's no use. No sooner do I move my hand away, more tears are waiting to cross the picket line. "Shawn, I feel like I need a drink. Would you mind making one for me? I just need something to take the edge off."

"Alright, Amber, I could use a drink, too. Anything to help me cope....help us get our heads right." Shawn walks down the stairs, and I think I hear the door bell ring. I'm so consumed with my own drama that I can't really tell or care.

My cell phone rings again and instead of avoiding the problem once more, I decide to confront my fears. I open the flip and speak.

"Hello?" The voice on the other end of the phone brings a smile to my face as well as some relief to my existence.

"Baby girl? What the fuck is going on? You okay? And why the hell is your husband calling *me* looking for *you*?" Scott's voice, although serious right now, relaxes me a little.

"Scott, please. Just slow down so I can explain."

"Explain?" Scott persisted. "Explain, what? How your husband interrupted my groove? I'm way over here at Chi-Chi's, in the village, when Khalil rings my phone, not once, but twice, looking for you. He sounded real nervous and not at all in control. Called himself questionin' me about you. Askin' me shit like, when was the last time I spoke to you or if I'd seen you today. But when I asked him what the problem was, he ain't wanna talk no more. So I politely told your *huzbin'* that if he couldn't answer my question, I damn sure wasn't answerin' his. Trust me, baby girl, the *only* reason I decided to call you is because Khalil *never* calls me so I knew something was wrong. I didn't call you for him, but for me. I had to make sure you were okay, so spill it." *Khalil really did call Scott.*

My tears well up again as I begin to confide in Scott.

"Scott, listen." I respond between sobs. "So much has happened and...."

"Hold up! Are you *crying*?" Scott interrupts me as I try to explain. "Did that black, fake ass Tyrese, Tyson Beckford wannabe put his hands on you? Baby Girl, just say the word and I *swear* I'll have my peoples hunt his ass down and have him assassinated. You hear me? See, this some bullshit right here. Let me get the fuck outta this club. Got me in here sweatin' like a whore in confession. Baby girl, gimme half an hour and I'll be right there!"

"Scott, no!" I yell, trying to get his attention. "It's nothing like that, Khalil would never put his hands on me."

"You sure, Amber?" Scott insists. "Cause you know us queens have been known to make muthafuckas disappear."

The thought of Scott and his *peoples* inflicting bodily harm on Khalil makes me smile. I know he's only looking out for me, but Scott knows he wouldn't hurt a fly. I try to reassure him that Khalil didn't touch me. Scott continues.

"And did you know Khalil even called that "N*egro spiritual*" Keisha looking for you. I know because Keisha called me so he must've made her nervous as well. Amber, where are you?"

"Scott, I'm at Shawn's house in Manhattan. Listen honey, so much has happened. Let me start at the beginning."

"Amber, did he hurt you?" Scott interrupts again. "I'll castrate that son of a bitch with the swiftness."

"Scott, *please*, let me tell you. Khalil and Shawn went to Virginia because Khalil's daughter Lex had a recital. I found out that he was going from Aaliyah, the morning of, which really upset me."

I should have known yet another interruption was due.

"What the fuck? See, I told you about that lily white bitch Aaliyah. She didn't smell right once I got to know her stinking ass. Bet she couldn't wait to call and tell you that shit. Some bitches just love being the bearers of bad news. To see Lex, huh? Oh, that lil' bastard chile of his? And he wasn't gonna tell you, huh? Oh see…"

I plead for Scott to hear me out.

"Scott, please. I encouraged Khalil to go, because you know he doesn't give that child enough time. He has not been anything near the father he should be to that little girl. Besides, she didn't ask to be here. She has two stupid ass parents that were irresponsible."

"Okay, so why didn't he tell you he was going? If it was only concerning his daughter, why'd you have to hear it from the fatal attraction?"

I smile again because Scott always has a way of defining people.

"I don't know, Scott. He said he was just waiting for the right time to tell me. And when I think about it, there's no way he could've left town without telling me. But when Aaliyah told me about it, it just threw me, because I never saw it coming. He barely even talks about Lexis."

"All the more reason he should of said something. I'm more than sure his trip wasn't no spur of the moment shit. He had to know about it for weeks and he ain't say nuthin'? Some men are so fuckin' stupid, creatin' unnecessary drama for no fuckin' reason at all."

"Anyhoo Scott, that's history. But listen. Keisha and I went to see Miss Beverly earlier today, you know, my favorite patient at the nursing home? She had a stroke and she's in UMDNJ. Scott, believe me when I tell you it's a small fucking world, because it turns out that Miss Beverly's granddaughter is Loreatha a.k.a. *Chyna*, your friend Eva's partner."

"What?!" Scott jumps in. "Chyna's real name is Loreatha?" Scott busts out with uncontrollable laughter. "Oh, no bitch! Just wait 'til I tell er'body this bullshit."

"Would you shut up and let me finish boy!" I respond frustrated.

"Long story short, Scott. Chyna saw my wedding photo that I'd brought to the hospital for her grandmother. Turns out, her and Eva fucked Khalil at his bachelor party!" The thought of them with my husband makes me cry again. No matter how hard I try, I can't keep from bawling my eyes out. To describe Khalil's indiscretions to someone else hurts like hell. It constantly replays in my mind, over and over again. There's dead silence on the other end of the phone.

"Scott? Hello? Are you still there?"

"Yeah, I'm here Amber." Scott's tone sounds almost as sorry as I am. "I just can't believe this shit. Honey, trust me, as of right now, Eva and Chyna are both officially out of business. See, them bitches didn't realize they were fucking with family now....and my sister at that? Oh, believe me baby girl, consider their lives officially ruined. They'll be ran out of Jersey by week's end. Their dick-sucking privileges have officially been revoked!"

"Scott?" I continue hesitantly. I know I can tell him anything, but I feel like what I'm about to say will destroy his faith in me.

"Please don't share what I'm about to say with anyone. Please? Not even Keisha, okay?"

"You know I won't say anything, Amber. What is it?"

"You know that you and Keisha are my best friends, and I love you both dearly, so please don't look at me differently once I tell you this."

I can hear Scott breathing heavily through the phone.

"Amber, what is it? You're scaring me!"

I hesitate for a moment, and then proceed with my confession.

"I was too embarrassed to talk to you and Keisha about the Khalil episode, so I called Shawn. Well actually, I came over here to his house. I didn't know what else to do. He's always been the shoulder I cried on with Khalil's madness and…"

The tears gush forward and make it too hard for me to continue. What do I say at this point? That I slept with my husband's best friend? That I allowed Shawn to love me in ways Khalil has never thought of?

"Amber, stop crying." Scott continues, trying to calm me down. "Whatever it is, baby girl you can tell me. What's so bad that it's making you feel this way?"

I suddenly get the nerve to continue. Scott's one of my best friends and maybe if I'd gone to him or Keisha first, none of this would have ever happened.

"Scott, I slept with Shawn." I blurt out between sniffles.

"I didn't plan it, Scott, it just happened." I continue. "I'm so sorry, Scott, I know this is not me. I don't know what came over me. But at the time, it just seemed right. Shawn found out some things about Aaliyah, and everything just came down on us at once. I guess he was vulnerable, feeling betrayed. I was vulnerable, feeling betrayed, and it just happened. I feel so ashamed. I've never betrayed Khalil, ever. This person in my body is not me, Scott. I'm not this woman. I'd never do anything remotely close to what I've done. It doesn't make any sense, nothing makes any sense. What have I done, Scott?"

"Listen, Amber." Scott responds gravely. "I love you like a sister, with all my heart and soul, bitch, you hear me? You can *always*, and *should* come to me with anything. And I'm sure Keisha feels the same way. Don't you *ever* feel embarrassed about anything with me. We've been a part of each other's lives for too long, been through too much. As for the Shawn episode, I won't sugarcoat anything and you know that. Yes, Amber, you were wrong. Dead fucking wrong! Despite the fact that Khalil is a dirty dick mutha fucka, you were supposed to remain true as long as you share his last name. Never allow the indiscretions of another, to force *you* out of character. Once you do, you've allowed them to win. I know you need me right now, and I'm here for you. You know me. I've always been a realist, and I never bite my tongue. You should know I'm not gonna start now. Girl, Shawn is a great friend to you and a superhero to your dumb-ass husband. And yes, if I thought I could get him, I would have taken a run at him by now. I've always admired the way he treats you with so much respect. He treats everyone that way, because he's a nigga with class. But baby girl, if all this has happened, the way you say it has, then Shawn has and always will be in love with you, Amber. Aaliyah was just the skank to make him realize that."

Damn. Scott is on a roll.

"From the first moment I met *good-ole Shawnny*, I could tell you were with the wrong man. You know I can smell any scent a person emits. Nothing gets pass me, especially when it comes to you. Shawn loves you honey. And as fucked up as it is, I think…you love him too. But just remember this little thing called karma. I'm a firm believer in it. What goes around, comes around, you hear me?"

Oh God! Scott's words add an even new dimension to the pain, betrayal and total confusion. *Could he be right? I would think that I should know who I'm in love with, right?* I can't tell anymore, not right now. *Where is Shawn with that drink?!*

I prepare to respond to Scott, when I suddenly realize that Shawn is taking a mighty long time to bring our drinks. I *really* need one bad right now. Still wrapped in Shawn's sheet, I head downstairs to see what's taking Shawn so long, still keeping the phone prompt to my ear. Funny how I don't give a shit if Aaliyah steps through the front door or not. This is really not like me, but I'm so fucked up at the moment, that I could really care less about anything. Not anymore.

I walk to the top of the stairs and prepare to walk down, when I suddenly drop the phone over the top railing. The phone crashes at the bottom and breaks into a million tiny pieces on the living room floor. It's funny, but I don't even hear the sound it makes when it hits.

My heart stops, then races. I feel faint, weak, dizzy even. I wanna die right now, no matter how I get there; I'm ready to meet my maker in the worst way. My heart has somehow managed to ascend to my throat. I'm shaking and in a cold sweat. I feel like I'm in one of those nightmares where you're running for your life, screaming, trying to wake up, but you can't. I'm crying, screaming, but no one can hear me. I'm dying inside. My words are forming but nothing's coming out of my mouth.

Apparently the door bell did ring, as Shawn and Khalil are at the bottom of the stairs talking. Khalil looks up at me, his wife, naked, wrapped in his best friend's sheet, in his best friend's loft, coming down his best friend's stairs, after making love to his best friend. Time stops. All I can see is the confusion and rage in Khalil's face as he looks up at me. His rage turns to sorrow as his eyes fill with tears. I see him lip sync the words, "*Amber! No!*" No sound escapes those lips, and I can't hear anything. All is happening in slow motion.

Shawn, shirtless, and wearing only sweats, tries to calm Khalil down but Khalil, in turn, just punches Shawn and he falls to the floor. My pace quickens as I rush to the bottom of the stairs. No longer do I feel the floor beneath me. All I can think of is reaching Shawn, reaching my husband, stopping the madness.

Khalil gets on top of Shawn and punches him repeatedly in his face, yelling all types of things. Again, I see his mouth moving, but I hear nothing. I'm deaf, I'm mute, and I wish I was blind as well.

Shawn breaks free of Khalil's hold. He overpowers him and pins Khalil to the floor. Severe blows erupt from Shawn's fists and lands on Khalil's jaw. Both of their noses are bleeding; lips swollen and busted. *Oh God, I can't believe this.* My hearing comes back to life, however, I hear only my own screams as I reach the two of them.

"No! Stop it! Shawn! Khalil! Stop it! No! Please!" I cry hysterically and try like hell to break the two of them apart. "Shawn. Khalil. Please stop it!"

Shawn looks up at me with hurt in his eyes, then looks back to Khalil. Tears fall from his eyes as he releases his hold on Khalil. Khalil has other plans.

Without warning, Khalil uses the lower palm of his hand and hits Shawn in his nose. Shawn falls backward onto the floor, holding his nose and shaking his head, trying to regain his balance. Khalil wastes no time in climbing back on top of Shawn and finishing where he left off. More punches are thrown.

Khalil stands and stomps Shawn in his abdomen. Shawn grabs hold of Khalil's foot and kicks him in the groin. Khalil falls to the floor and the two of them switch places yet again. Shawn climbs on top of Khalil, instead of hitting him, he pleads.

"That's enough, Khalil!" Shawn screams as he pins Khalil down by the arms. "I don't wanna hurt you, man! Just listen to me!"

Khalil ignores Shawn and tries to free himself. He's no match for Shawn's strength. Shawn continues to beg. "Please, K, stop! Let me explain, man. I never meant to hurt you! I love you, man, please, just listen to me!"

All the while, I stand idly by the two of them, I am frozen and unable to move. At this point, Niagara Falls is no match for my tears. I'm screaming, crying and making no sense at all. This is all my fault, no one to blame but me. Scott was right, karma is a muthafucka!

I will myself to move from the spot my feet have grown so attached to. I manage to take my arms and pull Shawn off Khalil, and he doesn't resist my force. Khalil stands and rage still consumes him and all I can see in his eyes, his soul. He takes a step toward Shawn, and I position myself between them. My back is against Shawn's stomach; I extend my hand as it touches Khalil's chest.

"Khalil, please." I cry out. "No more. Please stop."

Khalil looks into my eyes, then at the sheet I'm wrapped in. He then gives me a look as if he's never seen me before in his life. Tears run down his face. He grabs my hand from his chest and pulls me away from Shawn closer to him.

I don't know why but I'm not afraid. Something inside of me *wants* him to take me in his arms. And at the same time, something inside of me *needs* Shawn to pull me back.

"What did you do, Amber?" Khalil cries. "Please tell me I didn't lose you."

Inside, I scream, *No you haven't lost me, nothing happened, I love you Khalil, you're my husband, and I'd never betray you.* Instead, I don't speak. Somehow, I feel as if there's nothing left to say. How can I forgive him this time? Do I really expect him to forgive me?

"Amber, I love you." Khalil's voice intensifies. "I'm sorry baby, please. It was a mistake, it meant nothing to me. Baby, think about it, we weren't even married when it happened, baby, please. You have to forgive me. We weren't even married."

I remove myself from Khalil's grasp and take a step back. *Oh, No! He didn't just say that shit.* All of the hurt, the pain, the lies, the cries, the sleepless nights, the turmoil, the forgiveness, the unforgivable, and the entire process even, come back into play.

I take my right hand, with all the years of bullshit and betrayal behind it, and slap the living daylights out of Khalil. I smack the shit, the hell and the damn out of him! His head snaps to one side from my blunt force and remains there. I'm not sure, but I think his neck cracked. I wish I could find it inside of me to slit his throat for how angry I am. I do, however, manage to make this much clear.

"You weren't married, huh? So that gave you the right to fuck two bitches at once, the night before you married me? After all we've been through Khalil?" I slap him again.

"I've always been true to you. I've forgiven you for everything, every time. But do you know that this bitch, who by the way, knows your corny, childish-ass signature statement, "get your swallow on," even gloated about fucking you? Fucking my man? My husband?" She bragged about it Khalil! She boasted about drinking you down *to the last drop*! Do you know the humiliation I've endured behind your escapades? Do you? And you do this in the name of love? Go to Hell Khalil! Go to muthafuckin' Hell!"

Khalil drops to his knees, grabs my legs into his arms. "Amber, I'm so sorry. Please, Amber. Take as much time as you need, but baby, please don't leave me, I can't live without you Amber. You are the reason I can do anything, baby, please, Amber."

Shawn interrupts, still the gentleman he's always been. "Listen…"

"Fuck you Shawn!" Khalil interrupts.

"You s'posed to be my dawg, man, my right hand man. Fuck you, man!"

"Listen, Khalil." Shawn insists. "I love you like a brother, and I know I fucked up big time man. I know you'll never be able to forgive me, man, and I'm willing to live with that for the rest of my life. Bottom line is....you have the most beautiful woman here with you, who loves you dearly, and as much as it pains me to say it, she doesn't love me man. Not the way she loves you, anyway."

"What the fuck are you talking about Shawn?!" Khalil continues, "Are you trying to tell me about *my* wife? You think you know *my* wife better than *me*?!"

"I'm not saying that, Khalil. I'm just pointing out the obvious to you. What happened between Amber and I wasn't planned, it just happened. I never intended to hurt either of you, and I'll understand if neither of you ever want to see me again."

"You fuckin' right we never want to see you again, BITCH!" Khalil screams at the top of his lungs. "You can drop dead for all I fuckin' care! You call yourself my friend? My brother? You stood next to me when I took my vows and this is what you do? *Fuck* my wife? What did you do, Shawn? Invite her to cry on your punk ass shoulder, then abuse her when she was most vulnerable? Tell me, *brother*, did you make my wife cum? You a ladies' man, right? You treat 'em all with respect, right? Were you respecting my wife while you were fuckin' her? All that shit you talk about being a man and playing your position, was all bullshit, Shawn! You ain't shit to me....nothing! If I saw your ass layin' in a ditch, on fire, I wouldn't piss on your bitch ass! Fuck you, nigga, and if you ever come near me or my family again, I swear, I'll fucking kill you!"

The look on Khalil's face tells me he's serious. I don't believe I've ever seen this side of him before. Sure, I've witnessed him angry, but never like this. Suddenly, he looks at me with hate in his eyes, the epitome of all that is evil. His mouth is still moving, but my deafness returns. I can't hear what he's saying.

His arms are grabbing me, pulling me, but I don't know what he wants. I try desperately to focus, but I can't. Everything around me goes black, and I'm lost in space. I panic as I try to find my way back, but it seems so far away. Faintly, I hear Shawn and Khalil's voices calling me in the darkness. I can't get to them; I can't find them. I search desperately but it's no use, as I float further and further away.

"Amber." Khalil calls out my name; his voice seems clearer, closer.

"Amber, baby, wake up."

I open my eyes. Khalil is standing over me. I look around and see that I'm still in Shawn's loft, laying on the couch. But how the hell did my clothes get back on? Who dressed me? And why doesn't Khalil have a scratch on him? And where's Shawn?

"You okay, Amber?" Khalil continues trying to get a response from me.

What the hell is going on? I sit up on the couch. Everything in the room spins. My head feels as if Plymouth Rock has landed on it. I place my head in my hands and still can't help but wonder how I managed to get dressed without remembering. And again, where the fuck is Shawn?

Abruptly, Shawn enters the living room with aspirin in one hand and water in the other and hands them both to Khalil.

"Thanks, man, for looking out for her 'til I got here."

Khalil speaks calmly to Shawn, then looks at me.

"Here Amber, take this, it'll make you feel better." I take the aspirin from him and chase the pills with water. *What the hell is going on here?* Shawn doesn't have a scratch on him either. Why the hell are the two of them acting as if nothing happened?

"No problem, man." Shawn responds, fully clothed. "That's what friends are for. You know I'll look out for my baby sis anytime."

Okay, enough is enough. Something's going on here and I feel as if I've just woke up in the Twilight Zone.

"What's going on?" I ask both of them, hoping to get some sort of explanation. But instead of answering me, they both look at each other and laugh in unison. Khalil sits down next to me and rubs my hair away from my face.

"Baby, you passed out." Khalil continues while smoothing my hair back. "I called Shawn a little while ago, and he told me you were here. He said you showed up here, a mess, crying real hard and he couldn't make out a word you were saying. Then he said, you went into the den and started drinking like a fish, just mixing everything you saw, and drinking it. He said you were acting neurotic, like a crazed person, and he got scared. He said he tried grabbing you, tried to get you to calm down, but you wouldn't listen. Eventually, you stopped all on your own....well, you passed out here on his couch."

I take my focus from Khalil and look over at Shawn who's sitting on his loveseat. Is this shit for real? Was anything for real?

Khalil continues telling me his accounts of things.

"Amber, I know we need to talk. When you called me a few hours ago, asking me about the bachelor party, I knew you'd found out. But listen to me, Amber, please. None of that meant anything, you gotta believe me baby, when I tell you I love *you* and *only* you. It's *always* been you. I'm so sorry for anything I've ever done to hurt you, and if I could take it all back, I would. But please, Amber, listen to me when I tell you that I would do anything for you. Without you, there's no me, there's no place for me, no use for me. Without you, I don't exist, can't exist, won't exist. This past weekend in Virginia, I missed you like crazy, baby, I couldn't wait to get home to you. I told Shayla that there are going to be a lot of changes. Changes that involve Lexis and not her. Amber, baby, nothing matters more to me than you and my daughter, and if you'll allow it, I want us to be a family. Please, Amber, just think about everything I've said. I know it'll probably take time for you to really hear me out, but I know exactly what I want now, know exactly what I need, and that's you. I took a vow to spend the rest of my life with you, so please Amber, don't throw that all away."

Khalil finishes and kisses me on my lips. I swear I'm trippin'. An hour or so ago, I was upstairs making love to Shawn. Wasn't I? Did I dream all of that? The love making? The fight? I couldn't have been dreaming. It was all so real, so life-like. I felt Shawn inside of me, I still feel him, his kisses, his touch, his breath on my neck, his smell even. No, I couldn't have been dreaming. Am I going crazy? What's happening to me? I get up from the couch and walk toward the kitchen. I stagger a bit before I get my balance. Both Shawn and Khalil reach for me.

"Let me help you, baby." Khalil gets to me first as I stand up from the sofa.

"Why don't you sit down, Amber. Whatever you need, I'll get it for you."

"No, Khalil." I respond confused. "I need to go to the bathroom."

Shawn comes over and takes one of my arms, while Khalil holds the other. *Damn, what was I drinking?* I can barely stand and my legs feel like rubber. And why are my thighs sore? The two of them help me into the bathroom outside the den and I assure them that I can handle it from here. I manage to get my pants down and notice that my panties are on inside out. I sit down on the toilet and feel the moisture between my legs, but I have not yet done anything. I unroll the tissue and wipe myself, almost afraid to look at it, but I do. I bring the tissue closer into view and observe the remnants of Shawn. I exhale.

I stagger from the bathroom and find Shawn sitting in the living room alone.

"Where's Khalil?" I ask, wondering why Shawn has such a serious look on his face.

"He had to park down the street when he got here, so he went to bring the truck closer so you wouldn't have to walk. He said that he's going to order dinner for the two of you from the Jamaican restaurant down the street, then he'll be back."

Shawn gets up from the sofa and moves closer to me.

"Come on Amber, let me help you outside."

Shawn grabs me around my waist. I place one arm around his neck. I notice the scratches that are so deeply embedded in his neck. I stop in my tracks and turn to face him.

"Shawn, wait a minute." I proceed, still confused about the past accounts.

"What's going on, Shawn? A couple of hours ago, we were...."

"Amber, don't." Shawn interrupts me and kisses me passionately. His tongue tastes familiar as it swims around in my mouth

"If you don't leave now, Amber, I'm afraid I won't let you leave later. It's going to be hard for me to let you go."

"But Shawn, how did I....?" Shawn pushes me back into the bathroom. Closes the door softly and locks it. He bends me over the sink aggressively, but not forcefully.

"Shawn...!"

He parts my legs with his knees, pulls my pants down and proceeds to bite my ass, lick my cheek, trace his tongue up the small of my back. I feel the rain coming again. He takes his left hand and reaches around to grab my face gently, pulling me back toward him. I feel him solid thru his sweats as he presses up against me. He pulls me further into his chest and whispers in my right ear.

"Amber, I will always love you. You know that? I've loved you since the days I first laid eyes on you baby." Shawn takes his right hand, reaches around and puts his fingers in my wetness. He feels how saturated I've become. He exhales deeply and pulls his fingers up to both of us. "You see this. This is me all in you. And the remains of what you and I shared. I love it."

He places those fingers in my mouth to give me a taste. I lick them. I'm moaning.

"You love it too Amber, don't you?"

I can't help myself.

"Yes, Shawn, I love you. I love it. Everything about you, I do."

He turns me around so that now I am face to face with him. Licking my lips once, then twice, then kissing my neck, he pushes me away.

"Amber, go, now. Because I swear if you don't leave right now, I'll never, ever let you go. Just go baby." I try to speak, but Shawn places his finger over my lips. "Just go Amber."

"Shawn, what about…?"

"I dressed you, Amber." Shawn continues with explanation. "After we finished making love, we started drinking. You were crying so much, that it bothered me so I gave you something to help you sleep. I didn't want Khalil to find you like that, so I dressed you and carried you back downstairs. This is your life, Amber, and it's not for me to decide who you're going to be with. I love you, Amber. I meant that when I said it earlier and nothing's changed."

"But what about the fight?"

"What fight? What are you talking about?"

"You and Khalil." I respond. "You two were fighting right here in the living room. You were bleeding, he was bleeding, and I couldn't stop it."

Shawn looks at me and laughs.

"No one was fighting, Amber. When Khalil got here, you were laying on the couch fast asleep. You must've dreamt that."

Was Shawn serious? Did I really dream that? It does make sense, though, especially since neither of them have a mark on them. I guess it's true when they say your dreams are usually about your fears, and or, your fantasies. I guess I was afraid that that's what would ultimately happen, once Khalil found out what I'd done.

As Shawn walks me to the front door, in walks Aaliyah, more beautiful than ever. I look at Shawn and remember what he said earlier about Aaliyah being Shayla's sister. The look in his eyes tells me that this is his fight and his alone.

Aaliyah looks at me and takes a stab at conversation but I ignore her. The thought of her trying to get between my legs makes me feel sick, and I'd like nothing more than to tell Shawn all about it. Just as I'm ready to expose her for the trifling bitch that she is, Khalil walks through the door.

"You ready, Amber?" Khalil asks as he reaches for me. "I moved the truck closer, so come on." Khalil takes me by the arm, but I'm finding it very difficult to release my hold on Shawn. For some reason, I feel I need to be here with him, take care of him, and defend him against the evil that has just entered his home.

"Wait a second, Khalil." I hesitate before leaving. "Let me talk to Aaliyah for a minute."

Khalil obliges and heads back outside. I turn to face Shawn, with Aaliyah standing by his side. I stare at her but speak to him. "Shawn, if you need me, I'll stay."

Aaliyah's cell phone rings. I flicker it lightly so that she loses the grip, and it falls to the floor. Shawn reaches down to the floor to pick it up. He places her cell on the coffee table and presses the speaker button.

"Lee Lee. What's going on? Khalil and Shawn left here. Khalil didn't even want to fuck me! Talkin' bout he love his wife too much and shit! Lee Lee, our plan didn't work! Dummy! I should tell Shawn everything…Hello? Hello?"

Epilogue

I can truly say that I understand the pain that Keisha endured after Mrs. Lily's passing. I guess I understand as much even on a deeper level. I'm still in disbelief as Miss Beverly's casket is lowered into the ground. I still can't believe she's gone. I feel so guilty about having left her the way I did, when I did. Something tells me when I left that hospital room that things went down hill after that, sounds strange, but I believe in energy.

Amazingly, I'm not as bad off as I thought I'd be when this time came. I'm sort of at peace now. I know Miss Beverly's in a much better place, and I thank God that He gave me so much time with Miss Beverly, that He put her in my life even. She has touched my soul in such a way.

The horrendous sounds of Loreatha screaming and crying interrupts my pleasant thoughts of Miss Beverly. I've heard that the ones who scream the loudest at the funerals are the same ones who are the guiltiest. Loreatha knows that she could have and should have treated her grandmother, *my* grandmother, with much more respect, given her much more love even. Some people don't know how blessed they are, I've witnessed it a time or two.

I turn to look at Keisha, her hand in mine, clutching on for dear life, weeping the same weep I am. The tears are endless for the both of us. I guess we have a lot to cry about. We decide to leave and let Miss Beverly's family have their last moments with her to say their goodbyes.

Keisha and I walk away, hand in hand headed toward Keisha's car. She turns to look at me. Keisha opens her arms wide, hugs me with all the strength she can muster.

"Look at my best friend! They say when one life is taken away, we're blessed with a new one. I can't believe my best friend is having a baby! So how far along did the doctor say you are?"

I look at Keisha, I simply reply, "About six weeks."

Keisha smiles and hugs me again. "So, did you tell him about the baby?"

Over the last six weeks I've learned to take one day at a time.

I simply say, "No Keisha, I haven't told Khalil or Shawn."

We continue with our stroll to Keisha's car. I guess we'll go out to lunch or maybe just drive and let the wind blow in our hair. Yep, Keisha will love that sunroof open.

A Word from the Author

First, thank you for taking the time to read my debut novel. I hope you had a good time reading it, because I had a ball writing it. I wanted my debut to come out with a bang. I think that was accomplished. Although this book is much more light-hearted than the thought-provoking poetry that I'm known to write, there is still a message, a healing.

I'd like to take this opportunity to thank some very important people in my life. I send these big shout-outs to my supporters and my true friends, family and literary colleagues whom I know love me unconditionally. I love the way you love me, and the way I love you more.

Giving thanks and honor to the God for the endurance. My mother and father, my husband and my children for all that you are to me.

And the shout-outs begin…

Thanks to Papi, Ruth, Monique, Chynk, Deseree, Kevin, Kisha, Aunt Betty, Jim, Loretta for your encouragement and support.

My closest and dearest friends Larry, Paula, April, Regina and my cousin Shauna. I love you so much. You've been undeniably down. I couldn't ask for a better nucleus.

A special thank you goes to my literary colleagues and new friends. Jessica Tilles; sister, you are the real thing and have been such a blessing to me. Claudia Brown Mosley; you're an angel and I am grateful to have met you.

So, do you like the book? Do you want more? Because I've got more in store. I'll holla.

Stay Blessed.

Lyrically yours,
Elissa Gabrielle
September 26, 2006
10:20 p.m.